PRAISE FOR DE

Cold Waters

"A compelling story filled with evocative description, deeply drawn characters, and heart-pounding drama."
—Elle James, *New York Times* bestselling author

"Herbert's haunting language, gothic tone, and vivid portrayal of small-town southern life add layers to this intriguing suspense. I was hooked from the first word!"
—Rita Herron, *USA Today* bestselling author

"Herbert delivers a fast-paced mystery where nothing is quite what it seems. Family secrets and a cold-case murder are at the heart of her compelling novel, where the author masterfully paints the canvas of a sedate southern town with intriguing characters and a crafty plot. Readers won't soon forget the chilling thrill of *Cold Waters*."
—Laura Spinella, bestselling author of the Ghost Gifts novels

"Small towns hide the darkest secrets, and Normal, Alabama, is anything but in this southern gothic thriller that will keep you turning the pages until the very last. A twisted southern gothic family drama that will stay with you long after you've closed the book. A stunning, deftly written journey through the dark corridors of the human heart."
—Sara Lunsford, author of *Tooth and Nail*

"*Cold Waters* is an unforgettable suspense story steeped in decaying old houses, dark family secrets, and rumors in a small southern town."
—Leslie Tentler, author of the Chasing Evil trilogy

"A southern gothic mystery dripping with atmosphere. *Cold Waters* will leave you breathless."

—Amanda Stevens, author of the Graveyard Queen series

SCORCHED
GROUNDS

OTHER TITLES BY DEBBIE HERBERT

Cold Waters

SCORCHED GROUNDS

DEBBIE HERBERT

THOMAS & MERCER

Published by Thomas & Mercer, Seattle
www.apub.com

Amazon, the Amazon logo, and Thomas & Mercer are trademarks of Amazon.com, Inc., or its affiliates.

ISBN-13: 9781542005869
ISBN-10: 1542005868

Cover design by Shasti O'Leary Soudant

Printed in the United States of America

To my husband, Tim, who has always believed in my wild dreams. And to my parents, J. W. and Deanne Gainey, for their love and support in my life.

Prologue

Niggles of noise pierce through the fuzzy haze of sleep. I burrow into my Hello Kitty comforter, making a nest of warmth, a baby bird seeking safe shelter. But the noise grows louder. I recognize the distinctive edge of words, and the sound becomes familiar.

Mom's shouting voice. She and Dad must be back at it.

I wiggle deeper into the pink cheer of cartoon kitty cats. Maybe they'll stop soon. I'll fall asleep, and when I wake up in the morning, it will all be over. Dad will be at work, and Mom will smile and point to breakfast on the table—bacon and grits and orange juice. Then it's off to Normal Elementary School. Just another day, same as before.

Jimmy's door creaks open across the hall. *Bad move.* My brother, only four years old, pads his way across the upstairs landing. I know what he'll do, what he always does: jump between them and beg them to stop. As if that ever did any good. All it will land him is a sharp thump on the rear from Dad.

Should I try to stop Jimmy? That usually doesn't work, although sometimes he'll crawl in bed with me and go back to sleep. I lie there for a second, considering. It'll be really cold if I get out of bed. Jimmy might not mind me. Then Dad will get all red in the face at both of us when he spots us on the stairs. I think of his belt.

Reluctantly, I throw back the comforter. I'd rather get whooped with Jimmy than lie in bed and do nothing. I'm not a great sister, but

I'm the oldest, and certain things are expected. I hurry to my bedroom door. The moment of hesitation has cost me. Jimmy has already made it to the bottom of the stairs. A great wail resounds through our house.

"Moooommy!" he screams.

There's something about that scream. It chills me all the way inside, so deep my tummy hurts. Something is really, really, *really* bad. My mouth dries, and I can't move, can't make myself walk down the seven steps and see whatever Jimmy sees.

Another scream—but this time, it's Mom. Moaning rumbles through my chest, and I stand rooted. I press my fingers in my ears, but I can't completely block the screams.

The police! The answer flashes in my brain like lightning. Dad will be super mad, but I have to stop this. I race to Mom and Dad's bedroom and dial 911 on the phone by their bed, just like I've been taught in school. I tell them to come. To hurry. I give them the address, my name, my parents' and brother's names.

The screaming stops. It's over! The nice lady on the phone asks if I want to talk to her until the police come. I want to so badly. But if Dad comes up here and finds me on the phone . . . "No," I tell her, hanging up. I'll jump back in bed and get under the covers. I leave their bedroom, then pause at the top of the stairs. Listening. Waiting.

The dead silence begins to frighten me as much as the screams had done. Did they all go outside? But why would they? A footstep echoes on the hardwood floors below. A faint tinkling of bells cuts the silence.

I ease down the wooden steps, avoiding the spots that creak the loudest. The den's overhead light is on, and I see a man is dressed all in black, including gloves and a ski mask. His back is toward me, and he's scooping something up from the floor. This doesn't make sense. Is it Daddy? If so, why is he dressed like a Halloween monster?

And then I see them. Mom. Jimmy. On the floor, not moving. Dark red seeps from their bodies, forming huge pools of crimson. The same shade of red is splattered on the back wall. Like the weird paintings we've seen in art class. Abstracts, Mrs. Moody called them. The blood seeps into the rug in ever-widening arcs. An endless red-on-red-on-red that blinds me. I feel dizzy, and a trembling seizes my body. I can't look away from the blazing liquid. I know it's blood, but my brain is slow and thick and doesn't want to accept what that means. More wails break through the night. With a start, I realize they are coming from me. The man in black stiffens and begins to turn his head.

Danger! My brain finally catches on, and my body leaps to action. I race back up the stairs and to my room. Footsteps pound behind me. I slam my bedroom door shut and turn the lock. Maybe he'll go away now. I strain my ears, hoping to hear a police siren. The monster slams a fist on the door. Over and over. The cheap pressed wood splinters and cracks. Soon, he'll explode through the flimsy door. There is no one to save me but me.

I grab my Hello Kitty comforter and fumble with the window sash. The cracking behind me grows louder, and I dare not look back. I fling the window open and then punch at the screen until it breaks and pops off. The winter air is bitter and cold, a slap against my face. One of the few Alabama nights that will hit freezing.

He's almost broken through the door. If it's Daddy, it's a scarier, meaner version of him than I've ever seen and that I want no part of. I don't even hesitate as I climb out the open window and stare at the second-story drop-off to the frosty ground below. I jump.

A freefall of air, and then thump, I land on my right side, my ankle twisted beneath me. Pain burns and travels up my bare leg. My gaze rises to the window. The monster leans out over the sill, backlit by my bedroom light. He's staring down, searching, then seems to look straight at me, although it's too dark, and he's too far away for me to know for sure. He suddenly disappears, and I cry in relief . . . until moments later, when the back door swings open.

I scramble to my feet and limp toward the rear of the property. The wooden tree house looms before me, as though offering a safe hideaway.

But no, that would be too obvious. I keep running, my bare feet slick on the frost, and I feel like I'm half running, half skating to the tree line.

Tears ice my cheeks and the front of my neck. Another look back, and I see the man headed toward me. Moonbeams flash on something silver in his gloved hand. He'll never stop chasing me. I choke back sobs and run past the first copse of pines. The woods are scary, but that man scares me even more. I body-slam fully into the trees, and branches slap and claw into every inch of my chilled skin. I might as well be naked for all the warmth of my flimsy pink nightie.

Can't think about that now. Keep moving.

Dead leaves and twigs snap and crunch from behind. I blindly press forward, lost and confused. All I know to do is to keep going.

I'm tired, so very tired. There's a stitch in my side I can no longer ignore, and my right foot burns with pain. I lean against rough bark and pitch forward, clutching my tummy. My lungs are on fire, and my breaths form little puffs of smoke.

Where is he?

I try to breathe more quietly and focus. I hear nothing. I'm going to rest now. I violently shiver and then realize I'm still clutching my comforter. Quickly, I throw it over my shoulders and sink to the ground. I stare up at the crescent moon and wait. I shut my eyes and again press my fingers in my ears. I can't run anymore. If he spots me, if he's still out there in the darkness, then I don't want to hear and see him the moment he catches me.

Darkness settles on me, as thick and heavy as the comforter. All I hear is the blood pounding in my ears. Beneath my eyelids, red explodes—an ocean of hot crimson that threatens to drag me under and suffocate the air in my lungs.

The unexpected scent of smoke fills my nose and mouth. My eyes pop open, and I stumble to my feet, leaning against the tree to keep the weight off my right ankle. Orange and red flames shoot up in the air like the firecrackers we watch every year after the Fourth of July parade downtown. It takes me a minute to realize it's our house burning. The sky is scorched with the blaze.

I can never go back now. Not ever. Nothing is left of my old life. Mom. Jimmy. Dad? All gone. My mind floods with images of red—the fire and the blood that destroyed my world.

Chapter 1

DELLA STALLINGS

Eighteen Years Later

The graveyard shift at Normal Community Hospital held a lulling quiet, yet underneath, it thrummed with a taut pulse from a skeleton staff and over 200 patients. A quick glance at my monitor showed that we currently housed 232 patients, of which 97 were in the residential substance abuse program. Another 38 unfortunate souls were in the psychiatric ward. The rest of the population suffered from various diseases and emergencies of a physical nature.

If it were up to me, I'd choose physical over mental suffering any day. Those with physical problems were treated and released with relatively short stays. But those with mental health issues took much, much longer to heal. Of course, in both cases, the diseases could be chronic or fatal.

I shrugged off my musings and checked the time: 3:18 a.m., which left me nearly two hours to kill before my shift ended. Now that my work in-box was clear, I leaned back in my chair and stared up at the polystyrene-tiled ceiling, pleased with the familiar certainty of its monotonous square grid. I loosened my eyes' focus and allowed the random textured pockmarks of the tile to form patterns that rendered unique and strange faces that stared back down at me.

It had been a good night so far. No accidental run-ins with people, which was mostly the whole point of my choosing to work such odd hours at the medical data-entry job. The Human Resources manager was a kindly older lady who had once worked with my mother at this hospital and was willing to accommodate the peculiarity of Mary Stallings's only surviving child.

Out of my purse, I dug the plastic baggie that held the lotion I'd made for Libbie Andrews, a nurse who worked in the cardiac unit. I'd say she was my friend, but that was claiming too close a relationship. To put it another way, she was one of the few people whose company I could tolerate. As a nurse, her hands were often chapped from constant handwashing, and my lotion helped ease the red soreness. A faint scent of chamomile wafted from the bag, a welcome change from the hospital's undernote smell of bleach and formaldehyde. I wrote Libbie's name on a sticky note and attached it to the bag. With any luck, neither she nor any other employee would be seated at the nurse's station when I dropped it off.

I peeked out my office door before venturing out. The coast appeared clear, so I walked down the long, deserted hallway slick with wax. My ears buzzed with the background hum of machinery. Occasionally, a ping resounded from elevator doors opening and shutting.

I'd been here before during the day, when the place was electric with people rushing about. And as comforting as it was for me to operate in the lonely dark hours, there was also something a little creepy in the atmosphere. The redbrick building had once accommodated nearly a thousand patients in its heyday as a regional hub for veterans' services. Over the years, funding had slowly shrunk until the county had finally taken it over and extended services to the general public. Only the substance abuse and psychiatric beds were still used much by veterans.

This left lots of empty rooms with old signage, such as the now-defunct tuberculosis ward and smallpox quarters.

Despite upgrades and the pristine cleanliness in which the hospital was maintained, there was no denying that it was old, old, old. Aunt Sylvie would say it was haunted by the ghosts of its former occupants. I didn't believe in that nonsense, but I also didn't rule out the notion that the place might hold an energy from contained memories of misery.

Just as I rounded the corner by the elevators, one of them sounded a familiar ping that warned someone approached. Probably a janitor or one of the lab techs. I quickly slipped into the stairwell before the elevator door opened. The concrete stairs were steep but sturdy. Muted light cast eerie shadows on the walls. Like everywhere else in the hospital, there was a timeworn solidity in the structure. Ugly, serviceable, and clean.

As was my custom, I pumped my legs and began running up the four flights. My legs hardly burned anymore, thanks to this regimen and my private martial arts classes. Only my right ankle twinged, more uncomfortable than painful. The ligaments had never properly healed from the window fall when I was eight, leaving me with an almost unnoticeable limp.

Physical fitness was one of the few areas of my life where I maintained discipline. You never knew when you might need to outrun somebody, so you might as well be prepared to give yourself a fighting chance. Aunt Sylvie would have preferred I'd chosen some new age practice like yoga, but even when I'd first arrived at her home as a scared and scarred little girl, I'd been insistent on learning self-defense.

Three and a half floors up, I was caught by surprise at the sound of heavy footsteps descending. I lifted my gaze from the gray concrete stairs and spotted a pair of hot-pink, glittery sneakers. My head jerked up, and I stared straight into cat-green eyes shot through with a yellow starburst around the pupils. Those startling eyes were wide and stricken. The woman appeared about my age or slightly younger and as equally surprised as I was at the sudden encounter. Her shoulder-length brown hair was messy and highlighted with Kool-Aid shades of pink and purple.

Was she a late-night visitor? A mental health patient who'd slipped out of the ward? Occasionally, over the past six years at my job, I'd spotted a handful of the substance abuse residents sneaking out for a cigarette or alcohol—or stronger mood enhancers. I'd never run into a patient who'd managed to slip out of the psychiatric lockdown unit, but there was always a first. I slid my thumb along the edge of the cell phone gripped in my right hand, prepared to call security.

"Uh, hi there," she said uneasily, her voice pitched high and brittle. It rang with a false note of forced cheeriness.

My bullshit meter was fully activated.

"Didn't expect to run into anyone in the stairwell." She gave an uneasy chuckle and glanced over her shoulder.

"Running from someone?" I asked, giving her a wide berth as I reached the fourth-floor landing.

"What? No, of course not." Another forced laugh, and she eyed me warily.

I had the impression that she viewed me as a threat more than I did her. My heart, which had been hammering painfully in my ribs, began to slow its wild, erratic beat.

"I was just here visiting a friend," she offered brightly.

"This time of night?"

The cat eyes hardened, and she squinted at my name tag. "You're not security, are you?"

"No, but I can have them here in two seconds."

"Don't bother. I'm leaving."

I hesitated, then pressed the speed-dial button for a hospital security officer. The hardness in her eyes vanished, replaced by an expression of fear and pleading. "Please," she whispered, digging in her jean pocket and producing a rumpled pack of cigarettes. "I'm in the drug program and just wanted a little privacy and a smoke."

Oh, hell. What was the big deal if a patient sneaked out after hours for a smoke? Why should I get her in trouble with her counselors? Besides, I felt like a joke to the security guards. I'd made the mistake of reporting to them that I'd caught glimpses of a disturbing presence here at night—a man who furtively ducked away as I rounded a corner, a man who drifted about in the shadows and watched me from afar. They'd been skeptical yet polite at first. But the last time I'd spoken with them, I'd heard the head of security, David Nelson, say *kur-a-zee* the moment I'd left the room. My ears still burned from their snorts of laughter.

"Security," a deep voice boomed in my ear.

"Never mind. Wrong number."

She offered a relieved smile and skittered away, evidently worried that I might change my mind. I sighed and disconnected the call. Had I done the right thing? Uneasiness rumbled through my gut, and I squared my shoulders. Who did I think I was—the hall monitor in elementary school? Not my job to catch misbehaving mental patients. Normal Community Hospital—I nearly laughed at the name's irony— barely paid me a notch above minimum wage to enter patient data and billing codes in their computer system.

Still, I felt edgy as I continued on my foolish errand of playing Hand Cream Fairy for Libbie. That was what you got for becoming even a fraction involved with other people—messy emotions of guilt and confusion. All I really wanted was to be left alone—unseen, moving invisibly through life, with as few complications as possible.

I exited the stairwell and entered the cardiac unit. I kept my gaze focused on the ground, determined not to see into the open doors of patients' rooms, where I would catch sight of IVs and blinking red buttons on medical monitors.

At least luck was finally on my side. The nurses' station was deserted. Quickly, I left the cream on the counter with a note for Libbie and returned to the stairwell, which, mercifully, also appeared forsaken. Once back in my little cubbyhole of an office, I pulled up my favorite history website to pass the time, but even that failed to entirely distract me from the mild agitation remaining from my encounter. Finally, five o'clock rolled around. I powered down the computer and collected my purse. Time to get home.

But no—I groaned, remembering that I'd promised Aunt Sylvie I'd pick up groceries. She'd offered to do it herself, as usual, but I knew she was behind on filling her craft orders. I didn't like being a total burden on her. It wouldn't be fun, but I could handle the occasional chore in the real world.

Or so I lied to myself. By the time I turned onto the dirt road leading home, my limbs felt drained and my mind was clogged with near panic. Hints of coral streaked through the clouds, and I eyed the potential danger. Another twenty minutes or so, and the sky might lighten to a menacing crimson as the sun rose. I grabbed both sacks of groceries from the back seat of my old blue sedan and hurried to the house.

Wafts of cinnamon and sage scents greeted me as I opened the door. This meant Aunt Sylvie was in the midst of a cleansing. Someone had gotten under her skin.

"Can you believe the nerve of that man? After all these years?"

Her voice drifted from the den, and I raised a brow at her when she whirled around to see who had entered. She held a smoking sage stick in one hand, twirling it like a baton. As I suspected, she wasn't on the phone but rather was directing her questions at the ancestral altar. All seven purple LED candles on the fireplace mantel were lit. Framed photos of family who had passed away were interspersed among the battery-operated candles, along with a couple of angel bells and a discreet sprinkling of graveyard dirt from our family's designated cemetery plot.

Over the years, I'd grown accustomed to my aunt's unusual customs—a strange brew of hoodoo, hillbilly conjuring, and who-knew-what-else. They no longer fazed me. But who'd had the audacity to get her so riled, so early in the morning?

"Problem?" I asked.

She smothered the sage stick in an abalone shell, then fiddled with the chunky jade mala bracelet encircling her wrist.

Now I was really worried. Her style was usually direct and to the point. Unlike me, she tackled problems head-on with a confidence I envied.

"Big-time problem," she admitted with a sigh, walking to the mantel and ringing one of the bells to signal the end of her cleansing ritual.

The light plink of the bells never failed to shoot a bittersweet jolt in my chest. The angel bells had once been part of my mother's collection. Mom liked to believe their ring called in angels. "What's the problem?" I asked, but I immediately sensed where the trouble lay. Dear old Dad, per usual.

"Let's put up the groceries first and then sit down to talk about it."

If I were one to believe in the metaphysical, I'd say this day was cursed.

She relieved me of one of the grocery bags, and I followed her into the kitchen. Sylvie began unpacking and opened the fridge to store the milk and yogurt. I put up the bread and canned goods, the knot of dread in my stomach growing heavier.

"I'll make us a cup of jasmine tea before we talk," she said, switching on the stove burner under the teakettle.

"I don't want one."

"Well, I certainly do."

I sat at the kitchen table and watched as she prepared our tea. Her long silver hair—witchlike, I'd always thought—gleamed under the overhead light. It was her most striking feature, the first thing people noticed. It wasn't the coarse salt-and-pepper gray of many women her age. Sylvie's hair was a thick curtain of clear gray only a hue deeper than snow white.

When I'd first come to live with her, her hair had mesmerized me. She'd read me fairy tales in bed, and I'd tentatively stroked the silky tresses, not paying attention to the words. All that had mattered was that she made me feel safe. There, in the lamplight's glow, as I'd lain in bed under a homemade quilt, she'd made me believe everything would be okay. That no bad man would dare enter our peaceful haven. And that had been more astounding than any fairy tale.

Sylvie placed two cups of steaming tea on the table and sat across from me. Her fingers curled around a cup, absorbing the warmth. Three improbable words tumbled from her mouth: "Your father's out."

I blinked. "Out?" I repeated stupidly.

"They released him from Holman Prison yesterday afternoon."

"But . . . but . . ." I had been warned this was inevitable. The town, even the entire state, had been awash with the scintillating news that a death row inmate was about to be released by the court. My thoughts tumbled round and round, and I couldn't sort one from another.

"We've known it was a possibility for several weeks now," Sylvie said gently. "Some part of me didn't believe the state would actually go through with it. Certainly not with this speed. But I was wrong."

Good thing I was sitting down, because it felt like the world was spinning out of its predictable orbit. I dug my fingers into my scalp and pulled at my hair. "I can't believe this is happening."

Sylvie patted my hand, her eyes warm with sympathy. "We can thank Brady Eckeridge for this mess. Talk about a dirty cop. The man did it all. Witness intimidation and withholding of critical evidence in over a dozen cases. And since your father's case was circumstantial to begin with—"

"He's guilty," I insisted flatly. "I don't care if that cop was dirty or not."

"You know I'm no fan of Hunter Stallings, but his attorneys made a compelling case. After all, hon, they now have that security footage that proves he wasn't there at the time of the murders. Eckeridge should never have withheld the evidence."

My teeth ground together, and I fought the impulse to slam my fist on the table. None of this was Sylvie's fault. "I don't give a damn about the footage," I said tightly. "Dad found a way around those security cameras. Either that, or he paid someone to kill Mom and Jimmy while he spent the night with his girlfriend."

Sylvie cocked her head to the side and drummed her fingers against the table. "Maybe it's time to face the facts."

I started to object, but she held up a hand before I could utter a word.

"First of all, his car was parked at that woman's trailer park, and he didn't return to his vehicle until after the murders had taken place. Second, Carolyn Merton recanted her testimony and now claims your dad was with her during that same time frame."

"You can't be saying that . . . that you think Dad's not guilty. Are you?" I stared at my aunt in horror. Her argument felt like a betrayal. Had all the buzz around police corruption in the case changed her mind?

Sylvie's lips pursed in a tight line. "Honestly, I don't know what to think anymore. It would be easy for me to discount anything that liar Carolyn says. Could be she just wants to be the center of attention by jumping on the bandwagon and claiming Eckeridge forced her to give false testimony. But I have to admit, the tapes do give me pause."

I jumped to my feet and paced the tiny kitchen. "That woman's lying *now*, not way back then. Dad's gotten to her. Convinced her to recant her testimony. I just know it."

Sylvie arched a brow. "And the tapes?"

"That grainy tape is practically useless," I scoffed. "And it's just one camera at the entrance. Dad could have left the area on foot, avoiding the entrance, and then gone to a nearby parked car. Or he might have left a borrowed car in the trailer park earlier in the day."

"Nobody's ever come forward saying they loaned Hunter a vehicle."

"Of course they haven't. Would you? No, he's guilty."

I lifted my chin and glared at her defiantly. As a child, I'd tried to convince myself that he couldn't have done it. But Dad's callous treatment of me over the years had gradually eroded my faith, and I'd come to accept the truth. Nothing would change my mind now. Who else could have been the killer but Dad? All the circumstantial evidence had pointed his way. And no one else had had the motive that he had.

Sylvie lifted her teacup with trembling hands. Hot tea sloshed out into the saucer, so she set it back down. "Guilty or not, it doesn't matter. I won't let him hurt you."

Her face was flushed, and tears shimmered in her blazing eyes. "I'm going to talk to the district attorney about all this. See if we can get a restraining order to keep him away from you."

"Doubt that's necessary. He'll probably avoid me." I drew in a rush of air. I hadn't seen Dad since I was ten years old. Prison visits had been too hard, too stressful, and too confusing. I'd return home from them with long crying jags and nightmares. Sylvie, never wild about the idea of visitation to begin with, had decreed them traumatic and a hindrance to my healing. We'd stopped making the five-hour trek to south Alabama after less than a handful of awkward meetings. Can't say I hadn't been relieved about her decision, either.

Sitting in the crowded prison visiting yard with other families, struggling to find something to say to Dad, had been an ordeal. The yard had been set between two wings of dormitories. Old picnic tables painted white had been crammed into the small area. In the summers, it had been miserably sticky and hot, while in the winters, the cold and damp had seeped into my bones. There'd been no TV or distraction of any kind. Only me, Dad, and a silent Aunt Sylvie sitting on a picnic bench, her back ramrod stiff, seething with silent recriminations.

Surrounding us, other prison kids had run about screaming and playing while their parents sat with shell-shocked expressions. *How did we get here? How did our lives lead to this dreary place?* Occasionally, one of the roaming guards would chastise an overly amorous couple. As for me, I'd always been transfixed watching the tower guard walk the concrete patch up high, shotgun at the ready. In my ten-year-old mind, I'd been convinced that he'd shoot me once visitation had ended and we'd walked to the parking lot behind the tower. After all, I was the daughter of a murderer and the sole survivor of that bloody night. I'd had to be guilty of something terrible, no different than the inmates behind the razor wire fence.

An arm, heavy and warm, draped across my shoulders, and I was startled from my reverie. "Don't worry, Della. You don't have to see him."

I recalled her words as I'd entered the house. *I can't believe the nerve of that man.* "Have you spoken with him?" I asked sharply.

"He dropped by less than thirty minutes ago looking for you."

I reeled at the news. Dad? Here? If I hadn't stopped by the grocery store, I'd have run smack into him. I wasn't sure whether I was relieved or disappointed that we hadn't crossed paths.

"I told him to take a hike," Sylvie continued. "I made it clear that we didn't want to see him and that he wasn't welcome in our house."

A tiny burst of annoyance flared within. She could have at least checked with me before making such a final pronouncement. "How did Dad take it?"

Sylvie's jaw clenched. "Not well. Claimed you were his daughter and he had a right to see you. I told him he lost that right long ago. He's a horrible man. I'll never forgive him for the way he treated Mary and Jimmy and you. If only she'd filed for divorce earlier. Maybe none of this would have happened. That night . . . all that blood . . ." She broke off, unable to say more.

I recoiled at the mention of Mom's and Jimmy's murders, at the involuntary memory flash of our living room awash in blood, the hooded man brandishing a knife. The screams. An odd whimpering echoed in the kitchen, and I was startled to realize that it had originated from deep in my own throat, much as it had that night eighteen years ago.

"He can't hurt you anymore, love," Aunt Sylvie whispered in my ear. "It's okay. You're safe."

I cleared my throat. "Right. I know that." I turned away, needing to be alone, when a sudden thought struck. "Wait a minute. How did he get here? Does he have a car? Is he driving?"

"Vic drove him. Stayed in his truck the whole time Hunter was on the porch talking to me." Sylvie's lips twisted in a smirk. "Wouldn't want to enter the heathen's den of iniquity, you know."

"Right. Wonder how he feels about Dad's release?" I mused aloud. They were brothers but had never seemed particularly close, even though they'd lived less than a mile apart.

"I bet Vic and Mabel aren't too thrilled with his release either. Hunter will bum off them as long as they'll let him."

Did Uncle Vic mind being his brother's keeper? I had no clue—the man was a mystery to me. He farmed cotton and soybeans about twenty miles outside of Normal and only came into town on Sundays, when he served as a deacon at the First Baptist Church. He was a tall man, taciturn and hardworking, and I imagined his life was mostly driven by a rigid sense of Christian duty. I'd never seen him smile. His wife, Mabel, was a miniature version of him—always busy, heavily involved with the church, and equally reserved in manner. They'd offered their home to me after Mom had died and Dad had been sent away, but there'd been no warmth in their overture. I tried to imagine how different my life would be if I'd been raised on their farm. Much lonelier, I'm sure. But I could hardly fault them for their stern dispositions and isolated lives. I was pretty much the definition of standoffish behavior, and few were ever permitted to enter my world past the barriers I'd erected.

Either I had inherited Vic's personality, or that murderous night had stifled my emotional growth. It was one of the many questions I'd never have an answer to. Perhaps it was best that I didn't.

Chapter 2

DELLA

A riot of vermilion scorched my eyes every time my lids shut, brilliant cherry and scarlet swaths licking the darkness of my mind. I'd tried to sleep for hours but given it up. There was only one cure for my burning turmoil. Decision made, I hurriedly showered, dressed for work, and made a sandwich for dinner. I'd eat it on the way.

I donned dark sunglasses and climbed in my jalopy, depositing my sandwich and a thermos of coffee on the passenger seat. I'd need every drop of that caffeine to keep fueled during my night shift.

Main Street downtown was thick with people getting off work from specialty retail stores and others entering restaurants and bars. Luck was with me—I drove past the first two traffic signals shining green. One more and I'd be off scot-free without having to face a red glare boring into my skull. Cars and humans thinned as I neared the end of the strip.

The last traffic signal flashed yellow, and I accelerated. Still, my blue sedan shot through the intersection a good two seconds after the light changed to red. There was a squeal of brakes and the blare of a horn to my left. I flipped the driver a finger and kept going, breathing easier as I pulled onto the two-lane county road. Modestly sized brick houses dotted fields of corn and soybeans. Small buds of cotton were beginning to pop open. By Halloween, the grounds would be flooded with the white blossoms that I thought of as Alabama snow.

I quickly passed through a succession of small communities—Society Hill, Chicamagwa, and Tillman's Crossing—before hitting the slightly larger township of Hartsville, which sported a laundromat, a dive bar, a hamburger joint, a feed-and-seed store, and three churches. Long ago, Uncle Vic had suffered a falling-out with Hartsville Baptist—something to do with a new pastor who'd leaned toward a kinder, gentler New Testament teaching rather than the fire-and-brimstone sermons Uncle Vic had grown up on. For the last two decades, he drove past it every Sunday in favor of the Normal First Baptist Church, which stuck to the King James Bible and fiery warnings of hell—which, in his mind, every good Christian knew was the only correct way to practice his faith.

I hadn't driven out this way for months, but nothing seemed to have changed. A mile past the Hartsville town limits, I turned right onto the dirt road by the ancient oak whose giant limbs extended almost as far as a football field. The boughs sank all the way to the ground under their heavy weight.

The only change I noted was that the road ruts were a bit more frequent and deeper. Not far in, I spotted my uncle's home. Self-reliant man that he was, he'd built the sprawling homestead with his own hands. The place appeared serviceable, and that was the kindest description I could grant it. The house lacked imagination and charm, with its plain wooden exterior and small windows. I'd managed to put Dad out of my mind on the drive over, but now my heart pummeled wildly at the thought of facing him.

Coming here was the best way to do this, I reminded myself. Otherwise, I'd have no peace at home or work, always expecting him to show up at the oddest moment. Plus, in coming to Dad, I could hear him out and then be free to hop in my car and leave the second I wanted. An easy escape plan—and I always strategized an exit contingency.

I pulled into the driveway and then cut the engine, collecting my breath. It wasn't like I had much to say, if anything. Once Dad said his piece, I'd tell him goodbye and that I wanted no further contact with him. Even visiting today felt like a betrayal to Mom and Jimmy. And if Aunt Sylvie knew I'd voluntarily come out here on my own, she'd have a stroke.

The front door opened, and a small bit of a woman emerged, carrying a large bag of trash. She stepped off the porch and then came to a halt, eyeing my car with surprise.

I climbed out of the sedan, jingling my keys in my palm. "Hello, Aunt Mabel," I called out.

"Della? Didn't expect to find you just sitting out here." There was no welcoming smile on her face—not that I expected one. She always seemed faintly disapproving of me for no reason I could fathom.

"I'm here to see Dad. He knows I'm coming. I'm a few minutes early."

Mabel regarded me soberly before nodding. Without a word, she strode to the side of the house and dumped the trash in the garbage can. I hugged my arms and waited, not sure whether I should knock on the door or wait outside while she delivered Dad a message.

"Come on in," she said shortly, not even glancing at me as she climbed the porch steps. My lips twitched in nervous amusement as I recalled learning that the name Mabel came from the Latin word for *loveable*. I couldn't think of a more ironic moniker for my aunt. She was the type of person who, had she been a mother, would have relied more on punishment than nurturance in her children's upbringing.

I followed her in and cringed at the sound of dogs growling and barking. I stiffened and backed up against the wall, awaiting death by Doberman. I'd forgotten all about their pack of damn dogs. They'd trained them to be aggressive, and what little affection I'd ever seen flicker across the couple's faces had always been directed at the pack. As my uncle and aunt were childless, these animals were the center of their attention.

Two dogs rounded the corner of the den and started up the hallway. Mabel ignored them and disappeared into the kitchen. "Down, Adley," Uncle Vic's deep voice commanded from the bowels of the house. A loud clap of hands and snap of fingers ensued. "Shep. All of you. Get down. Now."

The clatter of dog toenails on hardwood stopped, but a disturbing rumble of protest remained. The two dogs in the hallway dropped to their bellies, baring their fangs and emitting low growls. I hated these new dogs as much as I had their predecessors as a child.

Uncle Vic appeared and came to an abrupt halt at the sight of me. He rubbed his beard, then called over his shoulder, "Hunter! Della's here."

We regarded one another soberly.

"Well, come on, then," he said gruffly. "Might as well have a seat."

Not the most gracious offer I'd ever heard, but I followed him into the den.

I couldn't tell that the place had changed at all over the years but for the TV, which was now one of those large-screen affairs that hung over the fireplace mantel. It was the one obvious indulgence in an otherwise drab room lined with dark plywood paneling and furnished in earth tones. I knew Uncle Vic must have purchased the set to watch the Crimson Tide. Football games were the only times when he ever showed much emotion.

I settled onto the geriatric sofa, whose leather cushions were worn white in the center. Uncle Vic evicted all five dogs from the den while I eyed the front and back doors, checking out potential exit routes. A door closed down the hallway, and Uncle Vic returned to the den, plopping into his recliner. Awkward silence weighted the room, which stank of dogs and boiled cabbage. Rattling pans sounded from the kitchen, managing to convey annoyance with each clang. I itched to leave as much as Mabel wanted me gone.

"How've ya been?" he asked at length.

"Fine."

Uncle Vic didn't attempt to further engage me in conversation. I shrugged and crossed my legs. My right foot twitched violently, and I clenched my jaws as I forced my body still. From somewhere deep in the house, a toilet flushed.

We both sat with our eyes glued to the TV and waited. Doubt assailed me. Had I done the right thing in coming here? Was it a betrayal to Mom and Jimmy?

"There's my girl!" Hunter entered the den, grinning widely and wolfishly, his voice too loud and forced in the small room. His familiar confidence had returned, evident in the expansive set of his shoulders and the proud lift of his chin. No more of that gray-white head-to-toe inmate garb stamped Alabama Department of Corrections #186409. No more downtrodden slump of his shoulders and furtive glances at guards. Hunter Eugene Stallings, a man to be reckoned with, was free.

I didn't return his smile. "You wanted to see me?"

He turned up the smile wattage and strode toward me, arms extended for a hug. I stiffened my back into the worn sofa and made no move to stand. As though not picking up on my physical withdrawal, Dad stepped in front of me and held out a hand. "I've missed you, Delly-girl."

Inwardly, I winced at his old nickname for me. I debated not accepting his overture but decided to play polite. Keep it light, quick, and as painless as possible, then get the hell out of Dodge. Uncle Vic slipped out of the room as I reluctantly shook Dad's hand. The hand that had repeatedly stabbed my mother and brother to death.

Or could he really be innocent? If the legal system entertained doubt about his guilt, shouldn't I afford him that same mercy? No! Only one minute in his company, and I was falling for the phony-baloney charm of an ex-con.

"Must feel good to be out," I offered stiffly.

He clapped his hands together and rubbed them. "Excellent, excellent. Let's step outside and talk." Without waiting for agreement, he clasped my arm and pulled me up from the sofa. "This way." He snatched a lighter from the mantel and strode to the back door.

I was only too glad to get away from the howling dogs, the stink of cabbage, and the ears of Vic and Mabel. I pictured them on the other side of the kitchen door, straining to hear the father-daughter reunion.

Dad sat on the porch swing and patted the seat beside him, flashing his salesman-white toothy grin. It was unnatural. Those teeth should be yellowed and stained with tobacco.

"No, thanks. I'll stand," I said, then leaned against the wooden deck railing and waited. Despite the lateness of the day, humidity still permeated the September air. I'd be sweaty underneath my shirt the whole shift, not that I guess it mattered. There were no coworkers to offend.

Dad set down the lighter he'd swiped from the mantel, pulled a cigar from his shirt pocket, and unwrapped it. Nasty habit. "How can you afford them?" I asked.

"These?" He twirled the Arturo Fuente before clipping the end. "Vic's loaned me a little money until I get a job. Get back on my feet."

"Uh-huh." Vic would never get his hands on that money again. But he knew Dad as well as anybody, knew that loaning money to him was a high-risk proposition.

"You've grown into a beautiful young lady, Della."

I shifted from one foot to another, uncomfortable with the compliment. I was no great beauty. Short, skinny, a chin that jutted forward a fraction too far, muted brown hair, and eyes a tad too wide set. I was completely average, right down to the smattering of freckles across my nose.

"You have your mother's eyes," he continued, either oblivious to my discomfort or uncaring about my feelings. "Same unusual leaf-green color."

I crossed my arms and felt my lips pinch together into a tight line. "What do you want?" I asked bluntly.

He flicked the lighter, and a small flame ignited. I looked away.

"Don't want anything from you," he claimed, a faint note of hurt in his tone.

I snickered and faced him. "Sure you do. From the time I started collecting babysitting money at thirteen, you'd write asking me to send you some."

"Just a few bucks to buy the occasional smoke from the canteen." He glanced briefly at his watch. "Didn't think you'd mind."

Of course I'd minded. But like a dork, I'd mailed him most of my hard-earned money until Aunt Sylvie had discovered what I'd been doing and put a stop to it. He inhaled on the cigar, and I couldn't help staring at the glowing tip.

"Look, I'm sorry I couldn't be there for you," he continued. "Not like I wanted to be in prison. It was hard serving time knowing that I was innocent while the real killer still roamed free." He took another drag on the cigar, and the fiery tip flared aggressively. "You could have visited more," he chastised. "It was lonely for me in there."

Terrific, Dad. Way to turn the whole situation around and blame me for our estrangement. I refused to let him sucker me into misplaced guilt. He might be able to sweet-talk his brother and sister-in-law, but I wasn't so weak and gullible.

"Why did they let you out?" I asked abruptly, wanting to hear his version of events.

"Haven't you been watching the news? If nothing else, Sylvie must have filled you in." Dad's polished charm loosened, and his lips twisted in a grimace. Antagonism hardened his boyish face. In spite of his age and prison stint, Dad still managed to look like a professional golf pro who'd be more at ease mingling at a country club than making license plates at a maximum-security penitentiary.

I said nothing and waited.

"For once, the State of Alabama got something right. That dirty cop always had it in for me."

"Why do you say that?"

"Brady Eckeridge was a former client."

Dad didn't elaborate, but there was no need. Two months before the murders, he'd been caught in a major flimflam operation. As an insurance underwriter, he'd pocketed people's premiums instead of forwarding their money on to the insurance companies for the policies they thought they'd been purchasing. Eventually, of course, it'd all caught up to him, and the house of cards had come tumbling down with surprising rapidity.

"So this cop was one of the ones you'd ripped off," I noted flatly.

Dad raised his arms in an exasperated gesture. "I'd intended to pay Brady back for the tornado damage to his roof, but he didn't give me a chance to make things right."

"Guy's a cop," I pointed out in disgust. "What did you expect?"

"Simple human courtesy."

His outraged indignation was laughable, but I found little humor in the situation. Stupidity, yes, in spades, but levity, not a single peep. Bad enough that I'd grown up with the stigma of having my dad in prison for murder, but to top it off, many of his former customers still hated the man and mistrusted me as his daughter. Hardly fair, but if the tables were turned, I'd probably be equally as suspicious of them.

"So you're saying the cop framed you out of spite."

"Not just spite." He took another long draw of the cigar and again glanced at his watch. "I'm not the only one he helped get falsely imprisoned. Eckeridge is one of those cops who thinks he can play judge and jury. Man has a real God complex. If he decides a person's guilty, he doesn't mind manufacturing evidence and tampering with witnesses."

The hand by his side tightened into a fist, knuckles whitening with suppressed fury.

But maybe this time, his anger was justified. He'd spent nearly two decades locked up for a crime based on lies and suppressed evidence. Despite my resolve to only hear Dad out and tell him to stay out of my life, an unexpected stab of sympathy knifed my guts.

Like any good con man, Dad seemed to sense my softening. "I didn't do it, Della." Tears filmed his eyes, and he leaned forward. "Do you really think I'd kill my own son and wife and then come after you?"

My lungs seized, and I couldn't breathe, couldn't speak. What if . . . what if he was telling the truth? I'd been so sure for so long that he'd done it. And now the very foundation of my belief was thrown into a hurricane of doubt.

"I . . . I don't know what to think," I admitted.

"Whoever you saw that night—I promise you, baby, it wasn't me. Surely you realize that now."

Did I? I pictured the masked man turning to stare at me, the bloody knife raised high, and then the sound of his footsteps as he gave chase. I stared at the stranger before me with his beguiling, clear-eyed expression. Hard to reconcile the two images. But that's how killers operated, right? The good ones, anyway. They knew how to erect respectable facades to mask their inner rage.

"Think, Della," he urged. "Wasn't the man you saw a different build than me? Maybe different colored eyes? There must be something."

I shook my head and hugged my arms close to my chest. "No. I don't know. Maybe. I can't remember."

"You *have* to remember. Please. For my sake."

"Your girlfriend might have changed her testimony for you, but not me. I told the police everything I knew years ago. Besides, you've already been released. You're a free man. What I believe doesn't matter."

"Of course it matters, sweetheart. I'm suing the state for false imprisonment. My lawyer says having you at the civil trial could be the deciding factor in swaying the jury, not to mention getting a large settlement." He levered himself out of the swing, tossed his cigar over the railing, and walked toward me with a tender smile, arms outstretched. "Can I count on you, Delly-girl?"

His words were a douse of cold water on my momentary sympathy. I jabbed a finger in his direction. "And *that*, ladies and gentlemen, is the real reason why my father came to see me this morning," I said to an imaginary audience. "It's all about what *I* can do for *him*."

He dropped his hands to his sides, and the corners of his mouth turned down in hurt disappointment. But was it an act? *Stop it. Of course it's an act. He's trying to worm his way back into your life just to use you.*

"At least think about it," he insisted.

Tell him what he wants and get the hell out of here. "Sure," I said, not quite meeting his eyes. I swept past him. It would be easier to walk around the backyard to the driveway than go back inside and brave facing the dog pack as well as my aunt's and uncle's curious stares.

I felt my father's eyes on me as I hurried to my car, careful to navigate the piled land mines of Doberman crap on the lawn. Did he really believe I was still some gullible kid who'd fall for his lies? Evidently, he did.

The front door opened, and Mabel rushed toward me, waving sheets of paper. She thrust one into my hands, and I stared down at it numbly. "What's this?"

"A flyer we've just had printed up. First Baptist is holding a fundraiser for your dad. He needs help paying his legal fees." Her small hooded eyes were beseeching. It was the most animated I'd ever seen the woman. Dad had reeled her into his net, hook, line, and sinker.

I let go of the paper as though it had scalded my fingers. "Thought he had plenty of free legal representation from fancy lawyers all over the country."

"That was to get him out of the penitentiary. This here's for a civil suit."

"Why are you so hell bent to help Dad? Has he promised you a portion of the cut? 'Cause if he has, I can promise you'll never see a dime of that money."

Mabel drew up as much as her five-foot-three-inch frame allowed and patted an errant curl from her bun. "I'm merely doing my Christian duty."

"Uh-huh. Good for you." I opened the car door, slid in, and then shut it with an emphatic bang.

Mabel still didn't give up. She leaned over and peered at me through the open window. "But he's your father. Surely you have compassion for all he's been through. Can we count on you?"

Time to be blunt. "Fuck no," I said, enunciating each word loud and clear.

Her jaw dropped open, and she affixed me with a horrified look on her plain face. Bet she didn't hear that word much in her Bubble-Wrapped world. I couldn't help it. Hysterical giggles welled up from deep within and spilled out as I backed out of the driveway. I laughed until tears ran down my cheeks. Damn if that didn't feel good.

But my mirth was short lived at the sight of a Channel Twelve news van approaching. I slowed to a crawl and watched as it zoomed past me and into Uncle Vic's driveway, where Mabel still stood, clutching a handful of flyers. So that's why Dad had kept glancing at his watch. Wouldn't he have just loved to have me by his side as he put on an act for the cameras. Mr. Nice Guy with his long-lost daughter. I'd escaped by no less than two minutes. I stopped in the middle of the street, watching the show. Dad emerged from the house, pulling at the lapels of a sport coat he'd hastily thrown on. He wore an aw-shucks expression as the reporter and cameraman approached, all innocence and humble gratitude for the opportunity to start over in life.

What about Mom? I wanted to scream. *What about Jimmy?* There were no second chances for them. A red haze of anger burned through my body, and I hit the accelerator. It wasn't until I'd turned onto the county road that my breathing returned to a normal, steady pace. *It's okay; it's done.* I'd met my dad, and the worst was over. There was no reason to ever run into him again. He wasn't welcome at Sylvie's house, and I damn sure wouldn't be visiting Uncle Vic again.

The nerve of that man, though. We hadn't even exchanged letters for a good six years. After the prison visits had stopped, we'd corresponded, but that communication had dwindled with each passing year until it had died from neglect and the weight of unspoken words.

We were strangers to one another.

Less than a mile from Uncle Vic's, I turned onto Dark Corners Road and pulled my car over to the side. I hadn't consciously realized that this was my final destination. When I'd left my uncle's place, I should have turned right instead of left.

And so I found myself staring glumly at the crumbling remains of a building surrounded by charred trees on the sides and back of the property. Last time I'd come had been early spring, but it appeared unchanged. Yet year by year, the remaining wood rotted further, and like the shore eroded by the tide, weeds unrelentingly inched forward and claimed ground. I got out of the car and trudged over to the desolate structure.

This was my inheritance. My past and my future bound in ash and destruction. Aunt Sylvie thought I should bulldoze everything and sell the land, but that felt sacrilegious. This was where I went when I wanted to feel close to Mom. I visited here much more than the cemetery where she and my brother were buried.

The fireplace from our old house remained, the bricks scorched an unrelenting black. Remnants of burnt studs and framing material peppered the ruined home. I entered through where the front door had once stood. Six steps forward and five to the right, I padded through

30

our former kitchen. Years ago, someone had carted off all the appliances in the hope they might still function. I left, strolling over to what had been the master bedroom.

Broken glass crunched beneath my shoes. I scuffed at the ground, then frowned at the sight of litter. Scooping down, I picked up a cigar band, the paper still crisp and unfaded. It featured two golden lions set against a red crest. Arturo Fuente.

Dad had been here, and recently. But why? Had he come to gloat, or had he come to pay his respects? A murderer or an unjustly accused man? My gut told me that he was guilty, and it killed me to watch him roam free, to see people like Aunt Mabel pitying him and believing he'd suffered for a crime he didn't commit. I wanted Dad to spend every waking hour holed inside a miserable death row cell, and when his sorry life was over, I wanted him to rot in hell.

"I'm going to prove he's guilty, Mom, Jimmy," I said bitterly. "There's got to be something I can do. I promise you, I'll get him locked back up where he belongs."

I crumpled the cigar band in my fist and let it drop into the weeds.

Chapter 3

DR. IRA PENNINGTON

I reviewed the patient's file notes before removing my glasses and gazing at the fidgety young woman seated across from my desk. She twiddled with her mousy brown hair, which she'd attempted to brighten with a dye job of pink and purple strands. She crossed her legs before shifting positions yet again, uncrossing her legs and placing her hands in her lap. Her thumbs began to twirl despite her best effort to focus and keep still.

"Do you know why your counselors arranged for this appointment?" I asked.

"I . . . I've been in a little trouble lately," she admitted. "Nothing serious. Not really." She barked a nervous laugh, and I glimpsed a flash of rotten teeth. From that alone, I'd have realized she was a meth addict without even opening her patient chart. "No need for me to see a psychiatrist," she continued, shifting in her seat.

"I'd say it's more than a little trouble, Miss Mickelson."

She gulped. "I only sneak out a bit late at night to go smoke a cigarette. Insomnia, you know."

"Lab results indicate that you imbibed more than tobacco."

"Only alcohol. No drugs."

"Only alcohol?" I replied sternly. "The rules of our program are quite clear. One strike, and you're out."

Her eyes filled. "Please let me stay. It won't happen again." From her lips burst a sound that was part sob, part moan. "Please," she added brokenly.

I regarded her soberly. An image of my mother arose, broken and defeated with tombstone eyes, her heroin addiction ravaging and relentless until it left her body emaciated and her mind obsessed with the raging desire for more. Always more. It killed her in the end. And after all these years of treating addicts, I've become jaded. I'm secretly frustrated with their impaired thought processes because I know firsthand the suffering they leave behind in their manic pursuit to get high at all costs.

"If you kick me out, I . . . I have nowhere else to go but the streets," she whined.

"Burned all your bridges, eh?" I'd heard it all so many times before.

"Yeah, my parents have had it with me. Said this program was my last chance. I can't go back to that homeless shelter I lived in when they kicked me out of the house last time. It was horrible."

"We have strict rules for a reason," I admonished. "We're trying to retrain the neural circuits in your brain to cope without substance interference of any kind. It's also essential that you learn to manage your emotions without the use of drugs and alcohol."

"I know, I know. It's just that the insomnia won't let me rest. I can't stand lying in bed all night." She cast a sideways, crafty glance my way. "You're a doctor. Maybe you could prescribe something to help me sleep?"

Like I didn't see that request coming a mile away. "I don't prescribe sedatives to drug addicts."

She swallowed her disappointment and gave a quick nod. "Okay. I get it."

I steepled my fingers and regarded the overly thin young woman. Kick her out or let her stay? The weight of my decision hung heavily in the air between us.

"Why should we allow you to stay?" I asked wearily. "You've already been here a week. Has there been any progress since your admission?"

Mickelson vigorously nodded her head. "I was clean the first two days. Kind of a record for me. I really like my counselor and the other patients. I've made a few friends—"

"Like whoever slipped you the alcohol? Is that who you call a friend?"

"It wasn't anyone from the program," she hurried to explain.

At my frown, the woman rushed on, extolling her love of the program and how, if only given the chance, she felt she could turn her life around.

Discreetly, I glanced down at the appointment calendar on my desk, my decision already made. Her parents had paid cash up front for the program, so I was willing to let their daughter continue, for all the good it would do. After two decades as chief psychiatrist for Normal Community Hospital, I recognized a helpless case when it stared me in the face.

I'd let Melanie Mickelson sweat it out a bit longer, though, before I sent her on her way, no better or more enlightened than when she'd arrived for the appointment, but certainly no worse. Hippocratic oath fulfilled. At four o'clock, I'd be interviewing Agnes Patel, a new patient admitted to the psychiatric ward. Those cases were always so much more interesting than the substance abuse ones—psychotic breaks, phobias, severe depression, bipolar—all unique in their individual pathology. Color me intrigued.

". . . and my counselor promised that if you let me stay, she's willing to book me a few extra sessions so we can work on alternative therapies to help my sleep problem. Like meditation and—"

"Have you always suffered from insomnia?" I interrupted abruptly.

"Yeah. Ever since I was ten and almost drowned in the ocean. I have nightmares about the tow pulling me under and water filling my lungs. I can't breathe, and when I wake up, I'm panting for air and in a panic."

For the first time, I sat straight up and took notice of this slip of a girl. The discussion had at last turned interesting, something different from the usual chatter of an addict.

"A fear of water, you say? That's not uncommon in people who almost drowned as children. It's a trauma the brain has trouble coping with."

"No, I'm not afraid of the water," she said quickly. "Only in my dreams, anyway. Like, I swim and stuff. Just not in the ocean or a lake. Pools are okay."

"Yet the fear must be there, deeply suppressed by your subconscious. Otherwise, the drowning wouldn't replay in your mind every night, interfering with sleep."

"I suppose." She shrugged and fiddled with her hair again. "So . . . can I stay in the program?"

"Yes . . ."

Her pale face lit with hope.

"But with a condition," I added. "I think we should explore the deeper issues of your addiction and insomnia. I recommend we start with three sessions a week."

"Yeah. Sure, Doc." She broke eye contact and surveyed the medical tomes that lined a bookshelf behind my desk. "If you think it'll help me."

In the short space of our time together, Mickelson's emotions had ranged from nervousness to desperation and now boredom. She was obviously itching to leave the confines of the room. Her legs recrossed again, and she swung the top one to and fro in her twitchy way. Pink glittery sneakers sparkled under the overhead light. They looked cheap and out of place in my tastefully decorated office.

"Speak to my secretary on your way out to book our next appointment," I instructed her, scribbling a note for Gayla. She'd been my administrative assistant for years and could be trusted to coordinate patient schedules with the various treatment teams. Maybe, just maybe, if I treated Mickelson's underlying trauma, she'd have a chance at true rehabilitation from her addictions. Absently, I rubbed my chin, thoughts drifting to my greatest challenge and my greatest failure—Della Stallings and my inability to treat her rare phobia.

Chapter 4

DELLA

I was procrastinating, avoiding the painful research I had to delve into if I wanted to prove Dad's guilt. It had been three days since our meeting. I'd been swamped with end-of-quarter work in my data-entry job and kept returning home late, then immediately falling into deep, disturbing nightmares. But tonight I was all caught up here at work. No more excuses.

I closed the spreadsheet I'd been working in and gazed at the screen saver—a photo of the doomed grand duchess Anastasia taken before she was murdered. In one of the last official portraits of the Romanov family, she was dressed in a white lace smock, a modest strand of pearls adorning her young neck and long hair pulled back in a large girlish bow. She and her hemophiliac little brother, Alexei, had their arms draped around one another.

Did she have any inkling of the danger that lurked beneath the glamourous facade? That her days were numbered, her fate sealed? In fewer than two years from the date of that photo, Russian revolutionaries had captured the imperial family and transported them to Siberia for imprisonment and, ultimately, their brutal massacre. I loved reading history, but this particular blip in all the eons of time past held a peculiar fascination for me. I didn't like to dwell on the reasons why.

I clicked on the screen and pulled up the internet. No time to dip into the travails of the Russian Revolution and the poor, doomed grand duchesses. No, tonight I'd delve into old newspaper archives detailing Normal's crime of the century, something I hadn't done since my early teens, and even back then, it hadn't been a thorough exploration.

Dad's unwelcome homecoming changed everything. I needed to pore over every public detail available online. I had no idea what I was looking for, only hopeful that some small clue or remembrance would spark ideas on who to interview or how to proceed. It was a starting place. From there, I'd study the legal technicalities that led to his exoneration. If only I had the cash to spare, I'd hire an attorney or paralegal to speed the process and issue a legal challenge. Would it be possible to find one willing to help on a pro bono basis? Hell, dozens of attorneys had clamored to help overturn Dad's death sentence; maybe one of them could actually help a real victim. No, what a joke to even consider the possibility. Bile threatened to choke me at the injustice. There'd been no one to come forward on my behalf. Not now and not then. Sylvie and I had been at the mercy of the local police and district attorney's office to conduct a bulletproof investigation and court trial. I pushed aside the bitterness and tried to focus.

The first article I retrieved sported a front-page headline, "Woman and Child Murdered in Home, One Child Escapes." There was a photo of Mom smiling confidently into the camera. She'd been chairing a hospital committee and was dressed conservatively, her bobbed hair neatly coiffed with small diamond studs glittering discreetly in her earlobes. Had Sylvie or Dad provided the photo? Or did the newspaper already have it stored in their archives? Next was a photo of Jimmy, all smiles in a studio portrait with merry eyes and chubby cheeks.

There was a photo of me as well. A fireman held me in his arms as I clutched my cartoonish comforter, eyes wide and wild. Strange that I had no real memory of the morning after. Only that I'd been cold and lonely and frightened until that unknown man had cradled me in his arms and shuffled me to an awaiting cherry-red ambulance . . . or had it been a fire truck? I only remember the red and then warm blankets heaped atop me and how very, very good they had felt.

Everything after that was all a jumble of uniformed cops, firemen, and doctors asking me a gazillion questions, for which I had no answers. I'd been poked and prodded and declared physically intact. Much, much later, Aunt Sylvie had bustled me to her home, and there I remained.

My temples throbbed as I read and remembered. Thank God the old photos were black and white, not a speck of red to contend with. My absorption in the past continued until I vaguely became aware of the hospital coming to life, awakening from the deep slumber of night. Cart wheels rustled against linoleum. Pings and beeps and footsteps invaded the quiet background hum of machinery. I checked my cell phone and discovered my shift had ended over ten minutes ago. Before I could close the computer, a shadow fell across the room.

"Working hard?"

I jolted away from my desk, nearly toppling over in my chair.

Dad slouched against the doorframe, looking way too cheery and dapper for 5:10 a.m. But why wouldn't he be? For the rest of his life, any morning that began with him waking up in his own bed, in his own room, was a gift from the gods.

I scowled, remembering too late Dad's manner of sneaking up on people. As a child, he'd managed to pop up on me whenever I'd least expected, as though sniffing out trouble or any whiff of intrigue. And there he stood in the doorway, effectively blocking my only escape route.

"How did you find me? What are you doing here?" I demanded.

"Can't I come visit my own daughter?"

He pushed away from the door and in three long strides loomed over me, peering over my shoulder. My face heated as though I'd been caught viewing donkey porn.

It was his turn to scowl. "Why the hell are you looking at that?"

I crossed my arms and dug in my heels. "Because I want to."

"Why? No point dwelling on the past."

I bet he'd never lost a minute of sleep mourning their loss. His tears and misery were for his own unfortunate circumstances. It was all about what had happened to him.

"Maybe I want to dwell," I argued, though nothing could be further from the truth. I did my best every day to keep the past buried.

"No point in that."

"There doesn't have to be a point."

He shot me an assessing look, tapping an index finger against his mouth. "You do this every night then? Reread old news articles?"

"None of your business. What do you want?" I resented that he'd invaded my work space.

"No reason, just—"

"You always have a reason. An agenda. Just get to the point. I'm ready to head home." I shut down the computer and gathered my purse from underneath the desk.

He stuck his hands in the pockets of his creased khakis. "Only wanted to see if you planned on going to the church barbecue."

"Barbecue?" I gazed at him stupidly until understanding dawned. "You mean that fund-raiser for your lawsuit?"

"It would look good if you were there, supporting me."

"But I don't support you. Not at all. Guess Aunt Mabel didn't pass on my subtle message."

He flushed, and a muscle in his jaw worked. An old fear washed over me, but I quickly stifled it. I wasn't a small kid anymore who he could bully around and overpower. I stood and watched carefully, practically bouncing on the balls of my feet, ready to strike. Today might be the day all those martial arts classes paid off. Or I could let him go on and smack me. That would put a huge dent in the public sympathy for his cause once word of that got around town—and I'd make sure that it did by pressing charges. I lifted my chin and smirked, goading him on.

"What are you going to do, Dad?" I taunted. "Hit me?"

He let out a long sigh and unclenched his fisted hands. "Of course not, Delly-girl."

"Don't call me your *girl*. Stay away from me."

"I see Sylvie has poisoned you against me."

"You did that for yourself. Always wanting money and writing one letter to every dozen I sent you."

"Is that what this is about? My lack of communication skills? C'mon, I'm a typical man with not much to say. What would I write about? My exciting days sitting on death row, twiddling my thumbs? You didn't need that."

I'd needed lots of things since I'd witnessed my mom's and brother's murders. I'd wanted—no, *needed*—him to assure me that he wasn't their killer. That he loved me and hadn't been the one who'd tried to chase me down and murder me. Whether Dad had been unwilling or unable to provide those answers didn't matter at this point. It was too late. And I still didn't believe he'd sought me out only to ask about the church fund-raiser. That was over a week away. No, he was digging around, trying to gauge my state of mind in order to ingratiate himself back in my life. Renewing our relationship would likely bolster community support. After all, if his own daughter didn't believe in her father's innocence, why should anyone else?

"Don't come around to see me anymore," I said tightly. "There's nothing more to be said between us."

"I disagree. We're going to be living in the same small town. We should make peace."

"Peace?" I yelled. My voice violently bounced around the walls of my tiny office. I picked up the three-by-five framed photo of Mom and

Jimmy I kept on my desk and thrust it at his chest. "What about Mom and Jimmy? Am I supposed to forget what you did to them?"

He reluctantly took the photo and glanced down at it. The knuckles in his fingers turned white as he gripped the frame, and his lower lip trembled. I hadn't seen him display emotion like this since the day he'd been convicted in the courtroom. And I'd been convinced those tears were for himself. Even at Mom and Jimmy's funeral he'd sat alone, self-contained and silent. Kinder folks had said he appeared to be in shock while the suspicious had noted his lack of tears and wondered.

"Poor Jimmy," he said at last, choking on the words.

I hardened my heart and waited. He swiped a hand across his face and then set the photo down.

"And what about Mom?" I demanded. "She was murdered too."

"Of course," he said, regaining his composure. "No one deserved to die like that."

I stared him down, trying to read the murky spaces of his heart. Was he really sorry for her loss? I wasn't some gullible townsperson with no inside knowledge. I may have been a kid, but I was old enough to remember dark things. All the tension between them that frequently erupted into shouts and slaps and tears.

"You never loved her," I accused.

"Don't say that."

"What's the matter? The truth hurts? Afraid I'll put a dent in your PR campaign? You know, the one where you play the unjustly accused man mourning the loss of his wife and child."

"I loved them. I didn't do it. What reason would I have to—"

"Over a million reasons," I interrupted, my voice rising again. "You took out hefty life insurance policies on all of us a month before the murders."

"I was an insurance salesman. It cost me practically nothing to pay those premiums."

"You have to admit it looks suspicious on top of everything else."

"All circumstantial. That's all they had on me. I wasn't home when those murders happened. The state's witness—"

"You mean your girlfriend?" I asked bitterly. "If you weren't the killer, then you should have been at home. Instead, you were out cheating on Mom."

"Okay, I might have been a crappy husband and dad, but I'm not a murderer. Don't believe me? Review the evidence. Go talk to Carolyn Merton."

My face scrunched into a hard knot of anger. "I don't want to talk to your damn girlfriend. I don't believe her any more than I do you."

Whistling sounded outside the door, and we both froze. It grew louder, and I became aware of the scrape of something dragging against the hallway floor. Knox was on his way to empty my trash can, a bit later than usual. A mop bucket came into view, followed by Knox in his blue maintenance uniform. He regarded us with raised brows before casting me a look of concern. "Everything all right in here, folks?" he asked.

"Fine. He was just leaving," I said, glaring at my father.

Dad held up both palms in an I'm-harmless gesture. "Okay, okay. We'll talk again later, Della. This isn't over."

I tamped down an angry retort. I didn't have my dad's agenda of presenting a facade to outsiders. As though we had any semblance of a normal father-daughter relationship. However, I did hate anyone seeing me as an emotional wreck. I'd grown up with the stares, the speculation, and the whispering. *It's the Stallings girl,* they'd say in hushed tones. *The one that got away. Poor thing. Wonder how it feels to watch your family be stabbed to death? Can you imagine?*

In the doorway, Dad crowded out Knox and then turned to me, the slick salesman smile back in play. "By the way, I'm applying for a job here at the hospital. Put in a good word for your old man, okay?" Without waiting for my response, he made a leisurely retreat, keeping his shoulders back and head high. I envied his calm confidence to emerge unscathed from any confrontation.

I rubbed a hand over my flushed face, trying to regain my equilibrium. Why did he have to come back to Normal? Maybe once his stupid lawsuit was settled, he'd leave. For the first time, I hoped he'd win it. I hoped he collected enough money to move far away from this place and never return.

"That man giving you trouble?"

I startled from my reverie and turned to look at Knox. Over the years, we'd gradually become friendly as he passed my office mopping or emptying my trash can. Occasionally, we'd even shared a coffee or two when the work was slow and the night long and lonely.

"If he is, you can report him to security. They'll bar him from the building if he's harassing you."

"No. I don't want to do that. Not unless he keeps bothering me. He's—he's only my dad."

"Ahh," he said, as though that explained anything.

He ran a hand through his silver-streaked hair, and I noticed his red chapped skin, which was worse than usual. Nurses weren't the only hospital workers who suffered the occupational hazard of dry, rough skin. Impulsively, I opened a desk drawer and pulled out a bottle of my homemade chamomile cream.

"Here," I said, handing him the jar. "It'll help your hands. It's got shea butter, glycerin, and other goodies. My nurse friend swears by it."

He nodded slowly and accepted the gift. "That's very kind of you. I'll give it a go."

"You do that." I stepped around him and glanced down the hallway. Dad was nowhere in sight. Quickly, I walked down the hall, holding my car keys in my palm like a weapon.

"Have a good day, Della," he called out from behind.

I turned and saw him place a hand on his lower back before straightening and resuming mopping. His work was slow and deliberate, as though he suffered from arthritis. I was terrible at guessing ages, but it appeared he might be in his late fifties. Old enough to suffer aches and pains but not old enough to collect a pension either.

As Aunt Sylvie would say, we all had our crosses to bear. And my particular cross at the moment was Dad. I proceeded to the restroom and splashed my face with water. Weariness overwhelmed me, so after patting my face dry, I rested my head in my hands. I waited a few minutes, giving Dad time to walk to his car and leave. Two confrontations in the last twenty-four hours were more than I wanted. Satisfied he'd had time to leave, I left the restroom.

Outside, the suggestion of dawn lay in the lightening horizon, and a quick scan of the parking lot assured me Dad wasn't around. I strolled to my car and was about to slip in when I heard my name called. I paused, hand on the door handle, and saw Linda Bowen rushing toward me, waving both arms in the air.

This was a surprise. As Human Resources director, she usually didn't arrive before seven o'clock in the morning. She reached me and leaned against my car, panting. Her gray bun was slightly askew, and she patted it back into submission.

"Morning. What are you doing here so early?" I asked. A sudden apprehension settled over me. Was I in trouble? Had someone in IT reported my nonbusiness internet usage? It wasn't like I abused work time. I never played on the computer until I'd finished all my assignments.

"Early meeting with the hospital's board of trustees today," she said, still a bit out of breath. "I wanted to come in early and go over a few reports."

"Oh, okay." I couldn't help glancing longingly at the car's interior. Small talk had never been my forte.

"How have you been, Della? We haven't spoken in weeks."

"I'm fine," I automatically replied with my standard response. *Show no weakness.*

"That's good to hear. This must be a challenging time for you, what with the change in your personal life."

I forgot to breathe for a moment, sure I possessed that deer-in-the-headlights expression. "Um, yeah. Challenging," I mumbled.

Her eyes were sharp but kind. I didn't believe her guilty of prying to get a scoop. No doubt plenty of townsfolk were bound to be curious about the reaction of Hunter Stallings's daughter upon his miraculous return. But Linda Bowen wasn't that type of person. It was probably what made her so good at her job; she was privy to all kinds of confidential information on every employee and never divulged any of it. I always felt a burst of pride that my mother had held the same position and had been so highly regarded by everyone.

"Exactly. Which is why I want your input." She pulled at the lapel of her navy blazer. "Your father called me yesterday, asking if we might have a position for him open here. Said you would provide a reference, along with Victor and his wife."

Of course. I should have seen this coming. Dad had even warned me he'd applied. Still, I felt blindsided. I didn't want him here. My little office and Aunt Sylvie's house were the only two places where I felt truly safe. And he wanted to take my safety away from me.

"Is that what he told you?" I asked between numbed lips, buying time to put together an appropriate response, one that didn't include profanity or reveal my utter condemnation of the last surviving member of my immediate family. What kind of job could Dad possibly be qualified for anyway? He had a financial background, but surely his unsavory history would preclude him as a suitable candidate for managing other people's money.

"He did." She gave a brisk, understanding nod. "No need to respond. I sense your hesitation, and it's perfectly understandable. If you want to discuss it further, my door is always open."

"Thank you, Mrs. Bowen." I always addressed her by her surname as a sign of respect.

She patted my arm, and in a rare display of emotion, confided, "Mary was a dear colleague and friend. She'd be proud of you, Della."

I wasn't so sure of that, but I was spared having to acknowledge the compliment when Linda cleared her throat. "Well, then. I've a stack of reports on my desk to review. Let me know if I can be of service to you."

Gratefully, I slumped into the car seat and headed home. I caught the green light on all three traffic signals and hoped they were an omen that the day would only improve. Whoever claimed that venting emotions was healthy didn't know me. The exchange with Dad had only left me shaky and churning with bitterness.

The house smelled of bacon, and I entered the kitchen, where Aunt Sylvie was cooking. Her long silver locks were messily clamped into a high bun by a turquoise barrette, and she wore a colorful kimono. Even without makeup, her face appeared stunning and fresh.

"I hope I inherited your genes," I said by way of greeting.

"Thanks, hon. Sit down at the table. Biscuits will be ready in a moment."

"I'm not hungry."

She frowned. "But you hardly ate anything last night. You should be starving."

"I'm not."

She turned off the stove eye and removed the pan of grease from the burner. "Just eat a little something for me, then?"

I sighed and sat down. "One piece of bacon."

I was rewarded with a sunny smile, and she fixed me a plate with two pieces of bacon and a large serving of cheese grits. I picked at my food as she slid into the chair opposite me. "How was work?"

"It sucked. Dad dropped by. Can you believe he wants me to provide him a reference to work at the hospital with me?"

"The man has no shame." Sylvie clucked her tongue. "I did speak to the victim services person at the DA's office. Apparently, we can't get a restraining order against Hunter until we can prove harassment."

I could have told her that to start with, but I kept my mouth shut.

"The officer suggested keeping a log of any harassment incidents. Might come in handy one day."

I pushed my plate away. "I want to see everything," I announced.

"What?" Her eyes clouded with confusion, then cleared. She understood my cryptic request. "You're sure you're ready?"

"I am," I said with a conviction I didn't feel. It's not like I wanted to examine the horrific details of the crime, but Dad had forced my hand.

Sylvie left the kitchen and returned less than a minute later carrying a large cardboard box printed with pastel flowers. Such a pretty container for such ugly words.

"Is that everything?" I asked.

She nodded grimly. "Even copies of the crime photos. It's all in here. At least, everything the police said was public record."

"I'll get started on it now."

"You need to sleep. I heard you tossing and turning all yesterday."

I shrugged. "When my body's burned out running on adrenaline, it'll shut down."

"That's not healthy. Here, I've got something else for you." She reached into her kimono pocket and pulled out a violet mojo bag tied with a ribbon. It smelled of sweet musk and hoodoo oil.

"What's this for?"

"A little conjuring concoction for peace. Dried sage and angelica leaves, plus chips of rose quartz and citrine. Keep it under your pillow at night."

A smile tugged the corners of my lips. I didn't believe for a second in that hocus-pocus, but the knowledge that she was on my side helped calm my inner turmoil. I held the bag to my nose and sniffed the pungent herbs. "I feel better already," I declared.

Aunt Sylvie regarded me solemnly. "There's only so much it can do. I'm afraid things will get worse for you in the short term. You do what you have to do, and I promise, Della, one day you'll be the stronger for it."

For the second time in fewer than two hours, unexpected kindness made my lungs burn with suppressed sobs.

"In the meantime," Aunt Sylvie continued, "maybe you should see a doctor or counselor to help you through this."

"You're right." Looking at everything would be hard in the short term, but in the end, it might be what I needed to gain peace and clarity.

Chapter 5
DELLA

I knew she was home. Her off days at the Dixie One Stop gas station were Sundays and Mondays.

From a distance, I'd observed Carolyn Merton my whole life. Even before *that night, that woman* had been a disruptor in our volatile home. I'd heard her name come up many times when Mom and Dad were fighting. As a child, I hadn't been sure what that meant exactly, but I'd realized it wasn't good. That she was the cause of pain and darkness.

I also knew where Carolyn lived as well as the highlights and low-lights of her existence—twice divorced, three adult children, and two grandchildren, one of whom she'd obtained sole custody of due to the inability of her daughter to provide a safe home for the child.

And today would be the day I finally spoke to the other woman in my parents' marriage. I steeled myself for the unwelcome meeting as I drove to her place. *Thanks a lot, Dad.* Never thought I'd initiate contact, but this woman held the key to where my dad might have been while Mom and Jimmy were attacked. I needed to watch her face as I asked for the truth.

My head felt as though it were being squeezed in an ever-tightening vise, the way it always did when I went too long without sleep. The doctor treating me for occasional migraines had explained that a sustained lack of sleep could affect the brain like a physical blow to the head—migraine proteins and other chemicals leaked into brain tissues in toxic amounts.

I extracted a couple of ibuprofen tablets from my purse and downed them with a swig of soda. This headache was entirely my fault. It had been over two years since the last migraine attack, and I'd grown careless about avoiding its triggers. For the past two days and nights I'd pored over the trial transcripts, immersed in a red opaqueness that saturated my brain whenever I thought long and hard about the murders. I'd never bothered explaining to the doctor my peculiar phobia of the color red, so I didn't know whether it had any bearing on the toxic chemical soup of my brain matter, but I'd read that human eyes have a quarter million color-decoding cones. By far, red commanded the heftiest use of them, taxing eighty-three thousand cones to decode its hue. As a result, the cones became overstimulated when you focused on the color, causing visual fatigue. I suspected that an intense focus, such as the kind I'd maintained, must have played a significant role in my headaches.

In way too short a time, I was on Carolyn's street. Twice I drove past the turnoff to her place, mulling over the unpleasant task. I had a headache and could return another day. What was the harm if I kept driving and didn't stop by? What made me think the woman would even agree to speak to me? And if she did, how could I expect the truth?

At last I managed to crush my resistance, turned onto her street, and pulled into the Merry Land Mobile Homes Community. There was nothing merry about the cluster of rusted trailers and the clutter of old cars, broken appliances, and other crap littering the weedy plots. Still, this wasn't my first rodeo. I'd swung by here several times over the years, just out of curiosity. I'd do a quick drive through, never stopping to speak with anyone.

At the second trailer from the last row on the right, I spotted her car parked haphazardly out front—an old compact that looked even more worn out than my own, which was quite the feat.

This won't take long, I reminded myself. A few pointed questions and I'd be on my merry way out of Merry Land, never to return. I left my car and walked up the three steps of sagging concrete, then rapped at the dented metal door.

From a two-inch gap between the door and the trailer frame, a child's wail and the loud noise of a TV sounded. I twisted my fingers together in front of me. I was really doing this. I was here, about to come face-to-face with Carolyn Denzel Fairhope Merton.

The Lady in Red.

The Scarlet Woman.

The Rouged Tart.

With a lusty creak, the door swung open. Carolyn's eyes narrowed at me suspiciously as she bounced a crying kid on her hip. He appeared about two years old, and he scowled at me as she spoke.

"Who are you? Whadda . . ."

Recognition lit her faded brown eyes, and her jaw dropped an inch.

"That's right; it's me. Della Stallings." I shifted my feet and added unnecessarily, "Hunter Stallings's daughter."

"He send you here?" The wary look returned on her face.

"No?" My voice rose as though my answer were a question. "Why would he?"

"Can't imagine you and I'd have anything to talk about."

The kid wiggled off her hip and stomped his little foot. Clearly, I'd stumbled in upon a tantrum.

"Want ice cream," he pronounced.

"I already told ya, not until after lunch."

He threw himself onto the floor, little legs and arms flailing as he screamed. Carolyn's gray-tinged face flushed. "Maybe you should come back some other time. Now's not good."

The door started to close, so I wedged myself into the small opening before she could shut me out. "This won't take but a minute."

Her scowl almost matched her grandson's in its intensity, but she shrugged and allowed me entrance.

A stench of fried bologna hung in the air. Carolyn ignored me as she stepped into the kitchen and pulled a carton of ice cream from the freezer. The screaming immediately stopped, and the kid climbed onto a chair at the table, all smiles and sunshine.

Way to go, Grandma. Kid will be an unholy terror by the time he hits his teens. But I kept the chastisement unvoiced and my disapproval hidden behind a neutral mask. Carolyn noisily pulled a bowl from a cabinet and plopped several dollops into it before ungraciously setting it before the kid. Not that it appeared to hurt his delicate feelings. He lit into the treat with gusto.

"That should keep Billy quiet a few minutes." She gestured toward the den. "We'll talk in here."

I obediently walked the few steps back into the den, not sure why it mattered where the talk took place. The short distance between the two rooms ensured we'd have no privacy anyway. And now that her grandson was stuffing his face, he paid us no notice.

Carolyn faced me, arms crossed above her huge paunch of a stomach and face set in an obstinate stoniness. Whenever I'd stolen looks at her at work in the gas station's store, she'd been heavily made up with foundation and thick eyeliner. Her hair was always teased into some kind of bouffant '60s-looking hairstyle and, while she most certainly wasn't attractive, she'd looked okay enough.

But here in the comfort of her home, with her hair pulled back in an unflattering ponytail and her unadorned face so pale and listless, she looked like a woman twice her age. And this was the woman Dad had been so passionate about? Mom had been beautiful, and that wasn't looking at the past through a rose-colored lens either. She was not only beautiful but also intelligent. This woman here was nothing like her.

"Out, devil, out!" the TV blared, and I glanced over at it. A red-faced, sweaty evangelist flailed his arms from a pulpit. "Sin no more."

I couldn't help quirking a brow at Carolyn, who didn't even have the grace to appear embarrassed.

Okay, so this was it. My moment.

"Why did you ask if Dad sent me?" There. I'd start with that.

"Hunter's been on a real PR campaign since he's been let out. Figured he sent you over to make sure I wasn't changing my story again."

I snorted. "I can assure you, I'm not Dad's PR campaign manager. Aunt Mabel has that dubious honor."

"Ah, the pious Mabel. Your dad must be her new cause—like helping the starving children or literacy programs."

She had my aunt-in-law pegged all right.

Carolyn gestured to the sofa in a resigned manner. "Have a seat if you'd like. Say your piece. Can't say I haven't been expecting it all these years."

"I'll stand." I took a perverse pleasure in being rude to this woman. After all the grief she'd caused me and my family, she had it coming.

Carolyn nodded. I had the floor. My mouth twisted to form words, yet no sound came. I drew a deep breath and pushed past the knot in my throat. "What really happened that night? Was he with you the whole evening or not?"

She flinched slightly and colored. "He was with me. All night."

"Then why did you lie during the trial? How am I supposed to believe that *now* you're suddenly telling the truth?"

"I'm sure you've heard the news. Officer Eckeridge bullied me, same as he did everyone else in this town over the years. Hunter was the obvious suspect, and he'd do anything to prove it. Quicker he solved the case, the happier the townsfolk. Made him look good to the public and his bosses."

"Bullied you? How inconvenient."

"You have no idea . . . that man is scary. He was a cop, for God's sake. He threatened to ruin me and my kids if I didn't sign the bullshit statement he'd prepared."

"Dirty or not, what could he do? You hadn't broken the law," I argued.

A slight smile lifted the corners of her thin lips. "You're still very young, aren't you?"

"Twenty-six," I snapped. "Not sixteen."

"No kids and never been married, right?"

"Listen, lady. Spare me how hard your life's been. You think I haven't been through some shit? Did you witness the two people you loved most in the world get stabbed to death?"

Her face paled, and she nibbled at her lips. "No," she breathed. "Point taken."

I fixed her with a cold stare. "I think you told the truth back then. Dad was with you a couple of hours, and then he left."

"No. He stayed the night. Ernest, my husband at the time, was out of town. He's a truck driver. I'm not proud of the way I used to be, but I'm telling the truth now."

"Uh-huh." I pointed at the TV, where the preacher pounded the pulpit. "Watch all the evangelical shows you want, and pore over your Bible twenty-four seven, but it doesn't change the fact that you're a liar and a . . ." I faltered, glancing over my shoulder at her grandson, who'd finished his ice cream and was watching us with wide eyes. I faced her again. "Well, you know what you are."

She swallowed hard. "Guess I deserved that. Reckon I'd feel the same in your shoes. For what it's worth, I am sorry."

"A little late, aren't you?"

"Right." She heaved a sigh. "After the trial, I did try and talk to your aunt. Tell her how mighty sorry I was for everything. She let me know right quick what I could do with my apology."

I almost grinned picturing Aunt Sylvie's disdain. She could turn it on like no one else when she got on her high horse.

"Your remorse means nothing to me." I opened my mouth to tell her that she'd made my mom's last year of life miserable but clamped my lips together instead. It felt like a betrayal to let Carolyn know she'd wielded that kind of power. What had Dad seen in her? Mom had all the right qualities—beauty, brains, and class. A total flip from this woman's vulgarity.

Peas in a pod. Dad had obviously felt the need to find a partner who wallowed in his own level of scum.

Carolyn lifted her chin. "Okay. You've said your piece, and I've said mine. I think we're through now."

"I'm not leaving here until you admit the truth."

"I've already told you the truth. We're done." She pointed at the door.

I dug in my heels. "Did Dad kill Mom for you?"

Whoa. Where had that come from? I hadn't planned on asking that question. The whys of the crime didn't matter in my digging, or so I had told myself.

"Wh—what? No!" Her mouth dropped open so far, she looked like a beached puffer fish gasping for air. "I had nothing to do with that!" Her loud protestation echoed in the tinny confines of the trailer.

An act? Maybe. Maybe not. I stayed rooted to the spot, staring her down.

Billy flew into the room and launched his little body against his grandmother's legs. She patted the top of his head and cast me a see-what-you've-done look.

"Guess it really doesn't matter, does it?" I said tightly. "Mom and my little brother are dead. Jimmy was"—I pointed at Billy—"not much older than him when it happened."

Carolyn stooped down, clasping her grandson in a protective grip. "That's enough."

I ignored her remark. "You're such a liar. That officer never intimidated you. The statement you gave eighteen years ago was true. Dad left you in the middle of the night. Because in the end, no matter what, he always came home."

She shook her head, her lips trembling. "No. He'd had way too much to drink and fell asleep. That's the truth, and I've nothing more to say on the matter." She stroked Billy's hair, and a sob caught in her throat. "I've given the police a new statement and made my peace with God. It's over."

Not for me. It would never be over. The violence of the stabbings had permanently stained every cell and tissue in my gray matter. I carried that night deep inside, where it colored my every thought and emotion.

Billy turned his neck away from his grandmother's legs to peek at me. His mouth and cheeks were smeared with chocolate ice cream, and his wide eyes regarded me with both fear and accusation. I was the one making his grandmother cry, and therefore that made me the enemy. Somehow, I'd been turned into the bad guy in the room.

"Do the right thing," I said stiffly. "Recant your latest testimony. Dad doesn't deserve to be out of prison."

She slanted me a curious stare. "I think he's paid long enough for a night of infidelity and drinking. I did the right thing, and the rest was up to the courts."

"But it's not—"

The cell phone on her coffee table rang and vibrated against its cheap plywood surface like an angry wasp. Buzz. Buzz.

A name and number flashed on the phone screen. *Hunter Stallings.*

"I knew it!" I cried out. "You two still have a thing going on. He talked you into lying for him."

"No. I want nothing to do with Hunter. He ruined my marriage years ago. I won't let him ruin my life again."

Seemed to me that she'd ruined her own marriage by having an affair, but I let that point go to focus on the larger issue. "Then why else would Dad be calling you?"

"I don't know." Carolyn made no move to pick up the phone. It rang three more times before falling silent. The TV preacher thumped his Bible. "Honor the Lord your God," he intoned. "For verily—"

"I've said all I can say on the matter," Carolyn said quietly. "Now it's time for you to go."

"Go, lady," Billy demanded, backing up his grandmother.

Choking frustration seized my throat, but there was nothing more I could do. Carolyn wouldn't change her story again unless I presented proof she was lying. I'd have to find another way to prove Dad's guilt.

I stormed from the ramshackle mobile home without another word, glad to leave the cheerless trailer park, mentally dubbing it *Merton's Merry Madness*. All I'd really learned was that she and Dad were still in touch—another point she was lying about. If he was listed in her phone contacts, and Carolyn hadn't blocked his number, then it was a safe bet the two maintained a connection of some sort. Was she only a booty call? Perhaps after being locked up nearly two decades, he thought any woman looked good. As for Carolyn, she might have been lonely and easily susceptible to a charming predator like Hunter.

I shrugged off all further conjectures, uncomfortable with the path my mind had trodden. One interview down, several more to go. At least I was taking action, trying to find answers, despite how it stirred the sleeping monsters in my belly. Somehow, I'd find a way to get through this trial of my own making.

But I'd be kind to myself in the process. Go home and eat a proper meal with protein and veggies and then take a long, long nap.

I made it past the first traffic light but hit the second one on the outskirts of town. Crap. From the corner of my eye, I caught sight of a truck speeding to get through the yellow light. Of course, he wasn't going to make it through the caution light and instead would barrel through the first two seconds of the light after it turned red.

I was good and stuck. I closed my eyes but a fraction too late as a beam of red exploded into my retinas. Dizziness clouded my brain, and I hastily shifted my car into park. Just in case. A wave of nausea washed over me, and I rolled down the window to gulp fresh air.

A car horn blared from behind, a steady scream of annoyance. The driver did not let up. I stuck out an arm and waved him around me. Tires screeched, and the car sped past me in a flash of dark green. The back of my throat grew numb, that miserable precursor that meant bile was about to rise and temporarily seize control of my lungs. I flung open the car door and let nature take its course. Once finished, I felt a marginal relief from nausea, but the pain in my temples was unrelenting, and I shut my eyes, blocking the sunlight and my blurry vision.

I had no idea how long I sat there wrapped in a miasma of pain nothing could penetrate, but I eventually became aware of voices growing closer. I was making a spectacle of myself, yet I didn't dare open my eyes against the sunlight and drive off.

"Ma'am?" a deep voice asked, so close I judged he must have been standing within arm's distance of where I sat. I tried to pry my lids apart, but it was too much effort. "Ma'am?" he asked again, a little louder. "Are you injured?"

Yes. I was broken, sliced up into itty-bitty sharp pieces that could never be rearranged into a pattern called normal. But he'd never understand. I drew a deep breath, opened my eyes, and faced him.

Damn. A laminated ID badge glinted in the sun's ray, bouncing like a laser beam into my sensitive eyes. Squinting, I made out the police insignia on the badge.

"I'm fine," I mumbled. "Just got a bit nauseated and had to stop a moment."

"Please step out of the car, ma'am."

I wasn't sure I could, but what choice did I have? I opened the car door wider and spilled onto the blacktop with wobbly knees, clutching the door handle to keep upright.

"Have you had any alcohol to drink this morning?"

He thought I was a drunk driver. I shook my head no, immediately regretting the gesture as stabbing needles pricked beneath my temples. An involuntary moan slipped past my lips.

He peered into my vehicle, keeping a wide berth from the small puddle of vomit by the door. No doubt he was searching for beer cans or other evidence of drinking.

"What's that?" he asked, pointing and frowning.

I followed his gaze to where the old ashtray had been pulled out. Crushed dried herbs overflowed from the sides of the container. If I hadn't felt like shit, I might have laughed. Aunt Sylvie's protection herbs were harmless. "Unless it's illegal to possess dried bay leaves and basil, I have nothing in my car that need concern you."

The man's eyes were hidden beneath dark reflective sunglasses, but the momentary pause in his routine questioning clued me in that I had indeed surprised him. He and his buddies would have a good laugh over this one at the station later.

"But why do you keep . . . ?"

"It's a long story, Officer. May I go now?"

"Detective," he corrected. "First, I'd like you to walk a straight line for me, miss. Think you can do that?"

He might as well have asked me to perform a backward flip on a balance beam. Maybe if I walked very slowly, I'd be okay. I let go of my hand leaning against the car and took a tentative step forward, then another. The haze in my mind evaporated and adrenaline flooded over me, giving me strength and clarity. Over and over he had me jump through hoops—balancing on one leg, reciting the alphabet, counting to ten forward and backward.

"Are we done now, Detective . . ." I glanced at the letters stitched above his left shirt pocket. "Detective Whitt? This has been fun, but I have a life to live."

"Just one more matter. Stay where you are."

He returned to his cruiser, returning with a manila envelope and a pair of latex gloves. I watched as he pulled on the gloves and slid into my car. Ah yes, the blasted herbs. I really needed to have a talk with Aunt Sylvie about her hidden charms and potions tucked everywhere. Detective Whitt gathered a pinch of herbs and experimentally held it to his nose. "Smells like spaghetti sauce," he noted.

I doubled over laughing, clutching my belly. Laughed until tears wetted my face. At his stern, reproachful look, I gathered my dignity and straightened, swiping my cheeks. All my laughter drowned in sudden bleakness. The guffaws had merely erupted from the inner turmoil rumbling in my gut. Maybe Aunt Sylvie was right. What could it hurt to seek counseling? Anything to help me keep my shit together until I'd proved Dad's guilt.

Whitt climbed out of my car and pulled off the gloves with a distinctive slap of rubber against skin. "You're free to go, Miss Stallings."

I nodded and started to walk around him before realization hit. I whirled. "You never asked for my driver's license and insurance information. How do you know my name?"

He removed his sunglasses, revealing vaguely familiar hazel eyes. Where had I seen him before?

"Tenth grade algebra class," he supplied. "Nathan Whitt. I sat across from you."

The smell of chalk and the dread of pop quizzes rushed through me. I remembered Nathan well. He'd been the star running back on the football team and had that kind of quiet confidence that had made him irresistible to all the high school girls. Me included. Not that he'd ever paid me any mind.

"Surprised you remember me."

"Why wouldn't I?"

Of course he was aware of who I was, for all the wrong reasons. Everyone knew me as the poor, unfortunate kid. Nobody brought it up, but classmates and teachers alike knew my background. It had been an invisible wall between me and others. Still was.

I shuffled my feet. "So I'm free to go, you said?"

"Sure. Hope you feel better."

He continued to watch me as I slid into the car. Thankfully, the light was green, and I drove through the intersection without any further trouble. I had to be more careful. There could be no repeat of an incident like this. If my driver's license was revoked, it would be a huge constraint on my already-compromised freedom. Bad enough that the trauma effects I suffered mostly limited my world to my aunt's house and a tiny office in a hospital basement. Even then, I chose to function as much as possible in the protection of darkness, cocooned from people.

Dad's homecoming ripped that cocoon wide open, forcing me out into a cruel sunshine that exposed every dark thing.

Chapter 6

DR. PENNINGTON

What a banner two weeks.

First, Melanie Mickelson had stumbled into my office and made an offhanded remark about a fear of drowning. I'd already met with her twice since then, extracting as much detail as possible on this fear. Not a true aquaphobe, one afraid of water, and not even a thalassophobe, one afraid of the ocean or large bodies of water, but I'd plumbed a few nuggets. I'd had her focus on the sheer enormousness of the vast sea and led her on a guided meditation where she'd drifted on a raft, gradually wandering from shore until land had only been a speck on the horizon— and then disappeared altogether.

Next, I'd had her imagine towering waves crashing from afar and then growing ever closer, a storm's primal fury unleashed. Finally, I'd had her, under deep hypnosis, imagine an approaching tsunami. The water had pounded her in a sudden, salty blast, and a powerful undertow had gripped her toes, then her ankles, then her legs, mercilessly claiming her for the sea's unfathomable depths.

"How does that feel?" I'd asked. "Are you back there now? Ten years old again and powerless against the sea's force?"

"Yes," she'd answered faintly, lips quivering and beads of sweat popping on her forehead. "It's pulling me under. I can't break free."

"Tell me more about that," I'd urged in a hushed tone.

And so she had. When she'd last left my office, Melanie had been shaking and crying. "I don't want to come back here anymore," she'd whimpered.

"Miss Mickelson, need I remind you that you are only here because of my generosity in offering you a second chance after you broke the rules?" I'd asked pointedly. I understood the reluctance to face her fears, but it had to be done for the best chance of success in beating one of the root causes of her addiction. "After you'd told me this was your last chance and you had nowhere else to go? But it's your choice, of course. If you want to abandon treatment, you are free to leave."

She'd opted to stay.

And today—out of the blue, after I'd given up all hope of hearing from the most interesting patient of my career—Della Stallings had called wanting an appointment. I'd quickly cleared my calendar and informed her that I could meet with her at once. To my delight, she'd agreed to an immediate session.

She was due within the next fifteen minutes. I pulled up her file on the computer monitor, saturating myself with my notes, reliving our past sessions. She'd been a thin, trembly ghost of a girl when we'd first met. Her custodial aunt had revealed that, after the initial questioning by the police, Della had refused to speak any more about the murders, not even to the excellent child psychologist that I'd recommended.

Desperate, her aunt had sought me out for treatment. Her niece had begun experiencing difficulty with sleeping, nightmares, and withdrawal from her classmates at school. But the most disturbing trauma symptom was that the aunt had repeatedly caught Della stealing kitchen knives and stabbing her dolls with them, gouging their rubbery latex flesh until they'd been either shredded or dismembered.

The aunt had also revealed that Della had sudden screaming fits for no apparent reason.

The case both challenged and excited me professionally. Such violence in such a young child. I'd researched treatment options, which mainly advised a mixture of counseling and cognitive behavioral therapy for those suffering with posttraumatic stress disorder. In persistent, severe cases, selective serotonin reuptake inhibitors could be prescribed for anxiety, but the antidepressant drugs were more effective on adolescents and adults than on younger children. With the aunt's blessing, I'd decided to focus on nonmedical options first.

As a child, Della had been withdrawn, sullen even, refusing to discuss with me what she'd witnessed. I'd only been able to elicit details after I'd placed her under deep hypnosis. I'd noticed that she'd been heavily focused on the massive amount of blood she'd seen from the victims. After one of these sessions, I'd happened to witness firsthand one of her screaming rage episodes. She'd come out of the trance and sat with her arms crossed, mutinously staring out the window. A secretary had then entered my office, and Della's eyes had largened as she stared at the red scarf draping the woman's neck. Angry screaming had begun and only ended when the woman had left the room.

I'd formed a hypothesis and tested it. After Della had calmed, I'd pulled a red file folder from a desk drawer. The screaming had renewed. I'd buried the file back in the drawer, and the screaming had stopped. I'd had my answer.

Chromophobia—a fear of color. More specifically, *erythrophobia*, which is fear of the color red. Such a rare, intense phobia. One I'd only read about in books. On the spot, I'd resolved to record every nuance of the phobia I could glean from this patient and publish it in psychiatric medical journals.

Over the next few years, I'd collected data while treating the patient and happily observed that she'd gradually improved enough to function, albeit with a few caveats. The custodial aunt had homeschooled Della until she'd reached high school. The county board of education sent an emotional conflict specialist to the home every week to monitor Della's academic progress. According to the aunt, the screaming episodes and acting out with the dolls ceased within a few months. Della eventually managed to enter the public school system, graduate high school, and obtain gainful employment here at the hospital.

But sadly, desensitizing methods to gradually expose Della to the color red and rid her of her chromophobia had been met with only limited success. In my published articles, I briefly noted this complete lack of success and the qualifying environmental modifications that turned out to be permanent rather than temporary.

Details can be such a downer.

Despite the progress made, the Stallings case haunted me. I'd done my best to cure her phobia with various treatments, and even though she'd learned to function in spite of the condition, it had remained during her adolescence. I hadn't seen her professionally since then, but as she'd booked an appointment, I assumed the phobia had never completely vanished on its own. Had she even attempted treatment with another doctor?

The intercom on my phone buzzed. "Your next patient has arrived," my secretary informed me.

"Send her on in." I leaned back in my chair and waited.

Della Stallings had at last arrived.

Chapter 7

THE CORRECTOR

I adjusted the straps around her torso, buckling her even tighter to the makeshift waterboard. My gloved hands were clumsy, but I needed the gloves to prevent leaving fingerprints. I double-checked the straps around her knees and ankles. All secure.

She groaned against the gag and mumbled incoherently.

"Promise not to scream?" I asked the poor girl, not unkindly.

She nodded frantically, eyes wide with terror. Satisfied, I loosened the gag. I am not a monster.

"Please don't hurt me," she begged. "I—I'll do anything you want. I won't tell anybody. Just let me go." Her rigid body shook with sobs against the old piece of plywood I'd bound her to. "Please."

"Let you go?" I laughed incredulously. "I can't do that. You have to face your fears, my dear."

A wave lapped against the side of my boat and spilled over its side, the frigid water splashing onto her flesh.

She didn't react to the cold, her eyes never leaving my face. "Wh—what fears?" she asked breathlessly. "What are you going to do to me?"

It was only fair to let her see what was about to go down. I lifted the waterboard, no small feat, and propped it up against the boat's steering wheel. That done, I leaned forward, hands on my knees and panting from the physical strain.

"Where are we?" she asked, whimpering like an injured puppy.

"Hatchet Lake." I stood and zipped up the collar of my sweatshirt jacket tighter. The wind was a bitch this evening. Whitecap waves dotted the water, a vast expanse of black glass.

She searched my face. Blood ran down her nose from where I'd punched her earlier. Not an attractive look. "Why are you doing this to me?" she cried.

I chuckled and wagged a finger at her. "Now, now. I'll be the one asking the questions. You were a very bad girl, Melanie. Sneaking out of the hospital to meet your boyfriend. Thought you were going to score some drugs tonight, did you?"

"How did . . . how could you . . . ?"

I grinned, shoving my face close, only inches from hers. "Because I'm the one who sent that text, not him." Understanding dawned in her panicked eyes. "That's right. He doesn't know you're here. Nobody knows you're here. It's just you and me and"—I waved at the deserted scenery—"all this lovely water that you're so afraid of."

Surprise flickered across her features. "What are you going to do?" she whispered.

I fished the tube of red lipstick from my jacket and applied another layer on my mouth. The wind and the cold chapped my lips so quickly.

"You, my sweet, are going to face your worst fear."

Melanie struggled in her bindings, thrashing wildly and tossing her head from side to side. She screamed after having promised not to do so. I clucked my tongue and shook my head at this lie. She could not be trusted. The girl deserved her punishment.

"You're weak, Melanie. We have to correct that."

I hefted the board to the edge of the boat, then balanced it so that three quarters of the board stayed on the inside while Melanie's head and chest angled downward. I sat atop her knees as though she and the waterboard were a child's seesaw. Then, I slowly rose, inch by inch, and the board slid forward.

"What are you doing? No!"

Moonbeams spotlighted Melanie's pale face, which appeared all wide eyes and a mouth agape with screams. She entered the water head-first. Her shrieks smothered instantly to silence. I crouched with my hands on either side of the waterboard, peering intently at the barely visible bubbles escaping to the surface and the ripples caused by Melanie's head thrashing about as she struggled for air. I left her submerged right below chin level. Wild pink strands of her hair floated atop the water, then gradually waterlogged and sank out of sight.

I'd done my research. The average person in good health could take a huge gulp of air and then hold their breath underwater for about two minutes. But I felt certain Melanie had been too panicked to think properly or even guess that she was about to undergo a trial by water. She'd been yelling instead of gulping needed air. She'd had no idea that a slow-motion suffocation would commence, one that would drag her to the brink of her mental and physical endurance.

I hummed tunelessly until the bubbles dribbled to nearly nothing, and her head bobbed lifelessly. It was time. I sat down atop her knees, and she sprang out of the water, gasping and dripping. A jet of ice water doused me across the face and flowed down the collar of my jacket all the way to my crotch. I shivered. Should have worn a windbreaker.

"This is no picnic for me, either," I assured her. "Do you think I enjoy hurting you? No, ma'am. But it's my duty."

"Please," she cried, coughing up lake water.

I waited until she finished coughing, and I had her full attention. "Tell me, Melanie. Are you scared?"

"Yes," she wailed. "Please let me go."

I did. The board plopped back down as I rose to my feet, and I barely managed to avoid getting splashed again. I watched the bubbles and thrashing while counting. *One Mississippi. Two Mississippi. Three*

Mississ . . . I frowned at the smooth surface where Melanie's head was submerged. I sank back down on top of her knees, and the board sprang up.

More water splashed my jacket, soaking me all the way through. Annoyance sizzled up and down my spine like an electric current. I should have sat down more slowly to avoid the splash. Melanie coughed and spluttered while I patiently waited for her to get ahold of herself. At last her head dropped forward to her chin, and she sniffled. "I want to go home," she managed to strangle through her stressed lungs.

"Why, Melanie?" I urged. "Why do you want to go home?"

Her sobs grew louder. "I'm scared."

Wrong answer.

"Back you go," I said with a sigh. "It's for your own good," I added, but she was already under and probably didn't hear me.

The next time around, when I'd granted her a breathing reprieve and asked if she was scared, Melanie bit her lip and appeared to consider her answer.

"Yes. No. Whatever you want me to say!" The wailing began anew. "I don't know what you want. Just tell me. Please."

I gently brushed back the wet locks of hair that obscured her face so as to better witness her pain and terror. "I want you to tell the truth," I explained. "To be strong."

She nodded, her head knocking against the wet wood. "I will. I promise. Whatever you want."

Could this girl be saved? Lord knows I'd done my best. But they never seemed to grasp the notion of my correcting. Only one girl ever had, but she'd tricked me and escaped. I wouldn't be tricked again by a pretty face.

"Please," she begged.

I felt sorry for her. She really was pitiful. Maybe I could take her home. Keep her awhile.

The unmistakable putter of another boat drifted toward us from the other side of a nearby large point. Melanie's eyes lit with hope, and her mouth opened. A shrill caterwaul escaped from her lips, piercing the darkness before I could stop the damage. I jumped to my feet, and the board began to crash into the water. I barely gripped it before it completely submerged. Thank God I'd had the foresight to tie a rope to the bottom ends of the board and to anchor the whole contraption around the base of the captain's seat.

A moment of silence and then, "Anybody out there?" a deep voice called out.

I swiveled and looked in all directions, furtive and panicked myself. What should I do? *Get the hell out of Dodge, stupid.*

I gunned the motor and headed toward the house. Thump, thump, thump. The board bounced against the sides and bottom of my boat. What if the rope attached to the board got tangled in my motor? I stopped the engine and quickly dragged up the crude torture device.

Melanie lay motionless, her pink-and-purple hair draped across her face.

She looks like a drowned mermaid, I thought, near hysteria. With unsteady hands, I unbuckled the constraints around her knees and ankles.

The sound of the other boat's engine grew louder. There was no time to undo the rope around her upper torso. I spared but a moment to lay my head on her chest. Nothing. She was done for. I started to toss her overboard, desperate to get away. I'd been so sure fishermen wouldn't be out on a night like this. Seemed I was wrong.

Only one task remained. From my pocket, I withdrew a tiny silver bell and stuffed it into the pocket of her jeans. With a large heave, I rolled her deadweight into the water.

I started the motor again and gunned it. Winter wind whipped at my face, and my wet jacket and jeans chilled my skin. I kept going at top speed until I was sure no one was near. I steered the boat to a small inlet and cut the motor.

No answering boat motor chased me down. After several minutes of listening intently, I took off the wet sweatshirt jacket and swiped it over my face, staining the gray material with red lipstick, rouge, and the black kohl lining my eyes.

No one could ever see me like this. No one could ever know.

And they wouldn't. That woman was dead, and there was nothing that tied me to her. Yes, her body would bloat and surface from the water in a matter of days, but all was well. I was invincible.

I still existed. I lived on.

Chapter 8

DELLA

I left Dr. Pennington's office feeling more unsettled than when I'd first arrived. My usual MO was to avoid directly facing my past and my fears. Nobody's fault but my own. He'd done a decent job when I was a kid, diagnosing my phobia and trying to treat my symptoms. It wasn't his fault I was still so . . . unnormal. Every doctor probably had at least one case like me—a patient resistant to therapies that worked for others.

I stuffed the antidepressants prescription he'd written for me into my purse. No way that was getting filled. I'd tried that route once before in my early teens and hadn't liked the weird sensation of numbness that had enveloped my mind. I'd resolved from there on out to own every bit of my anxiety symptoms, much as they sucked.

Three employees huddled in the hallway in front of the nurses' station, gesticulating wildly with their hands and their faces animated.

"Did you hear what happened?" one of the nurses asked. "She's gone. Just vanished."

I slowed my step, curious about what had them so riled.

"Snuck out in the middle of the night," one of them offered. "Packed up all her shit and left without a word to anyone."

"Heads are going to roll on night shift," another remarked, shaking his head. "Bet you anything they've been sleeping on the job. You gotta watch those substance abuse patients like a damn hawk all the damn time."

The male nurse turned to look at me, and I flashed him the employee ID badge hanging around my neck. He nodded and waved as if to say, *She's one of us and not one of the crazies.* Quickly, I picked up my pace and entered the stairwell, applauding my good sense to wear my badge even though my shift didn't start for another couple of hours.

Had it been a mistake going back to Dr. Pennington? A regular psychologist would have sufficed since I didn't want to pursue the medication route. As usual, I'd merely followed the path of least resistance in my choice, traveling down the lane of the familiar and known. Pennington intimately knew my background, and I reasoned that our past association would save time. I wouldn't have to rehash the old. Or so I'd assumed. Instead, Pennington had come down hard asking me to describe my damn feelings when I saw the color red. He outlined a treatment program that consisted of counseling and phobia desensitization. Neither had worked before, but I was willing to try again.

In the spirit of new resolutions and making progress, I decided to eat supper at the Dixie Diner instead of returning to home and safety. I'd kill an hour at the restaurant and then clock into work an hour early.

The diner was abuzz with chatter, the air thick with the scent of fried chicken. I spotted an empty booth and gratefully made a beeline for it. Nobody appeared to pay me any mind, and I slid into the comparative privacy of the booth, away from prying eyes. Baby steps. A menu was propped against the window, anchored in place by a jar of ketchup and pepper and saltshakers. I reached for it and then froze as I read the tacky flyer taped on the window:

"Hunter Stallings, unjustly imprisoned on death row for two decades, needs your help. A trust fund at Community Bank has been set up to help pay his legal expenses. Please support one of Normal's own! Thank you!"

Pasted above the text was Dad's black-and-white grinning photo, seeming to mock me. Dad's new celebrity was a real pain in the ass. I supposed I'd better get used to it.

"What can I get you?"

I nearly jumped at the sudden voice by my side.

"What's the special?" I asked, quickly opening and scanning the menu.

"Fried chicken, mashed potatoes and gravy, and collards," the waitress recited flatly. "Add a drink and pecan pie for only two dollars more."

"I'll take the special and a glass of water. No pie." I closed the menu with a snap.

She scribbled on a notepad, then shot me a polite smile. "Coming right . . . hey, don't I know you? Della, right?"

I studied the sharp beak of her nose and long red hair pulled back in a thick braid. "Ashley?" I asked tentatively.

"That's me." She grinned as though I'd solved a difficult puzzle. "We had the same gym classes in the tenth and eleventh grades."

I vaguely recalled her red hair flopping about as we played volleyball. She'd been good, a strong server. As for me, gym was the longest hour of the school day. I'd always prayed that the ball landed as far from me as possible.

"Surprised I haven't seen you around before," Ashley continued, as though we'd actually been friends back in high school. "What are you up to these days?"

I wished she'd skedaddle, but Aunt Sylvie had raised me to mind my manners. "I work at the hospital. Night shift. Matter of fact, I'm due there shortly." I picked up my cell phone and checked the time as though I was in a rush.

She didn't take the hint. Ashley pointed at the flyer with her pen. "Guess you're glad your dad's out. That's terrible he was locked up for so long for something he didn't do. Bound to make a man bitter."

"What makes you think he didn't do it?" I asked flatly.

Her blue eyes widened. "You think he did?"

I thought it none of her business but decided to pick her brain. "I can't prove anything one way or another." *Yet,* I silently added. "What's the gossip? Do most people think he's innocent or guilty?"

"Seems like folks are split down the middle on whether or not he did it. Lots of the First Baptists tend to believe he's not guilty 'cause of Vic and Mabel, I suppose. But plenty of folks believe he got away with murder."

Count me in the camp that believed he got away with murder. Either that, or Dad had paid someone else to do the dirty deed for him—which sounded like something dear old Dad would do. Too lazy to even commit murder.

Ashley slid into the booth opposite me and leaned forward, her face lit with animation.

"Old Man Brooks was in here the other day, and when he saw one of them flyers, he went *off.* You should have seen his face. It turned practically purple. I thought he was going to bust a vein. Anyway, he said Hunter Stallings had ripped him off of thousands of dollars in insurance money and was still ripping off gullible people who put their hard-earned wages into that there trust fund. Demanded to speak to the manager."

Dad had crossed the wrong person all those years ago. Levaughn Brooks was a surly old coot who nursed grievances like nobody's business, always threatening to sue people over the least little thing. Although, in this case, I didn't blame him for being put out. And by no means was he the only victim in town who harbored ill feelings because Dad had swindled them.

"So why are these still up?" I asked, cocking my head at the flyer. "The manager didn't cow to Brooks?"

"Nope. Not even when he threatened to sue. Asa—the manager here—has had a few rounds with him before and isn't afraid of the guy. Asa said if the preacher believed Hunter Stallings was innocent, that was good enough for him."

Garnering the support of the preacher of Normal's largest church was a real coup for Dad. Seemed he could charm the devil himself when he took the trouble. I'd heard all I needed to know.

"I get the picture," I told Ashley. "Thanks. Don't want to keep you from your job."

"No problem. I'll sit with you after I finish waiting the next couple of tables if you want some company."

"No, that's okay. I've got to eat quick and run."

In hindsight, I should have asked Libbie whether she wanted to eat dinner with me. As a single mom, she was always busy. Eating out would have been a nice break for her and her son, Calvin. I resolved to give her a call soon. It had been a couple of weeks since we'd had a nice chat. At least I had one semifriend in Normal. Not that I faulted the people here for that sad state of affairs. I was entirely to blame. Aunt Sylvie chided me all the time on how reserved and defensive I was around anyone who tried to get close.

She wasn't wrong.

It didn't take long before Ashley plunked down the day's special, and I set to eating. The ambience here was mediocre, but the chicken was fried crisp, the mashed potatoes homemade, and the collards seeping with large hunks of ham and fatback. Good thing I'd kicked ass for two hours this morning in martial arts class. Way I figured, I deserved every calorie of this meal. After gobbling down the food, I pushed my plate away and stared out the window, waiting on the check.

"You didn't order any pie?"

Detective Whitt—Nathan—stared down at me, amusement radiating from his hazel eyes.

"Don't have room for it."

"There's always room for pie." He gestured at Ashley a few tables down, holding up two fingers. "Two pies," he called out in the din before sliding into my booth.

I seemed to be a freaking magnet today for company. Annoyance stiffened my spine. "I told you—"

"They bake them from scratch every morning. It's a crime not to have a slice."

"Going to arrest me if I don't?" I challenged, frowning to drive him away.

"Still upset I thought you might be drunk yesterday? Or is this just more of your usual surly attitude?"

"How would you know my usual attitude?" I asked in genuine surprise.

It was his turn to look taken aback. "You're joking, right? In high school, you put out strong don't-you-dare-speak-to-me vibes. Appears you haven't changed."

The words were harsh, but he delivered them with a smile that took away their bite. I didn't respond immediately, torn between an unwilling flattery that Nathan had even noticed me back then and irritation with the notion I hadn't changed. I settled for shifting the focus back to him. "So why are you speaking to me now?" I asked.

He grinned as Ashley set down our plates. "Maybe I don't intimidate so easily now."

"As if. You strutted around high school like you owned the damn place."

"Sooo." He quirked a brow. "You noticed me then?"

"Hard to miss you and your jock friends." I frowned at him, then stared down at the brown sugary goodness nestled within a perfectly golden crust. I should get up and walk out. Escape the questions and the hundreds of pie calories while I could.

Nathan tapped the side of my plate with his fork. "Go on and take a bite. It's awesome."

I dug in and closed my eyes in pleasure as the warm, syrupy goo of the pecan pie exploded in my mouth. When I opened my eyes, Nathan was staring at me intently, and I swallowed, self-conscious and again annoyed. I knew what kind of vibes he was exuding with those hot hazel eyes, and I wanted none of it.

"Pretty good, huh?" he asked in a suddenly husky voice.

I took a long sip of water. "It'll do." I needed to change the subject. Quickly. I tapped at the flyer. "Have you seen these posters around town?"

He jerked his gaze from me and stared at it. A deep scowl settled across his features. "What a crock of shit. Hunter Stallings doesn't deserve . . ."

I snorted as his voice trailed off, and he faced me with chagrin.

"Oh, sorry," he said sheepishly. "I shouldn't speak ill of your father in front of you."

"No apology necessary. I feel the same way about him." I dug back into my pie and avoided his eyes.

A sudden static crackled through the silent tension running between us. Nathan unclipped the two-way radio from his belt and answered the summons.

"Ten-eighteen to 2423 Captain's Lane on Hatchet Lake," the disembodied voice rumbled. "Body found by hikers."

Body? The sweetness in my mouth soured.

"Ten-four." Nathan stood, his face set in hard lines. He spared me a quick nod and tersely spoke. "Catch you later." In two seconds, he was gone. I watched as he strode to the door, wondering whether he was rushing toward trouble.

Body didn't necessarily equate to murder, I scolded myself. Someone could have suffered a heart attack or stroke while walking around the reservoir. Damn it, nothing but bad news ever seemed to be connected with Hatchet Lake—so named because several generations ago, a man had cut up his wife, Irma, with a hatchet after he caught her meeting another man in the woods by the lake. Many claimed the lake was haunted—that Irma's bloody ghost roamed the land searching for her lover.

I didn't believe in ghosts, although it was right up Aunt Sylvie's alley. But a teenage girl had been murdered there for real, her body discovered a year ago when the lake had been drained for dam repairs. Now it appeared another body had been found at Hatchet Lake.

I signaled Ashley for the check. She strode over, carrying a pitcher. "More water?"

"Check, please."

"Oh, your bill's already been paid."

I stared at her blankly.

"Nathan," she said with a grin. Ashley waved to someone at the table behind me. "Coming," she called as she hurried to them.

Quickly, I retrieved a few bucks from my wallet, wanting to make my escape before someone else tried to join me. I'd at least leave Ashley a tip, though, since she'd been nice. I slapped a few dollar bills on the table and left the booth. Halfway down the aisle, I whirled around on a sudden whim and returned to the booth I'd just vacated. I reached over and ripped Dad's smiling photo off the window. Satisfaction settled in my gut as I balled up the flyer and stuffed it into my half-full water glass, hopefully saving some sucker from wasting money on Dad's greedy cause.

Outside, the sun was setting, offering a cooling respite from the day's heat. October in Alabama didn't even hint of the fall season—no snow or even crisp breezes. Only the weekend football games signaled a changing of the seasons.

Blue lights strobed the parking lot, and I watched as Nathan pulled out, tires squealing. What would he find when he arrived on the scene? A murder victim or someone who'd died from natural causes? I thought of the loved ones left behind and what a grisly evening it would be for them.

I started my car and glanced at the clock. Plenty of time to burn before my shift started. Maybe I'd ease on by Captain's Lane and check out what was going on. No harm in taking a quick peek. I headed in that direction out of town. At least three cop cars passed me en route, lights on and sirens pealing. This certainly didn't have the feel of an accidental death. By the time I turned off the main road onto Captain's Lane, a dizzying strobe of blue lights accosted me before I made it to the address.

Men and women in uniform swarmed in front of a huge floodlight that had been set up in a vacant lot. First responders were everywhere, all seemingly talking at once. Dogs barked excitedly and were tightly restrained on leashes. A few onlookers—I assumed they lived in the neighborhood—stood around the outskirts of the action, necks craning to glimpse what was happening. The place buzzed with an urgent energy.

A loud horn blared from behind, and I nearly jumped out of my skin. I hastily pulled to the side of the road. A black sedan came within inches of clipping me as it roared past and then drove onto the field. The seal of the county coroner's office was emblazed on the sides and back of the vehicle.

A man waved the sedan over to where a group of people were clustered by the edge of the woods. Another light show peeped out from deep inside the darkness, this time produced by the flash of cameras and flashlight beams. Shortly afterward, two men carried out a stretcher. The body on it was completely covered by a tarp. I searched for Nathan in the crowd of cops who were scanning the area with flashlights pointed to the ground. I was pretty sure I caught sight of his profile, but it was hard to be certain from this distance. Time for me to leave and let him and the other cops do their job.

I cut the steering wheel to the left and began to ease away when a shimmer of pink came into my peripheral vision. It seemed out of place, so I narrowed my eyes, trying to decipher the anomaly.

A police officer held up a pink sneaker bedazzled with pink sequins in a gloved hand, shining his flashlight on it. A shudder of recognition traveled up my spine, and I was transported back to that night nearly two weeks ago when I'd encountered the mysterious girl in the hospital stairwell, her hot-pink, glittery sneakers sparkling against the dingy gray concrete stairs.

I got out of the car and moved closer to the group until I picked Nathan out and then strode directly to him. He left the group he was standing with and approached me, frowning. "What are you doing here? Did you follow me?"

"Couldn't help overhearing the address back at the diner. Call me curious."

"You shouldn't be here. This is a crime scene. Go on home."

Not a trace of the interested guy from the diner remained in his brusque manner. "I didn't come here to gawk. Well, maybe at first. But I was fixin' to leave when I saw . . ." I glanced to my left and pointed. "Until I saw an officer over there holding up a shoe. One I recognized. I think I know who the shoe belongs to . . . or rather, *belonged* to. Is that . . . was it a young woman's body you found? Shoulder-length brown hair with streaks of pink and purple?"

"How could you . . . ?" His voice trailed off as he waved both his hands in the direction of an officer bagging evidence. When he faced me again, his jaw was rigid, his eyes skeptical. "You really think from that distance, in the twilight, you could recognize a mere shoe?"

"Not just any shoe," I quickly explained. "But it was a pink glittery sneaker. Very unusual."

"You tagged her description all right. Any idea who our Jane Doe might be?"

"I don't know her name," I admitted.

He frowned harder but turned his attention to the officer who'd reached us. Nathan nodded in my direction. "This person claims to recognize that shoe. Let her get a closer look."

The officer obliged, aiming his flashlight on the sneaker like a spotlight.

"How do you know what the victim looked like? Where have you seen her before?" Nathan asked.

"At Normal Hospital. I work the night shift, and a couple weeks ago I encountered a woman on the stairwell wearing sneakers like that."

"You'd never met her before? You don't know her name?"

"I don't. It was an accidental meeting. She told me she was in the drug rehab program and was sneaking out from her room to get a little privacy and a smoke."

"That'll be easy to check out. We'll get a patient roster from the hospital."

My mind leaped to the conversation I'd overheard today about the patient who'd left with no warning, and I filled Nathan in with this information as well.

"We're on it," he said, gesturing for the other officer to leave. "I need to talk to my lieutenant. We'll need a formal statement from you later."

"What happened to her? Did she overdose or what?"

"This was no overdose," he said grimly.

My throat grew dry. "A horrible accident?"

"No. Not that either."

Nathan's jaw set, and his lips thinned into a tight line. He didn't reveal the cause of death. But the word hung between us.

Murder.

I had to get away. The crowd of cops and strobing emergency lights were too much like the night I'd been found hiding in the woods, cowering from the monster that had killed my family.

"You know who I am and where to find me." I spun away, my duty done.

"Hey, Della," Nathan called out from behind me. "Thanks for the info. You've been a big help."

I threw up a hand, waving in acknowledgment of his words as I continued walking back to my car. Was it possible she'd stumbled into a killer's path while sneaking out for a smoke? I wished I'd reported the incident to security the night we'd met. If I had, maybe she'd have gotten in trouble and been watched more closely by staff. Should have trusted my first instinct to report her to security.

Who had killed this woman? And why? A sudden notion stopped me in my tracks, heart thumping wildly. We hadn't had a murder in Normal since Mom and Jimmy. But now that Dad had only been out of prison a week, a body was discovered. My scalp prickled, and I swallowed hard. Much as I despised Dad, I shouldn't jump to conclusions. What reason would he have had to murder this unknown girl?

Still, the coincidence didn't sit well with me, and I wondered whether the cops would make a connection between Dad's recent release and this woman's death. I balled my hands into fists and dug my nails into my palms so hard I felt a droplet of blood ooze out.

Chapter 9
DET. NATHAN WHITT

Dawn was breaking as I pulled onto Vic Stallings's property, noting the jon boat positioned beside the large shed in the backyard.

That answered one question. Hunter Stallings had access to a boat. But, to be fair, most folks around here did. Fishing was a popular pastime.

And yet the one piece of physical evidence we'd found on the victim's body indirectly suggested a link to Stallings—albeit a very tenuous one. I hoped for Della's sake that Hunter had a valid alibi for last night. I wasn't optimistic. After all I'd heard from my fellow officers, I was convinced he was guilty of murdering his wife and son eighteen years ago. Once someone crossed that line in taking a life, they proved to me that they were capable of doing so again. And the fact that the murder at Hatchet Lake had occurred only days after Hunter had returned to town . . . well, that was one mighty big coincidence. Even his own daughter believed he was guilty.

The image of Melanie Mickelson's drowned body hog-tied to a length of plywood was forever seared into my brain. Her death had not been quick but designed for a lengthy torture. Waterboarding was used as an interrogation technique, and I wondered whether Mickelson had seen something she shouldn't have, and the killer had tried to pry that information from her. Either that, or he was a sadist who'd enjoyed watching her suffer. Mickelson's nose had also been shattered, presumably from a punch to the face.

The coroner's initial assessment was that she'd been dead approximately twenty-four to thirty-six hours. Hospital staff had reported her as missing sometime between midnight and six o'clock in the morning yesterday. Cause of death was drowning.

I got out of the car, feeling the fatigue in my legs. I'd gotten no sleep last night after the discovery of the body. Before I even mounted the porch steps, the door swung open, and a tall bearded man watched me with a stoic set to his jaw. Dogs barked from somewhere in the house.

"You must be Victor Stallings. I'm Detective Whitt with the Normal Police Department. Sorry to disturb you so early in the morning."

He shrugged. "I'm a farmer. I've already eaten breakfast and was about to head to the field. Is there a problem, Detective?"

"I need to speak with Hunter Stallings. I understand he's staying with you?"

The man didn't look a bit surprised. "Come on in."

The barking was loud and incessant as Vic led me inside. "I put the dogs up in the guest room. Go ahead and have a seat while I get Hunter."

He stepped into the hallway, and I heard him order the dogs to stop barking. Surprisingly, they obeyed him at once. It took several minutes before he reemerged from the hallway, his brother in tow.

At last I came face-to-face with the notorious Hunter Stallings as he stumbled into the room, wincing at the bright overhead light. He was at least six feet tall with light sandy-brown hair that was close cropped and blue eyes shot through with red. Della and he didn't favor much. She was petite with dark hair and green eyes. Must have gotten her looks from her mother, I decided.

Hunter dropped onto the leather sofa, rubbing both hands over his face. A flicker of annoyance lit Vic's eyes. I suspected Hunter's temporary stay in his home was beginning to grate.

"I'll leave you to your business, if that's okay, Detective," Vic said, turning to me. "Got work to do outside."

"Of course," I assured him. I wanted to speak to Hunter alone.

At the door, Vic suddenly swerved around. "Excuse my manners. Would you like something to drink? My wife, Mabel, usually handles these things, but she's not home. Visiting her sister a couple days."

By *these things*, I assumed he meant hospitality duties. I waved him off. "No, thanks, I'm good."

"I could use a drink," Hunter grumbled. "I'm thirsty as hell."

"You know where the kitchen is," Vic said, not bothering to hide the irritated edge in his tone. The door slammed shut behind him, leaving me alone with Hunter.

I wasted no time. "Mr. Stallings, I'm Detective Whitt, Normal Police Department. I'd like to ask you a few questions."

"About what?" He narrowed his eyes and regarded me directly for the first time. "Should have expected cops to come round here sooner rather than later and start harassing me for no damn reason."

"No harassment," I assured him calmly. "Just need to know your whereabouts last evening."

He threw his hands in the air and snickered. "Yeah, I get it. Anytime something happens out of the ordinary, you people are going to show up on my doorstep asking questions."

"Isn't this your brother's house?" I asked.

His face darkened. "You know what I mean."

"I assure you that's not the case. However, I do need to know where you were all last night."

He stood abruptly. "If I'm going to be questioned, I need a tall glass of water and a couple aspirin first." He strode halfway to the kitchen before tossing his head over a shoulder and asking, "Sure you don't want anything?"

At least he had a modicum of manners. "No, thank you." I stifled my annoyance as I heard him open and shut cabinet doors, pour water from a tap, and finally return to the sofa. Once he settled back down, he popped two pills in his mouth, swigged water, then threw his head back and swallowed.

"About last night," I prompted.

"I was here. I'm sure my brother will vouch for me."

"All night?" I asked. I already knew he'd been out late drinking at the Triple K bar, but I wanted to see how much he truthfully volunteered.

"No, I had a couple drinks. But you probably already knew that."

I didn't confirm or deny it. "What time did you return here?"

"About . . ." He rubbed his jaw. "I'd say about midnight, maybe? It was late."

"Can your brother confirm that?"

Hunter set his glass on a coffee table and crossed his arms. "He was already in bed when I got home, but I'm thinking he must have heard me come in. Why all the questions, Detective?"

"Whitt. Did you go anywhere else between leaving the bar and coming home?"

"No. Why?"

I didn't answer, letting the silence stretch out.

"Ah, hell," Hunter said, his mouth twisting in disgust. "Let me guess. Somebody's got hurt or accused me of something." He leaned forward and picked up a cigar from the humidor on the coffee table and began to unwrap the cellophane coating. "Vic doesn't like me smoking in the house, but I reckon he can make an exception this once."

I caught the gleam of the red-and-gold cigar band. My pulse quickened. "What brand of cigar you smoke?"

"Arturo Fuente," he said, flicking open a lighter.

I suppressed my surge of excitement. "In that case, we need to continue our discussion down at the station."

~

I stood outside the holding room with Senior Detective Josh Adams. Impressive title until you learned there were only two of us in our small department and that Adams was the police chief's nephew. But that didn't stop Adams from acting as though he were smarter and better than everyone else on the force. It didn't win him any friends. As for me, I mostly let his air of superiority glide off me like water on duck feathers.

From the one-way mirror we observed Hunter pacing the small room, eyes downward as he strode back and forth like an agitated wild animal ready to pounce at the first opportunity.

"It's only been fifteen minutes," Adams noted. "He already looks ready to explode."

"After all those years on death row, I imagine this brings back bad memories. All the way down here, he yelled about how we're trying to frame him again." I shook my head, my ears still ringing from Hunter's loud screams of protest on the drive. "Local law enforcement aren't high on his list of people to be trusted."

Not that I blamed him. Brady Eckeridge had tainted the Normal PD's reputation so badly it might never recover from the blow.

Adams glanced at his watch. "Let's give him a few more minutes to stew before we go in. Maybe he'll get so pissed off he'll get careless during the questioning."

"Sounds like a plan. Any new leads while I was gone?"

"Nothing. Cops on the ground are still going door-to-door to see if anyone might have seen or heard anything unusual in the past forty-eight hours. Forensics experts are also scouring the area where the body was found."

"Maybe it will be easier going now that it's daylight."

"Let's hope so," Adams said. "I need to talk to the chief. Meet me back here in fifteen minutes."

"Ten-four."

While Adams went into Chief Thornell's office, I drummed my fingers on the desk and considered the significance of the matching cigar bands. It looked bad for Hunter Stallings. All we needed to do was find some connection between him and the victim to establish a motive. Without that, everything fell apart.

My thoughts again drifted to Della. How would she respond to this latest news? She claimed to want her father locked up again, but knowing he'd murdered another innocent person would certainly dredge up old memories for her. I thought of the stubborn lift of her chin, the way her unusual green eyes hardened at the mention of her father, at the way she'd cut everyone out in high school and held her head high at the stares and whispers.

The woman was tough, forged from fire and grief. She'd been through the worst and would survive this latest incident. Adams finally reentered our office.

"Anything new?" I asked.

He shook his head. "The cops in Robertsdale are still trying to find Mickelson's boyfriend for questioning. If we're lucky, the boyfriend might know Stallings or of some connection between Stallings and Mickelson. There has to be one. How else can we explain the engraved bell we found stuffed in her pocket? The M. & S. initials are the first letters of their last names. But don't bring that up with Stallings. Not yet. We'll keep it as our ace in the hole. You ready to see what Stallings has to say?"

I had my own idea about the initials, but I'd keep my mouth shut until I had time to ask Della about them. I picked up the file from my desk and followed him to the holding room. The moment we entered,

Hunter stopped pacing and glared at us. "You can't do this to me. I know my rights, and you can't hold me unless you arrest me."

"You're wrong, Mr. Stallings." Adams sat in one of the folding chairs and indicated for Hunter to have a seat. "The state allows us to provide you accommodation for up to seventy-two hours before we have to either release you or arrest you."

I remained standing in case Hunter made a sudden lunge at Adams.

"I want my lawyer," Hunter announced.

"That's your right, Mr. Stallings." Adams turned to me. "Take him to the public phone, and then tell the guards to prepare a cell."

"You can't do this!" Panic replaced the anger on Hunter's face.

"I'm going to do it unless you can convince me you had nothing to do with Ms. Mickelson's murder. Your choice."

"You bastards," Hunter said, hands clenching at his sides. "I just served eighteen years for something I didn't do. I can't take being locked up again. I—I just can't."

With that, he folded. His head hung down as he finally collapsed in the seat across the table from us. "I'll talk," he whispered.

We were in business. I sat beside Adams as he began to question Hunter further. "Now. You told Detective Whitt you were at the Triple K bar last night. How many drinks did you have?"

"A few."

"How many is a few?"

"About seven, I guess. I wasn't counting."

"Were you alone?"

"Yes."

"Why did you go there?"

Hunter's lips pursed together, and I didn't expect him to answer, but he surprised me. "I've been upset about my relationship with my daughter."

"Not going well?" Adams asked with false sympathy.

Hunter buried his head in his hands, and his shoulders shook. Adams kicked me under the table, and I glanced at him. Adams rolled his eyes. Clearly, he wasn't buying this sob story. "Show him the photos," Adams told me.

I opened the file and slid an enlarged photograph of the victim across the table. The edge of the photo brushed Hunter's forearm, and he glanced up, startled. Despite the earlier display of emotion, there were no tears on his face. His gaze slid down to the photo, and he gasped at the grisly image. He scooted back in his chair.

"No, no, no! I had nothing to do with this. I don't even know who this is."

"Her name is Melanie Mickelson," I volunteered, searching for a flicker of recognition in his eyes. They remained open and blank. Another acting job like the crocodile tears over his concern for Della? "Sure you didn't know this woman?"

"I'm positive. I swear I've never seen her before."

"Did you go on a little boat ride last night, Mr. Stallings?" Adams asked.

"What? No. I—I don't even have a boat."

"But your brother does," I said. "I saw it out by the barn this morning."

"That old thing? I'm not sure it even runs anymore."

Adams spoke up. "We'll have it tested, of course. And combed for evidence."

"Fine. You won't find anything."

"I've asked around," Josh continued. "People say you used to be quite the fisherman."

"That was years ago," Hunter protested. "Me and the guys used to do a little night fishing and drinking, but I haven't been on a boat for ages."

"So you are used to operating a boat at night, even while intoxicated," Adams pointed out.

Hunter's face flushed. "Why are you guys fucking with me? I told you I don't even know this Melanie person."

A triumphant smile crossed Adams's face. "Then how do you explain the Arturo Fuente cigar band found at the murder scene?"

Adams nodded at me, and I produced a photo of the evidence collected last night and slid it to Hunter.

Hunter paled, and his mouth fell open at the photograph.

"Same brand you smoke," I said. "I'm willing to bet there's not another person in Normal that smokes them. They aren't sold locally. You'd have to order them online or visit a specialty cigar shop in Huntsville to purchase them."

Hunter licked his lips and swallowed hard. "I—I don't get it." His voice dropped so low I had to lean forward to catch his words. "Someone must be trying to frame me."

"Who would do that? And why would they?"

"Plenty of people. Lots of folks think I ripped them off with their insurance policies."

I let the skepticism sound in my voice. "And so they'd kill an innocent person and frame you for the murder? That's a little far fetched."

"It wasn't me!"

Adams snickered, and Hunter kept his gaze on me. "Look, I'm not stupid. I'd never leave such an obvious piece of evidence behind."

"Not intentionally," I agreed.

Hunter momentarily shut his eyes and then opened them to regard us both wearily. "For all I know, you or any of the other cops on scene last night could have set me up. Eckeridge did it years ago, and who's to say it's not happening now? It's the past all over again. Take me to that phone so I can call my lawyer."

Adams and I left the holding room.

"Let's lock that bastard up," Adams said in a frustrated growl. Hunter's dig about the dirty cop had hit home.

"Say we do. How do you think the news media are going to cover this? It will bring up all the old Eckeridge news again. And since we have no definite connection yet between Stallings and the victim, let alone a motive . . ."

I let my voice drift, letting Adams reach the correct conclusion.

"Could have merely been a crime of opportunity," he grumbled. "Stallings was in the area, saw the woman, and something bad happened between them, so he killed her."

I said nothing. I could tell Adams had seen the risk of holding Stallings. If there was one thing he and his uncle feared, it was bad press.

Chapter 10

DELLA

The doorbell rang insistently, and I dragged myself out of bed. Through the slatted blinds, I spotted a lone cop car parked in the driveway. That sure cleared any remaining mental fog of sleep. Aunt Sylvie's car was gone, and I remembered she'd planned to drive into Huntsville today for more craft supplies. A major arts and crafts festival was slated for the end of the month, and it was one of her most profitable venues. People loved buying her homemade cinnamon-scented brooms for Halloween decorations.

What a crappy day, though, to have to drive so far. The sky was a damp pewter that eked out a steady drizzle that could only be described as miserable.

The bell rang again—Nathan, perhaps?—and I hastily donned a pair of jeans and a T-shirt. He'd mentioned last night he'd need a statement from me. Much as I wished, there wasn't time to even run a brush through my hair. I hurried to the door and slung it open.

Nathan stared back at me, grim faced and unsmiling. His hair and face trickled with rain. I hadn't expected a Hallmark moment kind of greeting, but his utter lack of friendliness caught me by surprise.

"Guess you're here for my statement," I said unnecessarily.

"Did I wake you?"

I ran a hand through the tangles in my hair. "Yeah. I work the night shift at the hospital and sleep during the day. Come on in, and let me take your coat."

He entered, shrugged out of a dark-blue rain slicker that looked department issued, and handed it to me. As I placed it on the hall hanger, he regarded me soberly. Flustered, I waved for him to enter the den. His cop eyes swept the room, no doubt expertly recording every detail. If he found all of Aunt Sylvie's scattered altars and crystals strange, he didn't comment on them.

"Have a seat," I invited again, sitting primly on the edge of the sofa.

Nathan nodded and sat in the chair opposite me and took a note-book and pen from his shirt pocket. "Tell me everything about your encounter with the victim."

Appeared we were getting straight down to business, which suited me fine. I hadn't exactly been warm yesterday at the diner when he'd tried to be friendly. "Not much to tell other than what I'd already told you," I began. "We met in the stairwell, and she seemed in a big hurry. Kind of furtive, you know what I mean? Jittery. Kept looking back over her shoulder like she expected someone might be following her." I shrugged. "At first, she claimed to be a visitor, then admitted she was sneaking out for a cigarette. She held up a crumpled pack that appeared half-empty."

"What brand?"

"Pretty sure it was Marlboro. It had a red-and-white design. I started to call security on my cell phone and then hung up. She seemed grateful that I didn't rat her out, and we went our separate ways. That's pretty much the whole story."

"Was she carrying anything else with her?"

I frowned, concentrating. "Not that I know of. Unless it was con-cealed in her jacket or something. Why?"

He tapped his pencil against his notebook and studied me. "Did you hear any unusual sounds in the stairwell?"

His question puzzled me. "No. Nothing other than the noise of our footsteps and voices."

"When she left you, did you hear a faint noise like a bell or chime of some sort?"

"Might have been a ping from the elevator doors. I can't say for sure. Why do you ask?"

Nathan evaded my question. "I take it from our conversation last night that you aren't exactly on good terms with your father. That you believe he's responsible for your mother's and brother's deaths. Correct?"

My pulse quickened, and my entire body flushed with heat. "Do you think that my dad . . . that he . . ." I couldn't bring myself to speak the words.

"Everything is mere speculation at this point."

Of course the coincidence of Dad's recent release and this latest murder hadn't gone unnoticed by the police. I stood and paced the room. Dad was a killer; there was no question in my mind on that score. He'd killed Mom because of their relentless, nasty marriage problems or for the insurance money, or for a combination of both. Maybe Mom had just stood in the way of him and another woman. You could take your pick of motives. As for Jimmy, he'd been a hapless victim who'd unexpectedly walked in during the crime. A boy who had to be silenced. I mentally recoiled at the image of the man in black plunging his knife into my little brother without a speck of hesitation. Jimmy's only mistake had been to run to my screaming mother, who was already covered in blood. Already dying. But perhaps he'd made the right choice in the end. I liked to think they found comfort in holding each other as their lifeblood drained from their bodies.

I'd only escaped by pure luck. And by my incredible selfishness in choosing to lay in my warm bed and not immediately go after Jimmy when he'd headed downstairs. Would my brother be alive today if I'd stopped him? Or would I also be dead now? Some days, I imagined death better than living with my memories.

I stood before Aunt Sylvie's ancestral altar, gazing at the smiling photos of Mom holding Jimmy as a baby. I trailed an index finger along the inch-deep layer of dirt sprinkled on the altar cloth. Graveyard dirt. I crumbled the grainy bits of orange earth between my fingertips until they were scraped raw.

Another body bites the dust. Ashes to ashes, we all fall down.

But why would Dad kill this woman? This stranger? What was his motive?

"Della?" Nathan asked. "Are you okay?"

Hell, no. I hadn't been okay in eighteen years. "Sure, I'm fine." I dusted my hand against my jeans and faced him. "Do you have any reason to suspect my father killed this woman? Other than the timing?"

"We found something highly unusual stuffed in the victim's jeans pocket. Something we aren't disclosing to the public."

I stared at him mutely, willing him to go on.

"I need your help to clarify a detail. Can I trust you not to speak of this matter with anyone else? Not even your aunt?"

"Yes. Of course."

"We found a silver bell," he said and then paused a heartbeat. "And it was engraved with fancy scrolled initials. *M. & S.* At least, that's what we're guessing. The etching is very faint and hard to read."

M. & S. The initials fit for *Mary Stallings*, but the ampersand in the middle would make no sense if the bell had belonged to Mom. The symbol suggested the first names of a couple engraved on it.

Nathan retrieved his cell phone and tapped the screen. "Take a look," he said, handing it to me.

The image was grainy and the bell tarnished with age, but I enlarged the section that had been marked with a circle. I frowned, concentrating. The *M* and the *S* were unmistakable, but the middle . . .

Sudden understanding spiked in my brain. The middle character wasn't an ampersand. It was the letter *B*—*M. B. S.*

Mary Baines Stallings.

Mom.

The world burst open under my feet. I was falling down a tunnel, spinning in a vortex of distorted images and sounds. Gongs chimed madly between my ears, great clangs that warned of doom and destruction. They jangled and jarred in a cacophony that surely came straight from an underground inferno. Hell's bells. Bells that had been wrenched from atop church steeples and were descending with me into a mad abyss.

"Della? Della?" Warm, strong hands brushed hair back from my forehead. "Take deep breaths. Everything's going to be okay. Concentrate on my voice."

I did. I closed my eyes and listened to the deep timbre of Nathan's voice as I felt myself slowly grounded again in the chilling present. I was sitting on my ass, my breathing rapid and shallow.

"Long, slow breaths," Nathan said. He laid a hand on my back and gently directed my head between my knees. "That's it. Easy now."

I don't know how much time had passed between my seeing Mom's initials and slowly rising to my feet, Nathan's hands around my waist, guiding me to the sofa. I sank into the familiar cushions and angrily swiped at my eyes, ticked at my pathetic display of weakness. I didn't like anyone seeing me that way, not even Aunt Sylvie.

"Want a glass of water?" he asked.

"Nope. I'm fine." I drew a breath. "That engraving isn't *M. & S.*—it's *M. B. S.*, my mom's initials. I recognize that bell. Dad gave it to her one Christmas as a stocking stuffer."

Nathan nodded. "Thank you. That will be a tremendous help to our investigation."

Had I just condemned my own father? "Are you going to arrest Dad now?" I asked.

Debbie Herbert

"No. It's still the early stages of the investigation. After the fiasco of his last overturned conviction, we have to be one hundred percent sure of the evidence this time."

"It had to be him," I insisted, ignoring the tightening in my chest. "How else did that bell get there?"

"I'm sure when questioned he'll contend that he was either framed by the real killer or that the cops are planting evidence to frame him again and send him away for good."

I closed my eyes, thinking about what the victim's family must be going through. "What was her name?" I asked gruffly. "The woman who was killed?"

Nathan raised a brow. "You really *have* been sleeping all day not to have heard the news. It's all over the TV and radio. The whole town is buzzing about it." He again sat across from me, resting his arms on his knees and leaning forward. "To start with, the victim's name is Melanie Mickelson, and she was a patient in Normal Hospital's substance abuse program. Age twenty-three and a longtime methamphetamine addict. Her family's from Mobile, and this was her third residential treatment program. Her parents had warned their daughter this was her last chance and they were through with her if she didn't kick her drug habit for good this time."

What a rough end to a rough life. Would the third time around have been the charm for Melanie to finally get her life on track? Despite her extreme thinness and jittery manner, there had been a vulnerability in her eyes, a certain likeability in her raw plea for understanding that had touched me. And heaven knew I was a tough nut to crack.

"Melanie," I said softly. Such a pretty name. Such a young girl. "Has her family already come to view the body? They must be devastated."

"They arrived early this morning and confirmed her identity."

Those poor parents having to witness the carnage. "How bad was her body? Was she stabbed to death or what?"

"No. She'd suffered a head wound and a few defensive marks on her hands and arms, but she actually died from drowning."

"Drowning?" I hadn't expected that. It didn't fit with how Dad had killed my mom and brother either.

"Coroner said her lungs were filled with fluid. Mickelson's body was found onshore by two fishermen."

"But you found her shoes in the woods." I struggled to fill in what must have happened to Melanie. She'd been in the woods, running from the killer, and lost one or both of her shoes. There'd been a physical struggle with her assailant, and then . . . "What about the rest of her clothes? Were they in the woods, too? Was her body found naked?"

"Only one of her sneakers was found along with a torn, bloody shirt. The shoe might have slipped off while she was attempting to run from the perpetrator. And we're speculating that the shirt may have been ripped from her during a physical altercation. There was a contusion on her left temple, and her wrists were chafed."

I pictured the horror of the bad man catching up to her, just as he'd almost caught up to me when he'd chased me into the woods eighteen years ago. I'd been the lucky one. I'd escaped. So the man had caught up to Melanie, maybe punched her face, and then bound her wrists and taken her to the water.

"Had she been . . ." I swallowed hard.

"Raped? We're waiting on the coroner's report. But the rest of her clothes—bra, underwear, and jeans—were on her body when it was found."

"Why? Goddamn it, why?"

"That's what we're trying to figure out. Could be she left the hospital hoping to meet a dealer to score some drugs, and the deal went bad."

"But then there's that bell you found." I rubbed my temples. "Dad's done a lot of stupid criminal shit, but he's never been involved with rape or dealing drugs." I considered my answer. "Not that I'm aware of anyway," I quickly amended. "I mean, a man who would stab his four-year-old son to death is capable of anything, I suppose."

"Lots of possibilities we're exploring," Nathan said. "Mickelson had a boyfriend. A fellow addict she'd lived with on the streets before the homeless shelter had a bed available for her. We're trying to locate him now to see if she'd contacted him to help her leave the treatment program. Maybe the guy drove up here, and they had an argument."

"Must have been one hell of an argument."

He shrugged. "Addicts can be violent and unpredictable."

Terrible as that scenario sounded, a small part of me hoped that was what had gone down. That there was an innocent explanation for the bell found on the body. That Dad hadn't further stained his rotten soul with more blood.

"But, of course, that doesn't explain what that bell was doing at the crime scene," Nathan said, echoing my thoughts.

"Have you questioned my father yet?"

At that, Nathan clammed up. I had my answer. It was surprising he'd divulged as much as he had. I abruptly rose, wanting to be alone to process these latest developments. "Well, you've got my statement. Anything else you need from me?"

"No. Got it." Nathan stood as well. "If you have time before your shift, come down to the station to sign a written statement. If we have any further questions, we'll be in touch. And if your father should contact you about this matter, we'd appreciate your relaying that information."

I shuddered, hoping like hell that he wouldn't. Why would he? Nathan headed to the foyer and turned to face me at the door. "Take care of yourself, Della."

"What will happen to Mom's bell?" I blurted, then felt my face and neck flush with heat. "I mean, I know it's evidence, but can I get it back one day? 'Cause, you know, it belonged to her. To my mom."

Tainted as the memento now was, it still meant something to me.

"I'll see what I can do," he promised.

As soon as the door shut behind him, I flipped on the local TV news channel. Sure enough, a reporter was on camera, huddled under an umbrella, the tall pines and oaks surrounding Hatchet Lake in the background. That lonely stretch of land on Captain's Lane was now teeming with news vans from Huntsville as well as state and local law enforcement vehicles. Yellow tape sectioned off an area near the tree line, and a couple of police officers stood guard, preventing reporters from getting too close. Cops and canines were scouring the area.

Shouldn't they have finished searching by now? Maybe they'd had to abandon the exploration early last night because of the rain and darkness. I barely paid attention to the reporter's droning voice, instead mesmerized by all the activity. Officers emerged several times from the woods, carrying opaque bags, their faces stern and their eyes warning bystanders and camera operators to keep their distance. What in the world were they finding out there?

"Unconfirmed reports are stating that there may have been more than one body discovered in this remote area," the reporter said.

My attention snapped to her animated face. She spoke with a crisp, controlled excitement as rain drizzled down her umbrella and fogged the camera screen. "Normal Police Chief Dan Thornell is expected to make a brief announcement here within the hour. In the meantime, we'll continue live coverage as police officers and state troopers continue their search of the area. As you can see, officers are emerging from the wooded area behind me, carrying what appears to be evidence bags of crimes that . . ."

No wonder Nathan had appeared so damn grim.

I had to be there. At the scene. To witness firsthand what was really going down. To hear what the police chief had to say. If I was lucky, Nathan might be there, and I could press him to provide more information than I'd ever get from the TV news. Screw heading to the police station first.

Unheeding of my appearance, I grabbed a raincoat and struggled into a pair of boots before collecting my purse and keys. Rain pelted my face as I ran to the car. I turned on the radio—sure enough, they were reporting on the death of Melanie Mickelson and speculating about other murders that might or might not have taken place at Hatchet Lake. They even brought up the old news report of the skeletal remains of a young teenage girl that had been discovered last year.

I sped along the roads with none of my usual caution of wet conditions. Muddy water splashed my sedan, and my worn tires slid ominously through every puddle. The rain picked up. My tricky windshield wipers, which I'd been meaning to replace for months, did a piss-poor job of clearing the window, but I didn't even care.

Dad, Dad, Dad—what have you done? They should never have let you out of prison. Never.

I made it to the crime scene with no clear memory of navigating the roads. Cars and trucks sloppily lined both sides of the main street. Yellow police tape blocked the entrance to Captain's Lane. Red-and-blue lights strobed through the darkened woods. *Shit.* I haphazardly pulled my vehicle over to the side of the road, as the rest of the curious bystanders—drawn to this violent place where screams and unspeakable deeds had been absorbed by sturdy, silent trees—had done.

I climbed out into the frenzy, determined not to let the flashes of red stop me. I kept my gaze down on my boots as I sloshed my way to the front of the crowd being held back by a line of cops. Snippets of conversation pelted me along with the cold rain.

"Nothing good ever came of this here place."

"Ya hear they found more bodies?"

"Who do you reckon . . . ?"

"I can't see nothing. What's happening?"

"What sicko coulda done this?"

Indeed. That's what I had to know. I walked to where the tape ended on the right side of the road and stepped past the line.

A uniformed cop immediately blocked my path. "Hey, lady! What do you think you're doing? Get back."

Her lips were drawn back in an incredulous smirk as she glared at me, hands on her hips.

"I've got business here," I snapped. "What are you going to do? Shoot me?"

I made a sudden move to veer past her, and she grabbed my arm and squeezed. Hard. "I said *get. Back.* Now beat it, or I'll arrest you for trespassing."

The crowd tittered behind me. Another cop standing a few feet away frowned at us and started over to where the woman still held my forearm.

"Let go of me," I said with a hiss, then louder, for the onlookers, "Ouch! Lady, you're hurting me!"

"What's the problem here?" the male cop asked, strutting forward and shaking a finger at me. "You were told to stay back."

The female cop dropped my arm, evidently satisfied I wouldn't get past the two of them.

"I'm here to see Officer Whitt," I bluffed, hoping he'd returned here instead of the police station.

His brows rose, but despite the skeptical glare in his eyes, he got on his two-way radio. "Officer Whitt? What's your ten-twenty?"

Nathan's voice answered.

"There's a woman here by the entrance claiming to have business with you." He paused and asked me, "Your name?"

"Della Stallings."

"Stallings, eh?"

My name had certainly caught his attention, and not in a good way.

"Any relation to Hunter Stallings?"

"Just let Officer Whitt know I'm here."

The cop turned his back to me and walked off. After a few moments of a staticky conversation, of which I couldn't decipher a word, he returned, clipping his radio back on his belt. "He'll be here shortly."

I couldn't stop from flashing a triumphant smirk at the female cop. "Told you," I said, rubbing my arm. "I think you've left a bruise."

"Tough shit," she grumbled, hands back on her hips.

"That's real professional." I turned to the crowd behind me. "Police brutality. You all witnessed it."

A few laughed, but one asshole yelled out, "She warned you to stay back."

I flipped him off, mad at the world and only needing the flimsiest of excuses to direct my anger at the nearest available target. One of my many not-so-endearing qualities. I strode past the female cop, my shoulder brushing against hers.

"Do you want me to take you down?" she asked, grabbing at the sleeve of my raincoat. "Right here, right now, miss? 'Cause I can, you know."

"Like I told you; I have permission to be here from Officer Whitt. Let go of me."

"You aren't going anywhere until he shows up. Now you get"—her words now spat out like hard pebbles—"behind. That. Line."

Her eyes dared me to cross her again. She'd love nothing more than to throw me facedown in the mud and cuff me in front of everyone.

"Officers?" Nathan's voice cut through the tension. "Thanks for alerting me that Miss Stallings arrived. I'll take it from here."

With childish satisfaction unbecoming to a supposedly grown adult, I stepped around the female cop and walked past the yellow tape. My momentary triumph was short lived.

"What the hell do you think you're doing, showing up here and claiming I sent for you," Nathan demanded in a low, hard voice.

"Why didn't you tell me more bodies were found here?"

"Nothing's official until Chief Thornell holds his press conference." His gaze roamed to a man I judged must be the chief. He wore a jacket shiny with a double-breasted row of brass buttons and a blue uniform hat set sharply atop well-groomed silver hair. The man strode importantly in front of a crowd of reporters with cameras on and at the ready. A posse of solemn-faced men in suits crowded behind him. "Appears to be showtime now," Nathan added.

We headed to the edge of the reporter crowd, and if anyone noticed a bedraggled spectator who was obviously out of place, they didn't point me out.

The chief cleared his throat. "As has been reported, the body of a young woman, identified as Melanie Mickelson, was discovered here last night. After a thorough search of the area by my officers"—he paused and gestured to the men behind him—"officers from the Alabama Department of Public Safety, the ABI division, and—"

I groaned with impatience. To hell with their self-aggrandizing need to mention every bureaucrat who'd shown up for a piece of the action. "Get on with it," I mumbled.

Nathan shot me a warning look, and I pursed my lips together and waited for the chief to say something of substance.

"—our joint investigation has uncovered the existence of at least two additional skeletal remains in the same area."

The official words slammed into me like a gut punch. I'd wanted to hear that the rumors of more deaths were wildly untrue. But I knew better. As they say—where there's smoke, there's fire. Cold rain pelted my bare face. The reporters hammered the chief with specific questions about the victims' identities and demands to know whether there was a serial killer among us. He deflected every question, stating that everything was under investigation and no further information would be released until the remains were identified and the families notified.

"Are the crimes related?" one insistent reporter asked. "Do you suspect a serial killer?"

"Again, everything's under investigation," Chief Thornell said. "At this point, all we can do is warn the community to be extra careful until this matter is cleared."

A volley of questions ensued. Nathan took my arm and guided me away. "Let's go somewhere warm and dry."

He marched me past the yellow line on Captain's Lane—and I didn't even spare a glance at the two officers who'd been my earlier adversaries. Curious bystanders peered at me as we passed, and I recognized several faces. Still, I kept my own face blank to discourage interaction. We continued walking past a row of cars until we arrived at a police cruiser. Nathan unlocked the door and gestured for me to enter. I quickly slid inside to the front passenger seat. He shut the door behind me, walked around to the other side, and spoke on the two-way radio for a minute before joining me inside. Nathan sat beside me and wordlessly turned the key to start the motor and blast on the heat. The interior windows fogged, and I felt more self-contained and safe again.

"Feeling any better?" he asked at last.

"Yeah. Thanks for . . ." I weakly lifted my hand and then dropped it. ". . . for everything. You know."

His hands gripped the steering wheel, and he stared straight ahead. "I was on the radio with detectives just now. They've uncovered more significant discoveries."

Now what? I waited for Nathan to explain. He faced me, his eyes grim. "I'd asked you earlier if you heard anything unusual when you encountered Melanie Mickelson in the stairwell."

"The bell. Right."

"Now I need you to search your memory way, way back."

Dread weighted me down. I knew where we were headed.

"Tell me what you remember about the night you witnessed the murders."

"Why?" I asked sullenly. "All of this is a matter of record. Just pull out the old statements on the case and read them."

"I've read them." He reached into his pants pockets, pulled out a pack of gum, and stuffed a piece in his mouth before offering me one. I took it. Maybe it'd help with the sudden dryness in my mouth.

"What we're wondering is if there's a specific detail missing."

"I've told the police everything I remember. I have nothing left to offer. Nothing."

"Please, Della. Think back again, this time concentrating on the sounds."

Those piercing death-throes screams. I clamped my hands over my ears in a childish attempt to block auditory memory. "I don't want to," I said with a groan. "What's the point?"

"Bear with me, Della. Just for a few minutes. You could be a tremendous help to our investigation."

He laid a hand over mine. I closed my eyes and absorbed the warmth of his calloused skin against my own, listened to the rain patter against the car roof and the sound of our merged breaths in the cramped quarters. "I'll try," I whispered.

Nathan squeezed my hand. "Now, about that night. Forget the screams, forget the voices, forget the police sirens. Forget all the obvious sounds, and concentrate on any background noises. Is something out of place? Some small noise that doesn't fit in with what was happening?"

My eyes shot open, and a new horror washed over me. "You want to know if I heard bells the night they were murdered. If I might have seen or heard the killer pocketing some of them."

He didn't deny it. "They might be trophies for him, or have some personal significance to him."

"My God, what the hell is happening out there?" I asked. "They must have found more than just the engraved bell you showed me earlier."

"I hope you understand that I don't have the authority to confirm your guess."

"Then I hope *you* understand that I don't want to subject myself to recalling my mom's and brother's murders for you."

Nathan sighed and removed his hand from mine to scrub at his face. For the first time, I noticed his skin was ashen, and there were dark rings under his eyes. Had he even slept last night? He drummed his fingers against the steering wheel, weighing a decision.

"They're going to call you to the station today or tomorrow anyway," he said finally. "You're the most likely person to be able to identify the other bells found. Doubtful your aunts and uncle paid much notice to the objects in your old home. Not the way you would have, even if you were a child."

"I want to see them."

He dug his cell phone from his pocket and pulled up a photo gallery on the screen. "Click on the first two," he instructed as he passed me the phone.

The first photo was of a small china bell, stained orange from the rust-colored soil by Hatchet Lake. I enlarged the photo and made out the faded words *Come visit Ruby Falls*.

"Mom had one like this," I confirmed. "She collected them. You know, she bought one whenever we went somewhere like Gatlinburg, Tennessee, or Gulf Shores, or sometimes people gave her bells for gifts—ones of angels and stuff like that."

At his silence, I proceeded to the next photo. This bell was a stained porcelain, the lettering plain to read, even after all these years. *NASA Space Center, Huntsville, Alabama.* I spoke around the lump in my throat. "Mom had one like this too. But there must be thousands of stamped bells like either of these two. How can I know for sure they were Mom's?"

"You can't," he agreed. "Not like you were able to identify earlier today that she owned an engraved one."

"I take it these were found buried with the other two skeletal remains."

"You didn't hear that from me."

I slowly nodded. "I owe you one. I'd rather hear it privately from you than in the middle of the police station from a stranger." I drew a deep breath. "And I'd rather try to remember that night with just you here beside me," I admitted.

"Unless you'd be more comfortable doing it with a family member or a counselor—if you're seeing one."

I thought of Dr. Pennington's impassive, clinical demeanor. It wasn't one that welcomed troubled confidences. "There's no need putting Aunt Sylvie through it again," I said, evading the issue of a counselor. "I'll try to remember."

I shut my eyes again and felt the warmth of his hand touching my fingers. I went through it in my mind with as much detail as I could muster—waking up, hearing Jimmy, going after him, the screams, the phone operator, and then the worst sound of all: the dead silence before the man in black had faced me, and then the footsteps growing closer and closer . . . but, wait. There *had* been something between the silence and the footsteps.

A faint tinkling of bells.

I drew in a sharp breath. "I think I remember hearing the sound of a bell this time."

"Is that where your mom kept her bell collection? In the living room, where she . . ." Nathan hesitated.

"Where she was stabbed to death," I supplied, surprised to feel the salty wetness of tears on my cheeks. I scrubbed at them. "She'd kept a collection in a glass-shelved case in the den, but there were too many to fit in the case, so the bells were also scattered everywhere in the house. As far as hearing a bell that night goes . . . I don't know, Nathan. How can I be sure? Maybe instead of really remembering that sound, the idea was merely planted in my brain when you told me what had been found."

"It's possible. Only you can answer that question," he said quietly. "There are no other witnesses."

Maybe Dr. Pennington could help after all. I'd always been resistant to his trying hypnosis on me, but it was time to try. Whatever it took to get to the truth was worth the anguish.

Chapter 11

DR. PENNINGTON

It was starting all over again.

Only this time, the scrutiny was much greater than before. The hospital had been teeming with law enforcement officials since Mickelson's body was discovered four days ago. When it had only been a single dead patient, that was one thing. But the uncovering of skeletal remains of two other persons in the same area drew in cops of all kinds from an alphabet soup of state and federal agencies.

This did not look good for the hospital.

"So tell me, Doctor." The detective seated across from my desk eyed me shrewdly. "Do you believe the victim left this hospital's treatment program with the intention of scoring a quick drug deal and returning later, or do you think she intended to leave the program for good?"

As if I would know. I gazed at the badge he'd laid atop my desk. Detective Josh Adams, Normal PD. So a local guy, and young too. I judged him to be in his late twenties, tops, and guessed he had minimal investigative training coupled with limited experience.

"I'm a psychiatrist, not a mind reader, Detective." I smiled slightly so as not to unduly antagonize him.

"But you probably knew Mickelson more than any other staff person," he insisted. "Maybe even more than her fellow patients. Word is, she was a loner and not one to open up in group counseling sessions or even to her roommates."

Staff person. The MD after my name should have granted me a bit more respect than a mere mention as a staff employee. Was Adams making a small dig of his own?

"I met with Miss Mickelson individually on three occasions. As I'm sure you're aware, she'd broken program rules and, in my professional opinion, needed more intensive therapeutic intervention than could be provided in group sessions."

"She'd tested positive for marijuana and alcohol on a routine drug test," Adams said. "Why wasn't she kicked out of the program? Isn't that what normally happens when a patient is caught using drugs?"

"Not always. We handle these infractions on a case-by-case basis."

"So why did you allow her to stay? Or was it your decision?"

"As head of the substance abuse and mental health programs, I have the final say in all patient admissions and withdrawals."

"Sooo . . ." He quirked a brow expectantly.

"It was my determination that Mickelson was sincerely remorseful for breaking her sobriety and was willing to undergo more intensive therapy to get at the root of her addiction."

"Why did you give her that opportunity and not others with the same type of violation? Just five weeks ago, a patient"—he flipped through his notebook—"by the name of Barry Angliers was kicked out for testing positive on a drug test. Couldn't he have also benefitted from individual counseling?"

This guy was seriously getting under my skin. Who did he think he was to question my professional decisions? I steepled my hands together and let a sliver of displeasure show through my demeanor.

"As I'm sure you're aware, I'm under no obligation to provide details on specific patient medical information. Suffice to say, Mr. Angliers was not a suitable candidate to remain in the program and, I felt, would be a detrimental influence on his peers. We have a long waiting list of people anxious for any available bed space in order to turn their lives around. Those willing to undergo the hard work of rehabilitation deserve this opportunity in our excellent program here at Normal Community Hospital."

"Sure, sure." Detective Adams waved a hand dismissively, uninterested in the plight of those awaiting treatment. "But let's return to the issue of Mickelson's medical records. Now that she's dead, there's no problem in us reviewing her hospital records, is there?"

I let out a long sigh. "Do any of you people in law enforcement ever actually communicate with one another? I already shared Mickelson's treatment notes with an FBI agent yesterday."

"Then you won't mind sharing them with me as well," he said.

"I'll ring my secretary. She can provide them to you on the way out."

I didn't care a fig who read what in the file. They'd find nothing in my notes of interest to their investigation. There was merely the usual documentation of doctor-patient dialogue regarding client needs and coping skills for anxiety. The specifics on Mickelson's fear of drowning? Not a trace of that was in writing.

Detective Adams slowly stood and strolled about my office, checking out my stack of medical journals and reading over my framed degrees hanging on the wall.

"Impressive," he said slowly. "How many years did it take you to become a shrink?"

"Psychiatrist, not *shrink*," I ground out from my clenched jaw. "After obtaining my college degree, it required an additional eight years of postgraduate study, four years of medical school to become board certified, then another four years of psychiatric residency."

"Bet you've seen a lot of crazy shit, huh?"

"We don't use the term *crazy*, Detective."

"Whatever." He pointed to my certification degree from Columbia University. "I've heard of that school. Where's it at? Is it one of them Ivy League places?"

A prickle of sweat formed at the back of my neck. "It's located in New York City and is universally regarded as one of the top five psychiatry programs in America."

"It's a long way from New York City to Normal, Alabama." He put his hands in his pockets and faced me with a grin that put me in mind of a predatory shark. "How'd you end up way down here?"

"My family's from Montgomery, so I have ties to the state." I rose from my desk. "Much as I'd love to chitchat with you, I'm sure we both have more important matters to attend to. Good day, Detective."

"I'll be in touch," he promised. "Don't forget to call your secretary to have those papers prepared for me."

"Of course."

I rang Gayla and instructed her to provide Detective Adams with Mickelson's case file. He sauntered out of my office with the insolence of someone staking a territorial claim. I didn't like this man one bit.

A couple of minutes later, Gayla Pouncey, my administrative assistant and number one fan at work, briefly knocked on the door and then entered the room. "That man!" she exclaimed, coming to plop down in the seat Detective Adams had just vacated. "He acts like he owns this place. Demanded the papers from me and then snatched them out of my hands without a proper thank-you."

"I'm sure he's very busy," I admonished, though secretly pleased she'd found him as irritating as I had. Gayla was in her midfifties and had trudged along in low-level administrative jobs her entire career. As a result, she easily took umbrage at the slightest whiff of anyone turning up their noses when she performed one of her tasks.

"Humph," she said, sticking out her rather pointed chin and peering at me through her bifocals. "That's no excuse for poor manners, though. You'd never do that."

She was correct. I never failed to meticulously thank Gayla Pouncey for her work. In return, the woman warmly defended me against any staff member who dared refer to me as a cold fish or criticized me in even the slightest fashion. But Gayla's real value to me was that she'd grown up in Normal, had worked here for decades and knew the scoop on everybody's personal and professional lives. She was only too happy to share her knowledge with me on everything going on around the hospital—including those underlings who'd felt either slighted by me over the years or had ambitions of replacing me as chief of staff. I never forgot or forgave an insult.

"If we're lucky, maybe we've seen the last of that detective," I said.

"I hope so. Josh Adams is the nephew of the current police chief, and Dan Thornell has been grooming him as a replacement once he retires. So Adams feels bulletproof against civilian complaints and eager to prove he's ready to move up. At any rate, I logged into my notes that he'd received a copy of Mickelson's records."

Gayla took pride in excellently performing every detail of her administrative duties.

"I'd expect nothing less from you, of course."

Her thin lips twisted upward as she smoothed the pleats on her polyester pants. "Too bad about the Mickelson girl. What do you think happened? Was she abducted, or had she made plans to meet someone outside of the hospital?"

The same question the detective had asked. Had my prim-and-proper secretary been eavesdropping on my conversation with the detective? I should always assume the worst about people. Never let them catch you by surprise.

I lifted my shoulders and held out my palms. "Who can say?"

"If anyone can figure out what was going on in that poor girl's head, it's you."

"If I were forced to guess, I'd say she was a confused, struggling addict who probably made a bad choice to meet with a drug dealer."

Gayla tsked and shook her head. "For the life of me, I can't understand what's going on with our young people today and all these addiction problems. What can they be thinking?"

"The subconscious mind rules over ninety-five percent of our lives without us ever realizing what's running our decisions," I began, taking her question seriously. "It's like a submarine stealthily navigating our thoughts and beliefs in the murky, unclear level of our minds. But it leaves magnetic signatures, which are evidenced in our behavior and which provide a skilled therapist like me with clues about the underlying beliefs directing a person's inner life."

Gayla gave me a long, slow blink. "You're so smart. This hospital is fortunate to have someone of your caliber."

Her words helped ease my ruffled feathers from Adams's visit. "Time for me to get back to work. All these meetings with the police have set my schedule far behind."

She took the hint and headed to her office. "You work so hard," she said sympathetically. "I'll leave you to it."

Once the door shut behind her, I stood and gazed out the window, my attention flagged by the old abandoned concrete pool two buildings over. A relic from days gone by, it had been used decades ago to assist in the physical rehabilitation of polio patients. It had long since been filled with concrete, but the old diving board had never been torn down.

The news media had reported that Mickelson had drowned, and the pool made me think of her meeting her worst fear as water filled her lungs, choking out oxygen and life. Had her mind returned to the blank canvas of a fetus in the womb? Had her life flashed before her eyes? When she'd had no choice but to inhale liquid, had the cold lake water burned her lungs like lava? What had those last few oxygen-deprived moments before death been like?

I shivered at the morbid questions plaguing my mind.

Chapter 12

DELLA

I stuck my hands in my oversized sweatshirt jacket and surveyed the not-so-festive activities behind dark sunglasses. Dad's barbecue fundraiser had all the looks of a disastrous failure. The venue had moved from the First Baptist Church, and I couldn't help speculating if the elders now feared too close an association with my father after recent events, no matter how much sway Uncle Vic and Aunt Mabel held with parishioners. Nobody had been arrested, but everybody knew Dad had been brought in for questioning. Never a wise move for a church to be seen as supporting a potential serial killer, I supposed.

So instead, the barbecue was being held at the lakefront park. There was no country band or cloggers to entertain and no impassioned speakers onstage to rile up the people about the injustice done against Hunter Stallings. A long table had been set up near the small stage with large bins of barbecued pork, white bread, coleslaw, and baked beans. Although the food was plentiful and the crowd large, only a few stragglers actually purchased plates. A couple dozen folks sat at picnic tables. The rest of the crowd, like me, hung out from a distance, and I sensed their mood as curious and uneasy. I didn't exactly get the vibe they were on Dad's side.

Vic and Mabel stood off to the side of the stage, stoic as always in performing their duties. And the star of the hour? Dad was smiling like a politician and working the picnic tables, shaking hands with people who were either one of his few supporters or hungry barbecue fans not picky about the social connotations of hanging out with a suspected murderer.

I wasn't sure whether I was proud of or disgusted at Dad's behavior—or why I'd even bothered to show up. I certainly didn't want him to spot me in the crowd. A couple of cops strolled on the fringes of the bystanders, and I wondered whether they were trailing Dad or were there to protect him should the event turn unruly. Maybe both. I searched for Nathan, but he wasn't around. Just as well. I felt raw and vulnerable in his presence since spilling my guts yesterday. My car keys dug into my palms where I had them clenched, ready for my exit at the slightest provocation. I had a clear shot from here to my parking space, less than fifty feet away.

Screw standing around here. I'd seen enough. I turned and headed to the parking lot, but before I reached my car, a loud microphone squeal nearly split my eardrums.

"Howdy, folks! Thanks for coming out today. I appreciate the support."

Dad stood alone on the stage, grinning from ear to ear.

"Delusional," I muttered, stopping in my tracks.

A smattering of applause was followed by several distinct boos from the back. His grin held as he continued speaking. "Just want you to know that with every plate purchased, I'm closer to my goal of hiring an attorney to file a civil suit against the State of Alabama for unlawful imprisonment."

A familiar elderly man dressed in coveralls stepped forward from the crowd and shook a scrawny fist at Dad. "You belong back in the penitentiary, Hunter Stallings," he shouted.

Old Man Brooks was righteously fired up. His weathered face was lined in a heavy scowl, his tall, lean body tight with tension. The man was spoiling for a fight. One of the cops started toward this lone vocal dissenter.

"Well, now, you're certainly entitled to your opinion, Levaughn," Dad said smoothly. "And I suspect you're not the only one here today who feels the same."

A murmur of assent passed over the folks like a wave.

Dad held up a hand, like a preacher in a pulpit, asking the congregation to pay close attention to what he was about to say next. *Jesus, Dad. Just get off the damn stage.* I wanted to go shake him.

"I'm here to tell you I'm an innocent man," Dad continued. "There's a killer in our midst, but it's not me."

"Liar!" Levaughn again shook his fist at Dad, then rounded on the approaching cop. "I have a right to say what I want. It's a free country, ain't it?"

I couldn't hear the cop's response but saw Uncle Vic take the opportunity to stop the train wreck of a speech. He grabbed the microphone and spoke.

"That's it, y'all. Again, we thank you for coming."

Dad frowned at his brother but had the good sense not to make another scene.

"Levaughn Brooks has more sense than the entire Normal Police Department," came a gruff voice by my side.

I whirled to face a stocky man with a messy shock of gray hair.

"You don't recognize me, do ya? Haven't seen much of you over the years." He held out a hand. "Brady Eckeridge."

The man had not aged well. As a child, I'd thought him tall and imposing. But he was only medium height, middle aged, and many pounds overweight. I could take him in a fight or outrun him any day. Unless my martial arts classes only provided me a false sense of badassery. I folded my arms against my chest, deliberately ignoring his proffered hand.

"So that's how it is, eh?" He dropped his hand to his side. "Can't say I'm surprised. Seems I'm the town pariah at the moment."

"Nobody likes a dirty cop."

He winced. "I expect people will change their minds about me once all is said and done."

"What's that supposed to mean?"

"No offense, but your dad's a killer. Won't be long before that truth is confirmed, and I'll be vindicated."

Hackles rose on the nape of my neck. Was Brady implying that Dad was going to be arrested? But Nathan had told me that the discovery of the bells was being kept from public knowledge.

"Do you know something that I don't know?" I asked.

Brady smiled with no mirth. "I might not be on the police force anymore, but I still have friends and sources on the inside. So you know damn well what I'm talking about. No telling how many murders Hunter Stallings has committed over the years. Your mom and brother were the tip of the iceberg."

"Says who?" I countered. My words were flat and tight. The scent of barbecue began to make my stomach roil.

"Me." Brady puffed out his chest. "And before much longer, everyone else will be saying the same."

"Maybe. Maybe not. But you aren't on the force anymore. Which means the ones who are on it will make a proper investigation without jumping to conclusions and falsifying evidence and witness statements."

Brady's skin mottled red, and his eyes hardened. "I'd think you, of all people, wouldn't support your dad. I've never forgotten Mary and four-year-old Jimmy. I was one of the first cops on the scene the night they were murdered. Did you remember that? Blood was everywhere."

I swallowed hard as my mind flashed back to the sight of their lacerated, ruined bodies. It took all my self-control not to stick my fingers in my ears and run to the safety of my car. You'd think I was eight years old again and reverting to my cowardly, childish ways.

"I was there. Do *you* remember *that?*" My voice rose, and I stepped toward him, jabbing a finger at his chest. "Don't you ever suggest that I don't remember my family. I think of them every day, you . . . you smarmy, dirty bastard!"

He drew back in shock. Too late, I realized I'd drawn my own crowd of curious onlookers. My whole body trembled. Nothing I hated more than having attention focused on me. I'd spent my whole childhood and adolescence trying to blend in and go unnoticed, trying to avoid all the whispers and stares about the *Stallings girl.* And here I was, making a spectacle of myself for the whole town to witness.

"Hey, are you harassing my daughter? Get away from her!"

I closed my eyes and groaned. Just when I thought it couldn't get any worse. I opened my eyes and faced Dad, who was bearing down on us like an outraged papa bear. "I've got this," I told Dad. "I don't need you."

He ignored me, of course, and shook a fist at Brady Eckeridge. "Bad enough you fucked up my life. Leave Della alone."

As if Dad cared. This was all an act for the good citizens of Normal. If he expected me to play the part of *defending daughter*, he had another thing coming.

Brady smirked at him. "Go on. You wanna take a shot at me? Do it. Right now in front of the cops. They're just looking for a reason to throw your ass back in jail. I'll be glad to take a sucker punch if it means getting you off the street."

Out of nowhere, Uncle Vic was between them, beating the cops—the current, real ones—to the volatile situation.

I did what I did best. I fled to my car and locked myself inside. My breath came in rapid, shallow gasps, and my hands shook so much I could barely get the keys in the ignition. I laid my head on the steering wheel trying to calm down enough so I could drive.

A gentle tap sounded by the driver's-side window. Oh, shit. "Go away," I said, not bothering to raise my head.

"Della, it's Vic. Open up."

I popped up and stared at his familiar face. At least this was someone I knew. Sighing, I hit the car's unlock button. At the sound of the lock release, Uncle Vic nodded and opened the door.

"You're in no good condition to drive. Scoot over. I'll drive you home."

"But how will you get back here?"

"I'll have Mabel pick me up. So. Do you want to go home or sit out in the parking lot where everyone can gawk at you?"

Home. And it wasn't even close. I climbed over the console and plopped into the passenger seat. "Keys are already in the ignition," I said.

Uncle Vic nodded, and we eased away. My breaths deepened and slowed as he called his wife. I stole a glance at him after he hung up the phone. His huge presence filled the car. He was so tall his head almost bumped against the roof, and his farmer hands gripped the steering wheel—capable, strong working hands.

"Uncle Vic," I began in a small voice. "Don't you believe that Dad killed them?"

He turned his attention from the road and faced me with raised brows. "Killed who? Those two skeletons they just found? Because, no, I don't. Hunter has his faults, but a cold-blooded serial killer? No."

But he didn't know about the bells that were found. He might change his tune then. The murders might have occurred prior to Dad's incarceration.

"Actually, I was talking about Mom and Jimmy."

He seemed to consider his answer carefully, in typical Uncle Vic fashion. "I know it looks bad, what with the additional insurance policy on Mary. It was no secret he was running around on her, and they had serious marriage problems."

"Then why do you think he's innocent?"

A rueful smile peeked from behind his bushy beard. "*Hunter* and *innocent* are two words that don't seem to quite go together."

I snorted in agreement.

"But I'll say this—I don't believe he'd ever kill in such a premeditated fashion. You know, get dressed up in a head-to-toe disguise. And I also don't believe he'd murder his own son."

"But what about the insurance? Pretty damning."

"Hunter's greedy, but he's not stupid either. If he planned to kill Mary, then why would he set himself up by increasing her policy?"

"Not like it hasn't been done before," I quipped. "Greed can trump common sense when you start seeing dollar signs."

"True." His eyes bored into mine. "But if you thought your dad was guilty, why get angry today at Brady Eckeridge? His methods were unethical, but they worked. He put Hunter away for a long, long time. Almost to the point that he'd run out of appeals on the death sentence."

"Good point," I admitted, the words sour in my mouth. "I've been reading over the court transcripts and doing a little digging of my own. I even visited Carolyn Merton."

Uncle Vic gave a low whistle. "That must have been awkward. For both of you."

"Yeah." I folded my hands in my lap and watched the familiar landscape of town as we drove by. We settled into a companionable silence. It felt good to talk to my uncle, and I wondered why I'd never really given him a chance before. I'd been more familiar with Aunt Sylvie, who visited Mom a lot at our old house. When my world had imploded, I'd latched onto her like a crab in a sea storm and never let go.

"If you're trying to get to the truth, maybe you should befriend Eckeridge."

His sudden out-of-the-blue comment caught me by surprise. "Why would I do that?"

"To see what he really knows. What convinced him to jeopardize his career by setting Hunter up for the fall."

"Dad wasn't the only person he'd ever framed," I pointed out.

"I know this man's type. He's a person in authority suffering from a delusional God complex. Thinks he can make final judgments on others and any action he takes justifies the means."

"Maybe," I said doubtfully. "I can see if he has any other information. But the idiot probably just jumped onto the most likely candidate. The one who had the most to gain from their deaths."

Uncle Vic left me to my own thoughts again, and the more I considered his idea, the more I liked it. If Brady Eckeridge believed he could act with impunity, who was to say he didn't plant those bells found on the newly discovered victims—all to make my dad look more guilty.

But if that was the case, where the hell did he get the bells?

"Here you are," Uncle Vic said, pulling into Aunt Sylvie's driveway.

I craned my neck and saw Aunt Mabel pull in behind us. "Glad you don't have to wait for your ride. This was really nice of you."

A rare flash of amusement danced in his eyes. "And nice of Mabel too. Especially considering your last words to her were a big ole *eff you*."

"Yeah." I sighed. "Guess I owe her an apology."

"She's not so bad, you know. Mabel tries to always do the right thing by people."

That didn't mean I had to like her, though. I couldn't speak for others, but I'd rather someone not do me a good turn if it filled them with resentment. What did he see in that uptight, plain woman who was so Holy Roller that she wore no makeup and covered herself with unflattering clothes designed for modesty rather than comfort or fashion? Still, I was raised to mind my manners and would do the polite thing and apologize.

"How were you and Dad raised in the same house and yet turned out so different?" I asked.

"No telling. Nature versus nurture. The classic conundrum. Could be biology, or it could be the series of choices we make with our own free will. Personally, I fall into the free will side of the debate."

"But why did Dad choose to be a thief and . . . whatever else he might have done? You didn't. And y'all were raised by the same parents."

"You never met our grandmother. Did Hunter ever talk about her with you?"

I tapped my lips, searching the far-off memories of my childhood. "No. I knew your parents died in a car crash when you and Dad were young, and your grandmother ended up raising you both. She died before I was born. Honestly, I was never even curious about the woman. Why? What about her?"

Uncle Vic gripped the steering wheel and stared straight ahead. "She was a horrible woman. Cold and cruel. Hunter and I would've probably fared better if we'd been shuffled off to foster care."

"That bad, huh?" I said, hoping he'd provide more details.

"Pretty gruesome. For better or worse, she shaped our personalities. That's all I have to say about that period of my life. As to why Hunter and I are so different . . . well, only God has those kinds of answers. We can only believe in—"

"Sorry. I've got to run and get ready for work," I interrupted, waving my cell phone between us. I sensed a sermon in the works. I didn't want him recruiting me for First Baptist in an attempt to save me from the devil. Or, even worse, preaching to me about rising above my unfortunate circumstances. Screw that. I'd done my best.

Quickly, I exited the car and leaned down by the passenger-side opening to say goodbye. "Thanks again for the ride. I'll speak to Aunt Mabel a minute."

A rare smile lit his somber face, and I felt a twist of guilt in my gut. Maybe the distance between us was my fault, not his. Because I felt sure now that Uncle Vic was one of the good guys.

Chapter 13
DR. PENNINGTON

"May I ask why you changed your mind about undergoing hypno-therapy?" I asked Della after we'd exchanged pleasantries. I indicated the chair beside me, and she sat down, her eyes scanning the small therapy room connected to my office. She'd never outgrown her childhood compulsion to find an exit. Understandable, given her situation, of course.

The furniture consisted only of a couch and several comfortable chairs. The flooring was a plush carpet that muffled noise and, hopefully, created a feeling of warm coziness.

She crossed her arms protectively in front of her and crossed her legs. Always on the defensive, this one. Della might prove difficult to hypnotize.

"You were resistant to hypnosis in the past," I reminded her. It had taken considerable convincing for Della and her aunt to agree to only a single session.

She hesitated a moment before answering. "I changed my mind because I've been under a lot of stress the past couple of weeks. My anxiety's notched up, and I'm finding it difficult to . . . cope."

"I see. Has this difficulty led to suffering panic attacks?"

"Yes." Her lower lip jutted out a fraction, giving her a sullen appearance. It was an expression she'd worn often as a child and adolescent.

"Care to elaborate?"

She sighed, clearly reluctant to share details. "A few days ago, I got stuck at a red light in town. I got dizzy and nauseous. When the light turned green, I failed to notice and caught the attention of a cop—not to mention several irate drivers as well."

"I see." I made a note on my digital tablet. "Was this an unusual occurrence for you?"

"Only in the matter of degree. I've always felt trapped and uneasy at stoplights. But it's never been this bad."

"Any other instances?"

"That was the main one."

"Any reason why your phobia has gotten worse?"

"My father." Her lips pursed together in a hard line. "You had to have heard the news. He's out of prison and trying to get back in my life."

"And how do you feel about that?"

I could practically feel Della struggle to keep from rolling her eyes at the trite psychological question.

"Obviously, it stresses me out. I don't want to deal with him. Can, uh, can we just get on with it?"

"Of course. We can delve deeper into your feelings on the next visit. But I do need to know what you hope to accomplish in this hypnotherapy session. I propose we work on your aversion to the color red. While you're in a deeply relaxed state, I'll offer a few suggestions that you can either accept or reject. The choice is always your own."

"Fine. And, while I'm under, I want you to take me back to the night of the crime and let me relive finding Mom and Jimmy."

My hands stilled over my tablet. I hadn't been expecting this request. "Why?"

"I just want to see if I've forgotten some detail. Okay?"

Della made me fight for every little nugget of information. But I was up for the challenge. "Have you had many conversations with your father since he's returned?"

Della regarded me stonily, her hands clenched into fists.

"Has he . . . been pressuring you to reexamine his innocence or guilt in the case?"

More stony silence.

"You know, Della, that this is a safe place for you to open up and share your feelings. Repressing your emotions doesn't make them disappear."

"Can we proceed with the hypnosis?" Her words were clipped and unyielding.

I stifled a sigh. But perhaps she'd let go of tightly held secrets in a calm, entranced state. "Very well. Would you like to lie on the sofa? It's more comfortable."

"Here's fine."

No surprise at her terse response.

"I want to remember everything I say while I'm under," she continued.

"Absolutely. You're in charge," I assured her.

"Okay, then. I suppose I'm ready."

I modulated the rhythm and pitch of my voice to a deep, methodical baritone. "Then we'll begin. Close your eyes, and take several deep breaths, relaxing your mind and body. Remember that you are safe here."

Della obediently closed her eyes, but her hands remained clenched in her lap.

"You have the power to end this session at any moment you choose. You set the boundaries."

Her fingers loosened.

"Your feet and legs are growing heavier, rooting you to the ground. It's a pleasant feeling, a letting go of tension. Your breath grows deeper as you focus on my voice. It's as though you are detached from your body. An observer of all that is happening."

Della's palms opened, and her lips slightly parted. I silently clicked on my cell phone recorder. "Your arms are also growing heavy. All tension floats away. You are relaxed and slightly drowsy. And now, if you're ready, we'll go back to the past." I paused. Della's breathing remained deep and steady. "Are you ready, Della?"

"Yes," she said softly.

"You're eight years old, asleep in your bed when something awakens you. What is it you hear?"

"Mommy and Daddy. They're downstairs, yelling."

"Do you hear anything else?"

"Jimmy. I hear his door open, and he runs to the stairs. He screams 'Mommy, Mommy!' I want to go to him, but I'm afraid I'll get in trouble. And I'm so warm and safe underneath my blanket."

"What happens next?"

"Mom is screaming. It's bad. Really, really bad. I don't know why, but it feels different this time. I don't want to get out of bed, but I do. I run to Mom and Dad's bedroom and call the police. I cross the hallway to go back to my room. It's so quiet now. I'm scared. Has everybody gone? Am I all alone? I creep down the stairs . . ." Her voice faltered.

"It's okay, Della," I said slowly. "You're safe. No one can hurt you. You're only an observer. What do you see?"

"I hear a bell tinkle. Then I see him. That man. All dressed in black. He scares me. He's bending over and picking something up off the ground. And then I see Mommy."

Tears ran down Della's cheeks. A moan rumbled in her chest.

My heart raced as though I'd been there with Della on the stairs. I strove to keep my voice slow and unruffled. "Go on. Describe what you see."

She shook her head back and forth. "No, no, no, no, no, no, no."

"It's okay, Della. Tell me what you see."

Her face and lips twisted in agony. Her chest rose with rapid, shallow breaths. I feared she was in too deep, and I'd have to stop. Evidently, she was not going to open up. And I was so damn close.

"Blood," she spat out, panting. "Blood's everywhere."

I wanted more, so much more. But I couldn't lose her by pressing for too much, too quickly. I'd give it one last push before quitting. "You are merely an observer, Della. You're safe here with me. Take a deep breath—in and then out. Again."

She obeyed. Ever so slowly, the anguished lines on her face smoothed out, and her breathing returned to normal. "So much blood," she continued. "It's flowing out in ribbons from Mom's chest and stomach. Jimmy's pajamas are all bloody. They are lying on the floor side by side, arms wrapped around each other." Della began talking faster, her voice raised. "There are red splatters on the wall and couch. Red seeping into the rug. Red and death everywhere I look."

"Deep breaths. In and out. What happens next?"

"I can't help it. I scream. The bad man turns around. A ski mask is over his face, and it has holes for his lips and eyes."

I leaned forward and whispered, "Who is it? Who is the masked man?"

Della shook her head back and forth. "I don't know. I don't know."

"Are you sure, Della? Is it your father?"

"I can't tell. Red is seeping in my brain. I can't think. I just want to run. I have to get away from the bad man."

I eased back in my chair, confident there was no more to be gained in reviewing the crime. Della continued on about running from the house and into the woods. A quick glance at my watch, and I saw our hour was quickly slipping away. I wanted to redirect her attention back to the instant her phobia first blossomed.

"You've done well, Della," I interrupted quietly. "But let's go back to that moment when you were on the stairs. Can you do that?"

She drew a deep breath. "Okay."

"Your mother and brother are lying on the floor. What do you see?"
Her face paled, and her whole body trembled. "Red. So much red."
"How does red make you feel?"
"Scared. Dizzy. Out of control. Like I'm falling down a well."
I urged her to better explain that sensation. "A well, you say?"
"Everything blurs. My legs want to give way. It's like the earth has opened up and wants to swallow me whole."

I felt her pain, her confusion. I gathered it deep within myself. Yes, yes. I saw what she saw. Red coating every crevice of the mind, driving one to delirium, a frenzy of panic. A black abyss from where there was no return. I closed my own eyes and breathed deeply. Time to guide her, and myself, back to the present.

"It's only a color," I said. "Like any other color—such as blue or green or purple. And colors can't hurt you."

"But . . . the blood."

"Lots of things are red that aren't blood. The two are not one and the same."

"Blood is always red." It wasn't said argumentatively, but more as a whine. As though she were a child again.

"But blood isn't always a bad thing, Della. It's a natural part of life, as is the blue sky and green grass. The next time you see the color red, immediately bring to mind an image of blue water."

"Blue water," she repeated.

"Exactly. Cool, refreshing water that soothes the skin and mind. And now, Della, take a few more deep breaths. On the count of three, you'll open your eyes again. You'll feel relaxed, as though you've awakened from a nap. You will remember everything that took place." I turned off the record button on my cell phone and slipped it in my pocket. "One, two, three."

Her eyes shot open, and she stiffened in the chair. "It's over? I feel weird. It's like we just started but also like it's been going on for hours."

"It's common to feel that way after hypnosis. Any dizziness?"

She yawned and shook her head. "Just thirsty."

"Ah, water. Refreshing, cool water." I suppressed the urge to wink. "You remember my suggestion on what to do the next time you see red?"

"I do."

"Let's put this to a small test. Shall we?"

The tension returned to her shoulders. "I guess so," she said without enthusiasm.

I removed a small piece of red felt I'd hidden in my shirt pocket and placed it between us on the coffee table. Della flinched and turned her head aside, then looked back again. "Maybe it's not . . . not quite so bad."

"Progress, already," I said, picking up the felt square and tucking it back into my pocket. "Every session we'll work on desensitizing your fear by gradually increasing your exposure to the color red."

"I can hardly wait," she mumbled, rising to her feet.

She annoyed me by being the first to signal our session was over. That was my job, not hers. The slight lapse of power reminded me that Della Stallings was strong willed. I'd be well advised to keep that in mind.

Chapter 14

DELLA

My hands tapped a steady peck at the keyboard as I settled into the familiar rhythm at work in the quiet hospital, my mind content with processing data. Occasionally, my thoughts drifted back to the session with Dr. Pennington before my shift started. When it did, I mentally repeated my new mantra: *Cold, cold blue waters.*

Could it really be so simple? I was skeptical but willing to keep an open mind. It certainly couldn't hurt. I pushed away from the desk and rolled my shoulders, aware it was past time for a short break. I clicked the mouse and pulled up my favorite Russian-history website.

"Della?"

I jumped at the deep male voice and turned sideways to find a familiar face observing me. Familiar, but unexpected. "Uncle Vic? What are you doing here?" A knot formed in my stomach. Something must have happened. "Is Aunt Sylvie—"

"Your aunt's fine. Sorry, I didn't mean to startle you."

My pulse immediately slowed, and I exhaled. "Then, what . . . ?"

"It's Mabel. She fell and twisted her ankle. They're going to x-ray it to make sure it's not broken."

"But it's . . ." I glanced at my computer screen. "Almost three o'clock in the morning. I know y'all awake at dawn, but—"

"She got up to go to the bathroom and tripped and fell," he explained.

"Hope she's okay," I said politely.

"We'll see. The bad news is there's no x-ray technician on shift, and they're having to call one in. So we've been waiting almost an hour."

"Might have been better off just driving to Huntsville," I said, albeit with a small stab of disloyalty for my employer.

Uncle Vic gave a rueful smile. "Next emergency, I'll keep that in mind."

I waved a hand around my tiny quarters. "Sorry. I don't have an extra chair in here for you to sit down. Office is too small."

"No problem." He leaned against the wall and pointed at my monitor. "What are you looking at there?"

"Nothing much." I laughed self-consciously. "Sometimes when I need a little break, I poke around on history websites. Guess you could call it a hobby. Nobody cares as long as the work gets done."

He left the doorway and leaned in toward the computer, squinting his eyes. "'The Last Days of the Romanov Imperial Family,'" he read aloud. "Tell me about them."

"They were the last ruling royal family of Russia and were executed in the revolution."

"And this interests you because . . ." He paused.

I shrugged. "Can't rightly say. Why do some people enjoy reading romance novels or watching football games? It's something to pass the time."

He regarded me curiously and remained silent. I rushed to fill in the void.

"I suppose it fascinates me because the family had five duchesses, all young and very pretty. On the outside, they appeared to have it all—looks, wealth, and the privilege that goes with it. Everything was all fun and games, yachts and debutant balls, until the evil that had been brewing underneath eventually caught up to the royals."

"You think the revolutionaries were evil?"

"Yes. Not that they didn't have a good cause. I'm sure that in their minds, they were fighting for social justice and the greater good of the country. But the ends never justify the means, and the revolutionaries weren't the only bad guys in this drama."

"Rasputin," he offered.

I nearly choked. "You know Russian history?"

"I may be a farmer, but it doesn't mean I'm uneducated."

"Of course not." My face flushed, and I rushed to explain my surprise. "I just don't run across many people who share my interest in history."

Uncle Vic winked at me. "I saw a documentary about Rasputin once on PBS."

I laughed, more surprised now by the fact that we were actually having a conversation that didn't feel awkward.

He sighed and straightened. "Guess I better head back to the waiting room. Hopefully, the x-ray technician's finally arrived."

"Tell Aunt Mabel I hope she's fine."

He waved farewell, and I smiled at his retreating figure. I should make more of an effort. Spend more time with him and Mabel. After all, they were family.

I stood and gathered my purse, determined to grab a drink before finishing my shift. Maybe I'd even stop over in the ER and check on Mabel.

The halls were quiet and unoccupied, just as I liked it. In the vending room, I dug out change and deposited it in the drink machine. Moments later, the machine spit out a rattle of change, the noise ricocheting like a bullet in the empty hospital hallways. I glanced back over my shoulders. *Stop being ridiculous,* I scolded myself. Every time I left my office confines, the hairs on the back of my neck prickled, and I was convinced I was being watched.

I snatched up my rejected coins in disgust. Damn machine didn't work right half the time, and tonight it was being extra ornery. My stomach rumbled. I'd been poring over Dad's court transcripts most of the day, and when I'd realized how late it'd grown, there'd been no time to eat supper before work.

Sighing, I stuffed the coins in my jeans pocket and headed back to work. My sneakers squeaked so loudly against the linoleum that I grew convinced the noise was loud enough to wake even the comatose patients a floor above. Squeak, squeak. I felt like a marked animal, easy prey for whatever lay in the silent shadows. I had half a mind to take off my shoes and pad around in socks. Only the unlikely event of running into Knox or a night nurse or lab tech held that impulse in check. How crazy would that look to anyone? I'd never live it down.

I passed by the open door of the outpatient waiting room and paused. It was dark and empty. A small table against the back wall held a coffeepot, foam cups, and a small wicker basket that volunteer staff kept filled with granola bars and crackers.

I could really use a cracker.

It's not like I'm stealing, I told myself as I checked both directions in the hallway before making my way forward in the darkness. Tomorrow night, I'd replenish the basket with whatever I'd taken. Greedily, I plunged my fingers in the basket and struck bottom. It was empty. Well, wasn't that just my luck tonight? I'd never known it to be empty before.

I pivoted on my heel and then froze, midturn. Later, I couldn't say which sensation had hit me first—the funky smell of cigarettes and musk, or some micromovement from the corner of my eyes. Something was there in the shadows. My eyes adjusted to the dark, and then I spotted him, sitting alone with wide, wary eyes. Our gazes locked, and he slowly stood.

I let out a shrill scream and stepped backward.

The man was tall and thin to the point of emaciated. His long arms hung by his side, pale and fingers twitching. He had thin, mousy hair pulled back into a ponytail, and his bloodshot eyes appeared huge in his unshaven face.

"I—I ain't gonna hurt you," he said, his voice rusty, as though it wasn't often used.

"Who are you?" I asked breathlessly. "What are you doing here?"

He pointed to the monogrammed pocket on his shirt, and I realized he was wearing a janitor uniform. "Myers," he explained. "Maintenance crew. I just came in here to rest a minute. Didn't mean to scare nobody. I'll be going now."

Myers backed away and nodded his head at me. "Evening, ma'am."

He exited the side entrance, and I rubbed my arms, where chill bumps refused to fade. My knees wobbled as I made my way to the door. Down the hallway, I saw a figure in blue run around the turn by outpatient surgery.

"Della? Are you okay?" Knox rushed toward me, concern widening his large brown eyes. He stood so close to me I smelled his breath, scented with the cherry antacids he habitually chewed. "I heard a scream."

"That was me," I admitted, my cheeks flooding with warmth. "Sorry I scared you."

"What happened?"

"I ran into a man unexpectedly. That's all. I overreacted." My face grew even hotter. I hated looking scared and ridiculous.

Knox frowned and gazed up and down the empty corridor. "Who was he? Where'd he go?"

I pointed at the room behind me. "He left out the side door there. Guess he headed toward the north elevators."

Knox ran a few yards and peered down the hall. "No sign of anyone." He returned to my side. "What did he look like? Did you speak with him?"

"Yeah, everything's cool. He's a janitor here. He was in there taking a break when I came in the room." I stopped abruptly, not wanting to explain why I'd gone in there. "Anyway, we startled each other. That's all. He seemed nice enough."

Even if sorely in need of a bath. I kept that unkind observation to myself.

"You get his name?"

"Just his last name. Myers. You know him?"

Knox's lips parted incredulously. "Myers? Are you sure that's what he told you?"

"Yeah. Even had his name stamped on the front." I pointed at his shirt. "Just like you."

Knox let out a long, slow whistle.

"What's wrong? Don't you know him?" Normal Hospital wasn't small, but I figured the handful of maintenance men on the night crew would know each other.

"Charlie Myers retired over a year ago. What did this dude look like?"

"Super skinny. Unhealthily pale skin. Tall. And he had brown hair pulled back in a ponytail."

Knox regarded me somberly. "Charlie Myers is a short, stocky black man."

"Then why . . ."

"I don't know. But whoever you ran into, the man was up to no good."

My flesh itched as though it suddenly crawled with lice. "He lied," I said through numb lips. "Why?"

"Exactly." Knox rubbed his chin and fixed his gaze in the darkened outpatient room.

"I'm calling security," I said quickly, pulling out my cell phone. "Maybe they can—"

"Don't," Knox said, briefly laying a hand on my wrist.

"Why not? They might find him. They can block the exits and search the building."

"They'll only tip the guy off. I've got a better chance searching on my own."

"You can't do it alone. What if he's dangerous?"

"I've got this. You go on back to your office. Might not be a bad idea to lock yourself in. I'll let you know when it's safe to leave."

Knox left without waiting for my response. "Call me when you find him," I said to his back as he started around the corner. I slowly walked back to my office and resolved that if I didn't hear from Knox by quitting time, I'd notify security to locate him and make sure he was okay. I sat at my desk and tried to read more about the Romanovs, but my heart wasn't in it.

Ten minutes before quitting time, footsteps squeaked outside my door. Knox popped his head in.

"Did you find him?"

He shook his head. "Guy got away."

"Will you call security now? This should be reported. The guy might be dangerous."

Knox ran a hand down his long face. The shadows cast by his sunken cheeks appeared darker, giving him a haggard expression. "Sure. I'll file an incident report. They may want to question you later."

I nodded, relieved it would be investigated. "There's probably a logical explanation. Maybe a new employee who hasn't been issued a uniform yet and got Myers's old one." Even as I offered this explanation, it didn't ring plausible.

Knox frowned. "There isn't any new employee. I oversee the maintenance crew and would be the guy hiring and supervising them."

So much for that theory. "It'll get sorted," I said, not wanting to believe the guy meant any real harm to others. He'd looked more pitiful than dangerous. I shot Knox a nervous glance. "Do you think I'm overreacting?"

"Hell, no. You saw someone who has no business being here."

I smiled with relief. "David Nelson won't agree with you. He shrugs me off whenever I report anything to him. Like he thinks I'm making things up in my head."

"Nelson's an idiot," Knox retorted. "This was no figment of anyone's imagination."

I cocked my head to the side, studying him. It was so nice to have someone to talk to on these lonely nights. "You ever wonder why I work these crazy hours?"

"Who says they're crazy?" He grinned at me. "I like working nights. Fewer idiots like Nelson to deal with."

"There's that," I agreed. "No one breathing down your back." I drew a deep breath, wanting to share more. "But there's more to it in my case. I guess you know who I am, right? About what happened to my family?"

He nodded, eyes warm and kind. "Yeah. Can't help but hear gossip in this small town."

I picked up a paper clip from my desk and twirled it between my fingers. "The thing is, I've never really gotten over what I saw that night."

"Don't reckon anyone could ever get over a thing like that," he said.

I stared down at the paper clip, unbending the coiled metal and avoiding Knox's gaze. "It left me . . . damaged. I developed a weird phobia of the color red. Anytime I see it, I begin to panic. Like, full-blown anxiety where my heart races, and I struggle to breathe." I risked a quick glance, but his kind expression had not changed.

"So that's why I work nights. I'm less likely to encounter anxiety triggers, like people dressed in red clothes. For me, it's like waving a red flag at a bull—it sets me off."

"Must be hard for you. Red's still everywhere."

My lips ruefully turned upward. "Yeah, it's a dominant primary color. Did you know that red is the first color babies perceive after black and white? All languages have words for black and white. If they have a name for a third color, it's red."

"So you can't completely avoid it."

"No. But working in such an isolated environment helps. And if I do have a panic attack, it's unlikely anyone would witness it." The paper clip broke in two where I'd bent it back and forth, and I tossed it in the trash can. I cleared my throat and shrugged. "Anyway, that's my deal. In case you ever wondered about me."

He nodded thoughtfully. "Thanks for telling me. I'm sorry to hear it. I hope you're working on getting over this phobia?"

"I am." I shut down my computer and prepared to leave, unwilling to talk about it further. Knox offered to walk me to my car, and I wasn't fool enough to refuse the offer. Outside, the air was chilly, and I shivered inside my heavy sweater. Knox slowed down and rubbed a hand at the small of his back.

"All this running around isn't helping your back. Hope you'll be okay."

"Couple of aspirin and I'll be fine," he assured me.

"Thanks for everything," I said as I opened the car door. Knox stood in the cold darkness, watching me as I started the car and then backed out of my parking space. I waved goodbye and sped down the road. I'd make Aunt Sylvie and me a huge breakfast before I crawled into bed for much-needed sleep. I'd even suffer one of her bitter brews of kava kava tea for a good day's rest.

The caution light in town glowed yellow and then blinked to red. The familiar anxiety drenched my mind. What was it Dr. Pennington had advised? Think of water. I slowed to a stop, closed my eyes, and imagined a blue hot tub frothing with bubbles. I sank into it, liquid warmth penetrating the chilled flesh of my legs, then waist, then chest. Actually, that felt good. Was I overcoming my phobia? Could it really be that simple?

I opened my eyes and stared into the unrelenting red light. My stomach knotted, and my heart rate accelerated. *Water, water, water. Blue, blue, blue.* My hands tightened on the steering wheel, and when the light at last changed to green, I was swallowing bile. Guess it was unrealistic to expect treatment to take effect that quickly and easy on the first attempt. But for a few seconds, thinking of water had helped. I was learning a new skill; this would take time. Sure beat what had happened last week when I'd been held up by the light—which made me think of Nathan. I'd only heard from him once since the night the human remains were unearthed. He'd called to ask how I was doing and to thank me for my cooperation with their investigation. Had I imagined his interest in me at the diner? Not that it mattered. I didn't have time for any entanglements. Between work, helping Aunt Sylvie with her crafts, and trying to uncover the truth about Dad, I barely managed to get enough sleep each day to slog through my waking hours.

Uncle Vic's old truck was parked in the drive. I groaned. Since Uncle Vic refused to enter our "heathen" household, Dad must have borrowed the car again. On the bright side, if he was hell-bent determined to talk with me, at least he wasn't hounding me on the job. I dug my keys out of my purse and walked to the front porch. Angry voices drifted through the closed door.

"—not true! And even if I did, so what? Do you blame me?" Aunt Sylvie yelled.

"I'm her father. I have rights."

"Della's way past eighteen. She's free to avoid you if she wants."

"She wouldn't be avoiding me if you hadn't poisoned her mind."

I quickly opened the door and entered the foyer. No need for them to argue. It would only upset Aunt Sylvie and serve no purpose. The past was gone.

"You turned Della against me just for spite," Dad accused. "You found out I was seeing Carolyn, and you snapped. You were jealous."

Jealous? I stopped walking, my legs paralyzed by shock. He couldn't mean . . .

"Don't flatter yourself, bastard! I was all set to end it before I found out about Carolyn."

End what? My ears heard the words, but my mind refused to accept their meaning.

"I don't believe that for a second. You always were a clinging, selfish—"

An explosion of glass sounded from the den. I walked in to find shards from an orange vase scattered against the fireplace ledge and on the floor around Dad's feet. In the shocked, tense aftermath, I spoke.

"What's going on here?"

They both faced me with wide eyes and mouths ajar.

"How—how long have you been there?" Sylvie asked, fingers nervously clutching her mala necklace. I'd never seen her look so nervous. Her normally composed features were crumpled and her long silver hair wildly tangled.

"Long enough," I answered shortly. "Did you have an affair with my dad?"

"Della, let's discuss this later, when—"

"I want to know *now*," I interrupted. I couldn't live with lies another minute.

"Yes," she whispered, the outline of her lips pale around her full mouth. "But—"

I didn't want to hear the buts, the useless justifications. There was only one more question I had to ask. "Was this going on while Mom was still alive?"

Her mouth opened and shut with no sound. I had my answer. I turned to Dad, who had the grace to appear embarrassed. To think that my heart had begun to soften toward the bastard.

"You son of a bitch," I growled, jabbing a finger at his chest. "Did Mom find out about the two of you?"

"Never. We were careful."

I wanted to believe that. The gut-punch betrayal bruising my heart would have been nothing compared to what Mom would've felt discovering that Dad had cheated on her with Sylvie, her own sister.

I threw my hands up. "Why am I even asking you anything? The truth isn't in you." I whirled to Aunt Sylvie. "Or you, either."

"Della, honey, I'm so sorry." Her eyes reddened, and she lifted a hand to her neck. "I never wanted you to know."

"Yeah. I bet you didn't!"

The need to get out of there, away from the two of them, pressed down upon me, a smothering blanket. If I stayed a minute longer, I'd suffocate under its weight.

I rushed to my bedroom and flung the closet door open. The only suitcase I owned was pushed to the back, buried under a mountain of old clothes and board games that Sylvie and I used to play for hours when I was a kid and had awakened screaming from bloody nightmares—a vermilion red spreading through my mind, threatening to coat and obliterate every inch of my sanity.

In a blinding panic to leave, I dragged the suitcase to my bed and proceeded to toss as many clothes as I could stuff inside it, including the rest of the court transcripts I hadn't had time to finish reading. I didn't have to turn around to know that Aunt Sylvie stood in the doorway, blocking my exit. Back in my closet, I found an empty duffel bag I could dump my toiletries in.

"Let's talk, Della," she pleaded. "Don't leave like this. I can't bear it."

"Well, I can't bear being around you, knowing what you did. How could you?"

"I was in love with Hunter long before he married your mother. And when their marriage went bad—"

"You were there offering him comfort," I said bitterly. "Is that it?"

145

She swallowed hard. "Something like that. Yes. I'll never forgive myself. I can only hope that one day you'll forgive me, Della."

I stared at the stranger before me, the muscles in my throat painfully constricting with all the hateful words I wanted to fling at her face. But they wouldn't take shape and push past my lips. No matter what, this woman had raised me through a hellish childhood, had opened her home to a broken child. And I was nothing if not brutally honest with myself that she'd provided a home for the broken adult that I still was.

"I can't talk to you right now," I managed past the lump in my throat. "I have to get out of here."

"But where will you go?"

I shrugged. "I don't know yet. Maybe a motel. Maybe over to Libbie's house." I brushed past her with the duffel bag, crossed the hall, and packed my basic toiletries from the bathroom. At the front entrance, Aunt Sylvie stood by the door, holding out a credit card.

"I don't need your money," I spat.

"Take it. Please."

She tried to slip the card in my purse, but I shuffled out of reach and left, banging the door shut behind me. I took to the road, speeding away, my mind racing as fast as my car. Libbie's or a motel? One look in the car mirror decided the matter. I didn't want anyone seeing my red eyes and the tears flowing unchecked down my face. I bypassed downtown and traveled a circuitous route out of Normal. Eight miles outside of the Huntsville city limits, I started to pull in at a cheap fleabag motel. At the last minute, I decided to splurge on something nicer. Not Ritz Carlton nice, but a decent chain motel with room service.

If I had to hole up and hide from the world a few days, might as well be comfortable and well fed. I found what I was looking for and donned dark sunglasses before heading into the lobby. The room I paid for was serviceable and much larger than my bedroom back home, with the added bonus of a bathroom sporting a whirlpool bathtub. With relief, I noted the decor was neutral. The only bit of red to contend with was in an abstract painting by the desk. I found a spare blanket in the closet and covered the offending artwork. Dr. Pennington might have preferred I just deal with it as part of his treatment plan of desensitization, but I felt bad enough without the added pressure.

Dad and Aunt Sylvie. It still threw me for a loop. Belatedly, I wished I'd stopped at the liquor store on the way over. Too bad I wasn't a big drinker. I could've used a few drinks to take the edge off and help me sleep. Maybe I'd venture out later.

I collapsed on the bed and thought about my mother, in a way that I had not for a long time. My knees curled into my chest, and I clasped the pillow tight. My stomach cramped with nostalgia and loss. As I had when I was a little girl, orphaned and alone in bed, I squeezed my eyes tight and imagined Mom's arms wrapped about me, inhaling the citrus floral scent of Jean Nate as she stroked my back and murmured that everything was going to be okay.

How I wished she were here. Despite all the knocks that had laid me low in life, or maybe because of them, all I wanted was for someone to hold me and assure me that all would be well. To just hang on and believe in that promise. For years, Aunt Sylvie had provided that comfort to the best of her ability. But in the wake of her betrayal, I felt like the earth had opened beneath my feet and ripped apart that solid footing. I wobbled on a precipice, my toes gripping shifting sand as I stared down into a gaping abyss that threatened annihilation.

Stop. That kind of thinking was madness. An indulgence of self-pity that served no useful purpose. I had only myself to rely on, and it would have to be good enough. I tossed the pillow aside and got out of bed, pacing the motel room. Before I totally lost the grip on my emotions, I had a phone call to make. Linda Bowen's assistant put me straight through, and I explained that I needed a week off due to an unforeseen family emergency. Hadn't she always told me she was willing to help me if I needed her? True to her word, Mrs. Bowen promised to speak to my immediate supervisor. "Take all the time off you want," she urged.

That done, I kicked off my shoes and crawled into bed. My churning emotions, coming on top of everything else, exhausted me more than if I'd dug ditches for eight hours straight. I sank into sleep's dark oblivion, praying for the peace rendered by a total void of consciousness and unremembered dreams.

Chapter 15

THE CORRECTOR

I missed the woman who'd suffered from ancraophobia—a fear of the wind. I'd kept Ellie Ingram the longest of anyone—twenty-six days. Every night I'd unlock her basement cell door below the abandoned tuberculosis ward and take her for a walk outside. The windier the better. If there was no wind, I'd tie her up in a chair by an open window, causing a mild anxiety prelude in Ellie before taking her to a deserted restroom and shoving her face under the blast of a hand dryer. In a pinch, even a breeze from fans or overhead air vents served to ramp up her fear.

After Ellie's death so many years ago, I'd ceased administering corrective treatments, discouraged over my inability to cure their weaknesses. I'd pushed Ellie over and over until she'd died from not taking her insulin correctly. That death was on her, not me. I'd provided her nutritious meals and the correct diabetic medicine. It had been her choice to stop taking the medicine and lie to me that she had.

I shook my head as I recalled opening her cell and discovering her body lying on the concrete, out cold from a diabetic coma. She had died less than an hour later. The woman was so mentally fucked up she'd committed suicide rather than undergo more correction to face her fears and become strong.

What was wrong with people these days?

I'd endured years of corrective treatment, and look how strong I'd become as a result. How powerful.

Nonnie had corrected me almost daily as a child. And it hadn't stopped during puberty either. There'd been no peace until at last I'd taken measures into my own hands at age fifteen. One snowy afternoon, she'd scolded me for leaving a spot of grease on the stove after I'd cleaned up after our lunch.

"If you don't take care with the little things, how can you expect to ever conquer the important tasks of life?" she asked that fateful day, grabbing my arm with bony, arthritic hands that could still dig deep into my flesh or pack a wallop upside my head. Like a chastised puppy, I offered no resistance as she guided me to the dark closet to be locked in darkness. I willingly shuffled my way into the cramped area that smelled of urine no matter how many times I'd scrubbed it down after being forced to relieve myself because Nonnie wouldn't let me out to use the bathroom.

And just like that, in a powerful surge of understanding, I realized that submitting to this frail old lady was a form of weakness on my part. Hadn't she tried to teach me to be bold—assertive? Electric energy crackled through my body, sparking neurons in my brain, lighting up every cell until I swore my very fingertips glowed from the charge. It was as though I'd lain dormant until a switch flipped on.

The door began to shut behind me. I swirled around, placing a hand on its battered wooden surface to stop it swinging completely shut, blocking my encroaching doom. I stepped forward from the doorway. Nonnie's wrinkled lips parted into a wide O of surprise. Not once had I ever before defied her corrections.

"No," I said firmly in a voice that I hardly recognized as my own.

"No?" she echoed, nearly choking with surprised disbelief. "You get right back in there—"

"I said *no.*"

She tried to push me then, as though I were an inert piece of baggage to be stuffed into storage. I stayed as rooted as one of the many trees that stood sentinel around the wooded property.

Confusion flickered over her frail features before she resorted to more drastic action. She raised her right hand, palm facing me. Once more I blocked her move, gripping her soft, toneless arm. And squeezed.

Nonnie whimpered, and the sound filled me with satisfaction. I was invincible. No one would ever hold power over me again.

"Let me go," she choked out, her tone half-pleading, half-demanding.

I pushed her away from me. We stared at one another, both startled at the abrupt shift in the balance of power between us. Nonnie rubbed her arm where I'd restrained her. "Get out of my house," she rasped, rheumy eyes bright with hate and fear.

I started to turn, then stopped. "No. You get out, old woman."

"Wh—what . . ." Her thin lips twisted, and she shook her head. Long gray hair fell from the messy bun.

"That's right. This is my house now."

"But I . . . I have nowhere else to go. This is my home." She defiantly lifted her chin. "You get out now before I call the cops."

"No cops." I stepped forward, thrusting my face only inches from her. She'd smelled of talcum powder, the corned beef hash we'd eaten for lunch, and underneath it all, a rank undernote of perspiration. Nonnie was sweating bullets. She was afraid. Of me.

Excellent.

I whirled her around and shoved her into the closet so hard that she fell headfirst into the drywall. It splintered and crushed. Nonnie screamed and tried to make a break for the door. I slammed it in her face and turned the lock.

The pounding began immediately. "You open the door right this minute," she demanded.

"Don't beg. It's a sign of weakness," I scolded, taking a seat on the floor. I crossed my arms and smiled as the pounding resumed. Nonnie screamed and cussed until her voice grew hoarse and her attempts to break down the door grew more and more feeble. She changed tactics.

"Please, dear," she entreated. "Open the door. We'll forget this ever happened."

I laughed.

A beat of silence, and then, "I'll bake your favorite chocolate chip cookies."

"That all you got, old lady? Ain't gonna work."

The cussing resumed. I grew bored and strolled to the kitchen, grabbing a can of soda from the fridge before heading to the den for a little TV.

The noise from the closet ceased altogether. I spent the remainder of the day eating and drinking whatever the hell I wanted, creating a huge mess in the process. I didn't care. I snoozed on the couch, and when I awoke and looked out the sliding glass door, moonlight glowed on the accumulated snow. So peaceful. So serene. I glanced from the closed door in the hallway to the blanket of snow on the lawn. Snow could cover a multitude of sins, including a freshly dug grave.

My day of liberation had arrived. From that day forward, I vowed not to be the one corrected, but to be the Corrector.

Chapter 16

DELLA

I ordered room service just as the motel restaurant was closing for the evening and gobbled it up the moment it arrived. Finally sated, I pulled out the box with its thick stack of court transcripts. As painful as this would undoubtedly be, at least going through them might push away thoughts of Aunt Sylvie and Dad's affair while Mom was still alive.

I rifled through the yellowed pages, eager to get to Dad's testimony near the end. The state's last witness before Dad was called to the stand was one of his former friends, Luke Billings. My heart pinched as I read that only a week before the murders, the two of them had gotten rip-roaring drunk together and that Dad had told Luke, *I'd kill Mary before I agree to a divorce.* When Luke asked why, Dad had explained that with his legal troubles and firing from the insurance company, he'd been unable to find another job. *Bills are piling up,* he'd reportedly said. *Money's tight, and Mary's the one pulling in the steady paychecks. Without her, I'd be on the streets.*

I slammed that page down beside me on the bed, resisting the urge to crumple it into a ball and throw it in the trash. It would do no good. The damage had already been done. Finally, I read Dad's interrogation by the state prosecutor. He'd claimed that there'd been nothing unusual at home that day before the murders, which occurred later in the evening. They'd all enjoyed a pleasant dinner before he left the house a couple of hours afterward.

"Liar!"

I scrambled off the bed and paced the room, needing to work off my fury before reading further. His statement was nothing like what had actually happened. My parents had argued, nothing new there, but their argument had been more bitter than usual. And when Dad had announced he was leaving to go out for a couple of drinks, Mom had told him she knew where he was really going and not to come back. That she was through with him.

Had that finally pushed Dad over the edge? Had he really meant it when he'd drunkenly told Luke that he'd kill Mom before agreeing to a divorce?

I quit pacing and returned to the bed, determined to finish the transcripts. There were more lies. Dad had tried to cast himself in a better light, fudging on how absent he'd been from their family home in the weeks leading up to the murders and glossing over his obvious drinking problem. When asked about his extramarital affairs, he'd only admitted to being with Carolyn Merton and made no mention of sleeping with his wife's sister, Sylvie Baines.

I lay still on the motel bed, papers fanned all over the comforter. I'd done it. Read through the meat of the bulky transcript. I clicked the TV on to a home shopping channel and watched in a semicomatose state, fantasizing that my woes could be cured by a trendy pair of shoes or a new lipstick.

I must have drifted off again because the next thing I was aware of was a pounding on the door. Some unknown God had answered my prayer for unremembered dreams, and I was grateful for the small mercy. I struggled to a seated position, my throat dry and my eyelids sticky. The knocking continued, steady and demanding. A quick glance at the alarm clock on the nightstand showed it was 9:21 a.m. I lurched onto my feet and peeked through the heavy curtains, squinting as sunlight pierced my just-awakened eyes. A white Impala was parked in the downstairs lot, and from my position at the window, I could make out a tall male in a suit standing at the door, but not his face.

Nathan, perhaps? I ran a hand through my hair and made a futile attempt to smooth my wrinkled clothes before opening the door. But instead of Nathan's familiar face, I stared into the eyes of a stranger.

"Della Stallings?" he said, flashing a badge. "I'm Detective Josh Adams with the Normal Police Department. I'd like to ask you a few questions."

What had I done wrong? I tried to recollect whether I had unpaid traffic tickets, but nothing came to mind. "What's wrong?" I asked, my heart thudding. This could only be bad news. "Is—is anyone hurt?"

"Hurt? No. Dead, yes."

My knees turned to jelly, and I slumped against the doorway. Aunt Sylvie? And to think I'd left in such a huff. My last memory would forever—

"Surely you're aware of the skeletal remains found last week out by Lake Hatchet?"

"Of course. Have there been . . . even more bodies?"

"Not yet. Although digging continues, and we've begun dragging the lake."

Air whooshed from my lungs. "The way you talked, I thought something else bad had happened."

He folded his arms across his chest, unrepentant. "If we don't get to the bottom of these murders, more people will die."

"How did you know I was even here?" I grumbled.

"I went by your home, and your aunt speculated you'd probably be at a nearby motel. Wasn't hard to track you down."

"What do you want from me?" I pinched the bridge of my nose. The sooner I answered his questions, the sooner I could go back to bed.

"Forensics has identified the skeletal remains. The victims were both women who had once been patients at Normal Hospital."

"Is that really so surprising? I imagine lots of people in this town have been a patient there at one time or another."

Adams shifted from one foot to another, but I sure as hell wasn't inviting this stranger into my motel room.

"But neither of them were local. Same as the latest victim, Melanie Mickelson—they were all from out of town."

"What does all this have to do with me?"

"I want to run the names by you. See if they sound familiar."

"If they weren't from Normal, I wouldn't have known them," I argued.

"But perhaps you would've heard your father speak their names? You were a child back when these women went missing, but in my experience, I've found that children pick up lots of information that adults aren't aware of."

I didn't care for the detective's insinuation that Dad might have had affairs with these women and that he and Mom had argued over them. Nor did I care for the smirk on his face that plainly stated he didn't hold any daughter of Hunter Stallings in high esteem. It wasn't the first time I'd encountered that expression, yet the injustice always infuriated me. Nevertheless, I thought quickly. There'd been fights aplenty, with vague accusations about "other women." Carolyn Merton's name had also been frequently bandied about. I hoped Aunt Sylvie was telling the truth when she'd said Mom never knew of her affair with Dad.

"The only name I'd heard my parents discuss was Carolyn Merton," I informed him, moving to shut the door.

Adams held up a hand to stop the door from swinging shut. "Wait a minute. I haven't even told you the victims' names yet."

"No need." I glared at him, wishing he'd go away.

"Should have expected you'd be uncooperative," he said with an ugly sneer on his boyish, handsome face.

I turned on my cell phone and hit the video record button. If he wanted to act like a jackass, I'd get it on camera. "If you have any further questions for me, I'll be glad to meet with one of Normal's cops at the station," I said sweetly.

Adams removed his hand from the door and shot me a tight smile. "See you around then, Miss Stallings."

He managed to make it feel like a veiled threat.

I slammed the door shut and bolted the lock chain. Immediately, I turned off the camera and dialed Nathan. Hell yeah, I wanted the victims' names and the whole scoop on what was happening, but not from someone like Detective Adams. Nathan answered almost at once, and we made plans for lunch. I took a long, slow shower, pondering why Adams had come to see me.

Despite the disturbing lies I'd read in the transcripts, I didn't want to believe Dad was involved with any more killings. I'd set out to prove him guilty of murdering Mom and Jimmy, but now my mind inexplicably reversed course.

I didn't want Dad to be guilty. Even I, who had every reason to hate and mistrust him, didn't believe him capable of committing a string of murders—which probably earned me the honor of Most Stupid Daughter Ever.

~

The country-cooking restaurant near the motel had more dirty dishes than customers by the time Nathan and I met there at 1:30 p.m. The lunch crowd had vacated, as I'd hoped, which meant less chance of anyone overhearing our conversation. Another plus for the otherwise bland meat-and-three place was that it was situated far enough from Normal that I'd be unlikely to run into anyone I knew.

Nathan surveyed the messy tables stacked with the lunch-crowd detritus. "There's a pizzeria a couple miles over. Want to go there?"

No pizzeria, too much red. "I've been here before with Libbie. This place will do."

He shrugged, and we both placed our orders.

The moment our server left, I began speaking. "Detective Josh Adams is a jerk," I said without preamble.

"Tell me something I don't know. He's generally despised by everyone at the department. Except for his uncle, who's the police chief and is grooming him to take over his job one day. Nothing like a little nepotism at work to bring down morale." Nathan sat back in his chair and took a long swallow of iced tea. "I see he charmed you like he does everyone else he meets."

"Charmed. Right." I snickered. "He's awful cocky. Did you know he was coming by to question me?"

"No. Technically, he's my boss, but we pretty much go our own way and share information on an as-needed basis."

"The man seems determined to prove that Dad killed all those women. He wanted to run the victims' names by me to see if I'd ever overheard my dad mention them."

Nathan's gaze sharpened on me. "And did you recognize the names?"

"No." I shook my head ruefully. "I never even heard them. I turned on my cell phone video recorder, and Detective Adams left me alone."

"He'll be back," Nathan warned. "Guy never leaves unfinished business."

I ran a finger around the rim of my iced tea glass. "So who were the victims?" I asked.

"Susan Battles and Willow Forsyth."

"Nope. They don't ring a bell." I grimaced at my unfortunate choice of words. "Willow's such an unusual name, it would have stuck with me if I'd heard it before. I know you can't tell me everything that's going on with the investigation, but is there any information you can share?"

"Only what's been released to the public. The victims' next of kin were notified, so we provided the news media with the names and the approximate dates of their deaths. It was in this morning's paper."

Should buy a copy before returning to the motel. "How long ago were the murders?"

"The forensics team estimates that Battles has been dead approximately seventeen to nineteen years and Forsyth about sixteen to eighteen years."

Disappointment rounded my shoulders. "Meaning that my dad can't be ruled out as a suspect, right?"

Nathan didn't confirm or deny my question, instead fixing me with a stoic expression.

"Bet you're great at poker," I complained.

"I'll throw you a bone."

We both grimaced—this time at his choice of words, not mine.

"Eventually, reporters will figure this out on their own fairly quickly. So here's a heads-up. The only connection we can find between the two women is that at one time they were both patients at Normal Community Hospital."

"Right. Just like Melanie Mickelson," I confirmed. "Detective Adams already told me that. What else you got?"

"All three were out-of-towners too. They came from different parts of Alabama to stay in the residential drug treatment program. In another interesting coincidence, none of the women had close family ties, which meant that there was no immediate cry of alarm when they went missing. Forsyth's family never bothered filing a report, and— just between us—Battles's family seems more interested in filing a civil lawsuit against the hospital than they are upset over their daughter's confirmed death."

"That's awful." I sighed and drank more iced tea, mulling over everything. "There's such a huge time gap between the older deaths and

Melanie Mickelson's," I observed. "If there was a serial killer, seems like there'd be more bodies in between."

"Which is why we're continuing to search the area and dragging part of the lake by Captain's Lane. If we don't find any more skeletons, we'll have to seriously consider that the killer might have been physically incapacitated for a period of time."

"Because he was locked up for eighteen years?" I rubbed my temples. "This puts me in the uncomfortable position of hoping you find more human remains from the time frame that Dad was in prison."

"Or," Nathan drawled, "the older murders might be unrelated to Melanie's. Could be we have a copycat killer."

"But then you have the problem of the bells left with both the old and new victims," I pointed out.

"Unless the copycat killer had knowledge of the older murderer's method of operation."

Nathan sat back in his seat, rubbing his jaw. "Theoretically, our mystery suspect might have known the original killer, who then bragged to him about his crimes. Or the copycat guy might even have been an accomplice for the original killer."

I threw my hands up in the air. "I still say the simplest solution is usually the correct one. There's even a scientific law or logic principle or some such thing that addresses that. What's it called?" I quickly googled on my cell phone. "Occam's razor," I said, triumphantly answering my own question.

Nathan didn't appear suitably impressed. "Yeah, I've heard of it. But help me understand. When we spoke at the diner, you were so down on your father. Has that changed? Are you hoping he's innocent or guilty?"

I fiddled with the paper napkin in my lap. If I said *guilty*, Nathan might think me a monster. What kind of daughter wanted her dad to be guilty of such horrific crimes? On the other hand, if I told Nathan I hoped Dad was innocent, he might find me gullible. A complete fool. And I hated to be seen as foolish or vulnerable.

"I want whoever is killing these women to be caught and punished," I said.

He quickly covered the flicker of disappointment in his eyes. "Good nonanswer."

"What about you? Do you think my dad's the killer?"

"What I think doesn't matter. Like you, I only want justice for the victims and to prevent any further deaths."

What a diplomatic, bullshit response. One that told me absolutely nothing I didn't already know. Oh, what the hell. How could I expect to form friendships, a real connection to others, when I kept my own emotions so pressed below the surface? I could use a friend these days.

"At first, I wanted him to be proven guilty again and thrown back in prison," I admitted. "I was angry about his release. But after those bones were found by the lake, it made me wonder. Years ago, I learned to accept that Dad must have been the one to kill Mom and Jimmy. But for my dad to be capable of a string of murders? I don't see it."

Nathan started to speak, but I held up a hand.

"Look, I'm under no delusions where Dad's concerned. He's a thief, a liar, a master manipulator, and a terrible husband and father to top it off. Terrible. But I'd like to believe he's not a serial killer. That there are limits as to how awful a person he is."

Nathan covered my hand with his own, and I almost jerked it from his grasp, my reflexive response to unexpected touch. But I didn't. His thumb stroked over my knuckles, and I momentarily closed my eyes, soaking in the comfort. I filled Nathan in on the lies I knew my father had told during his trial.

"But there's another side to him as well," I explained. "He could be lots of fun. He used to take me out fishing. Mom wasn't interested in it, and Jimmy was too young. So the two of us would head to Hatchet Lake alone. Dad taught me everything, even let me steer the boat sometimes. Called me his *little helper*." I smiled at the almost-forgotten old memory. "I'd do simple tasks like hooking bait or tying the rope to the dock while he got the truck and backed it down the lake's public landing ramp."

Nathan carefully set down his drink. "Tying rope?"

"Yeah. So what?"

"I want you to see something." He retrieved his phone from his pocket and scrolled through it. "There," he muttered, showing me a photo on his screen. "Did you tie it like this?"

Laid against a plain white piece of cloth was a length of blue cord tied into a bowline bight, its signature double loop formed in the middle. In the right corner of the frame was an evidence tag labeling the date and case number.

"Looks ominous, laid out like this," I mumbled, my mouth suddenly dry. "But yeah, that's what he taught me. And this came from . . . where?"

"The body of the first victim. Mickelson."

"The girl who drowned. The one I'd met days before she died."

Nathan kept his eyes fixed on me as he took his phone from my hand. "Bowlines are common, but not the bowline bight."

"Surely it's not *that* rare," I argued.

Nathan didn't defend his position, instead letting the silence gather between us. "Here's your food," our server announced. I jumped, then settled back in my seat as she laid out our plates.

As soon as she left, Nathan flashed me a warm smile. "Let's try to enjoy our food and talk about something other than crimes."

"Deal," I agreed. Despite the unsettling day, I dug into my meal with gusto, glad we'd shared information, even if it was only a crack in the door. Even if Dad appeared more guilty every day. At least we might be moving closer to the truth.

"Good to see you still have an appetite," Nathan teased, digging into his food.

Conversation lagged as we ate, but it was a companionable silence, interspersed with talk of former high school acquaintances and what they were doing these days. I hadn't kept up with anyone, not having been especially close to my schoolmates, but Nathan still maintained friendships with his former members on the football team.

"You had any more dizzy spells like the one you had in your car downtown?" Nathan finally asked, pushing away his plate.

Heat flushed the nape of my neck. "Nope. Everything's fine."

"Mind me asking what that was all about?"

"Must have been something I ate."

"Uh-huh." Skepticism laced his eyes, but he didn't probe deeper. "So how long are you staying at the motel?"

"At least a few days. I'm taking a much-needed break from work." Good thing I had so much money saved over the years. I almost never took vacations and had lived rent-free at Aunt Sylvie's.

Nathan laughed. "Then why hang around this place? But maybe the better question is, *Why* are you staying at a motel?"

"Aunt Sylvie and I had a bit of a falling-out."

"Does that happen often between you two?"

"This is a first," I admitted.

He raised a brow, silently urging me to confide everything. Strangely enough, I wanted to do so, but it felt like too much of a betrayal of my aunt and father to air their old secret. I despised what they'd done behind my mother's back, but I didn't despise them. Not Aunt Sylvie anyway. Yet I still couldn't face her. I needed this time to myself. Perhaps the whole sorry business coming to light would at least have served a purpose. It was a needed kick in the ass. A woman my age should be independent, live out on her own and act like an adult.

You can do this, I chided myself. I was back in therapy to deal with my phobia, I had steady employment, and I had more than enough money to get my own place.

"Anyone ever tell you that you ask too many questions?" I said brightly, evading the topic.

"I'm a detective. It's the nature of my job." But he smiled and changed the subject. "About this digging around you mentioned earlier—be careful, Della. Leave the investigation to us. We'll catch the killer."

Instead of arguing with Nathan, I merely smiled. If he wanted to interpret that as agreement on my part, so be it.

"I'm concerned about your working nights at the hospital," he continued. "Why do you have to work nights? Can't you switch your hours to daytime?"

"You mean like a normal person?"

"That's not fair," he said quickly. "I'm just concerned about the goings-on over there. The connection between the three victims is weird."

"I'll be careful."

"Have you noticed anything strange happening at the hospital?"

I started to shake my head no, then remembered my encounter with the mystery man roaming the halls and the eerie feeling I was being watched at the hospital. In light of my shock at learning of Dad and Sylvie's affair, the matter had been pushed to the back of my mind. "Actually, yes, there has been an incident. It may turn out to be nothing, but it was weird."

I filled Nathan in on the man sitting in the dark waiting room who'd worn the uniform shirt of the retired Myers.

"Did you report this?"

"I didn't. My shift was ending, so the janitor I mentioned, Knox Wilkes, said he'd file a report with hospital security for me. Plus, to be honest, I didn't feel like dealing with David Nelson, the guy overseeing security."

At Nathan's raised brow, I sighed. He was bound to find out sooner or later anyway. Might as well hear it from me first. "I've reported to security in the past about feeling stalked at the hospital. They didn't take me seriously. Instead, they made me feel like I should be a patient in one of the mental health wards."

Nathan dug out his cell phone and began texting.

"You think it's important? That this man might be a suspect in the murders?" I asked, wondering if I'd unknowingly encountered a serial killer. A chill slithered down my spine.

"Absolutely. Can't believe I haven't heard of this incident until now."

His phone buzzed and vibrated against the chipped Formica. Nathan picked it up and read the new message. "Okay, good. A report's on file with hospital security. But the bad news is that they didn't bother to notify us at the station. Incompetence, that's what this is," he grumbled.

"What are you going to do?" I asked.

"For starters, I'd suggest making a sweep of the place. Alert everyone to be on the lookout for the guy."

"Sounds like I couldn't have picked a better time to take work leave."

"You bet." Nathan picked up his iced tea glass, as though proposing a toast. I raised mine as well, and we clinked them together.

"Stay safe, Della. And leave the detective work to us."

I gave another noncommittal smile and sipped my tea. Now that I'd begun the search for my family's killer, I'd never be satisfied until I had answers. No matter the cost.

Chapter 17

DET. NATHAN WHITT

After lunch with Della, I immediately headed to the hospital to speak with David Nelson. It didn't sit well with me that Della, or any employee for that matter, should be made to feel embarrassed about reporting unusual incidents or asking for any kind of help in order to feel safe in their work environment. After all, this was the man's job. Sounded to me as though he needed to be reminded of that fact.

Nelson greeted me pleasantly enough when I'd entered his office, but I sensed the resentment behind his smile as he pulled the various reports I'd asked to review.

"What's this all about?" he asked, setting the paperwork on the vacant desk I'd commandeered.

"I understand that two employees witnessed an intruder in the building a couple of nights ago. Did you receive a report on it?"

"You referring to the one the janitor filed? Yeah, sure."

"Would have been helpful if you'd mentioned it to me or Detective Adams. We've told you we're interested in anything unusual happening at the hospital since the victims have a connection to this place."

Nelson shifted uncomfortably on the balls of his feet. "Sorry," he said stiffly. "We've been swamped the last couple of days, as you can imagine. Place has been running over with law enforcement officers, and everyone demands our time."

"I'm sure you're happy to comply with all requests to prevent any future patients from becoming victims," I noted dryly.

"Of course," he mumbled.

I began rifling through papers and skimming the text. "No one else has reported seeing a person on the grounds who has no business being here?"

"No. Only those two. Recently, anyway." He grimaced before adding, "Della Stallings has complained before that she thinks there's somebody roaming the place."

"And now you have an additional employee to confirm it."

I had Nelson pull up his department's security records and began skimming reports over the past few months. A curious pattern of theft emerged.

Missing: petty cash, bottles of Tylenol, snacks . . .

Those miscellaneous items had been reported missing from nurses' stations and administrative offices.

There were other reports as well. Cafeteria workers had reported minor thefts of food and drink. Laundry room workers had reported several blankets, gowns, and socks missing. A few patients had filed complaints that clothing items and books had been stolen.

Certainly, none of this was major stuff. It would be abnormal if there weren't occasional petty crimes reported in any organization. The key question was whether these incidents were on the rise. I kept scrolling through records and was rewarded by a series of monthly graphs depicting numbers of incidents reported. "Thank you, hospital security," I mumbled in appreciation.

Beginning in April of this year, the number of thefts had risen by 10 percent. A noticeable uptick, but nothing that would cause security officers to believe a potential crisis was brewing. I sat back in my chair and pondered the implication. Could these thefts be attributed to the man Della had seen dressed as a maintenance worker? The nature of the stolen items made me wonder whether the person who had stolen them was destitute, perhaps even homeless. My mind leaped to unusual cases where these types of thefts were committed by people later found to have lived surreptitiously in the company's building.

The mystery man, or woman, might have decided one of the vacant hospital buildings was an improvement over living on the streets. Maybe this person had even been a former patient and, upon release, had no other place to go. No welcoming home or family.

He or she might be harmless, but desperate people did desperate things when eventually discovered or cornered. I'd have to be careful. I tapped my lips, pondering how the mystery man evaded capture, if he was indeed living on the premises. Perhaps he'd scouted where hospital security cameras were mounted and knew the blind spots where he could scurry about like a rat, collecting bits of food, clothing, and other necessities.

He might be clever and brash, but if he was here, I'd find him. The more days that passed without his detection, the more he'd grow complacent—or just plain unlucky.

Chapter 18
THE CORRECTOR

As far as fears go, ophidiophobia was one of the most common, with nearly a third of adults fearing snakes. Experts estimated that as many as one-third of the population had herpetophobia, a fear of reptiles in general. They speculated the phobia might be evolutionary, that our ancestors had learned to fear them as a survival mechanism. These ancestors had passed on the learned behavior as a fear network in our amygdalae.

Not that I'd ever been afraid of snakes. I feared nothing and no one. Not anymore.

But pickings were getting slim around here with so many patients fleeing, so I couldn't be too choosy. I softly treaded up the stairwell, a large cardboard box violently pulsating in my arms. It was a long walk to the rooftop, but every elevator on every floor, even the service elevators, now had cameras pointed at them.

I was taking a risk. I knew that, of course. But I had been so good for so long. Years, actually. Yet being around Della Stallings's rare phobia had constantly triggered my urge for doling out corrections. Della was off limits, though. She was too risky, and try as she might, Della drew too much attention, especially since she'd become so chummy with Officer Nathan Whitt.

So I had to turn to another.

Melanie's death had been a reminder of how satisfying the process could be. As always, I learned from my mistakes. While Hatchet Lake's cold depths had served as an underwater cemetery for several of my failures, it was now too risky. That was what happened when you did everything the same way for too long. Time had a way of catching up to you.

I started panting, part from the exertion of stair climbing, part from anticipation. On the seventh floor, footsteps had sounded near the stairwell, but the person had continued walking past the exit door. I had a story planned about trapping an animal in the box and carrying it outside for release. My guess was that anyone would be repulsed by the whacking thumps emanating from the side of the box and would hurry past without close examination. Hopefully, they wouldn't notice the rattling and hissing noises in my special package.

One more flight remained. The door to the rooftop was locked, and I set down my cargo while I retrieved the stolen key. A final glance behind, and I pushed open the door.

Chilly wind blasted my face as I picked up the box and headed to the portion of the roof facing the woods. This area was perfect. No cameras, and the view from the front of the building was obstructed by the large metal air-conditioning unit. I set the box down.

"Be warm, my little friends," I said with a chuckle. "I'll set you loose soon."

My hand slipped inside one jacket pocket, and I palmed the hard plastic of the lipstick tube and the outline of my kohl liner pencil. Unfortunately, those toys would have to wait until the last minute. The other jacket pocket contained a damp washcloth for washing up once the session was over.

Satisfied with my preparation, I reentered the building and left the door unlocked. The first part of my night's mission was fulfilled. Now came the tricky part. Waiting to see whether Penny showed up.

Whether she did would depend on whether she wanted to—motive—and whether she could manage to slip by the nurses' station on her ward—opportunity. I checked my cell phone pocket: 1:58 a.m. I'd instructed her to meet me here at two o'clock. From a distance, I heard the faint padding of steps below. I leaned over the top railing and looked down.

Penny Thorpe waved, her smile tentative yet hopeful, the way she'd always greeted me. I'd earned her trust over the last few weeks, got her to confide in me about her fear of snakes and heights. And yet those phobias were the tip of the iceberg in her troubled mental landscape, which included a bipolar disorder diagnosis coupled with suicidal tendencies. Her last suicide attempt, slashing her wrists, had landed her a court-ordered stay at Normal Hospital.

"Why are we meeting up here this time?" she asked, barely out of breath from the trek up eight flights of stairs. Oh, to be young again.

"You've made so much progress with your snake phobia, I thought we could go ahead and make headway on your fear of heights."

Penny glanced apprehensively at the door from the corner of her eyes, clearly uneasy about moving a step closer to confront her fears. Thus far, my corrections had been passive. I'd shown her photos of snakes, and she'd gradually increased the amount of time she could view a photo before the crippling anxiety overcame her, and she had to avert her gaze.

But I'd quickly grown bored of that game. I had no patience for weaklings. Sink or swim, as Nonnie used to say. An image of Melanie's soaked, lifeless body flashed into my mind. That whole affair had been sloppy. The night fishermen had been unforeseeable bad luck, but I'd panicked by ditching her body to be found ashore.

"I was afraid that was your plan," she said, interrupting my thoughts. Penny hugged her sweater closer. "What if I don't want to?"

"That's your choice." I steeped my voice in reproving disappointment. "But I thought you wanted to get well. To get back home to your family. You said your son needed you."

Her lower lip trembled at the reminder of her six-year-old child, and her eyes darted again toward the door. "You really think this will help?"

"One obstacle at a time," I reminded Penny. "Phobias are the easiest mental disorders to cure."

I had no idea if this were true or not.

Skepticism flashed in her pale-blue eyes as she surveyed my casual attire. This was why I preferred my targets to be a little younger than Penny's age. The younger girls were more gullible and inexperienced with deception.

She waved a hand. "You have to admit, this is all extremely unorthodox."

"The best methods usually are," I said with what I hoped was a reassuring smile.

She took a step down. "I'm not ready for this."

"Of course you are." I closed the difference between us, sensing her sudden urge to flee. "You wouldn't be here if you weren't ready, and I wouldn't have proposed it otherwise."

She stood still, biting her lip.

"It'll take less than five minutes. I promise. A quick walk to the edge of the building for a look down, and then we'll leave. We start with short exposure, just like we did with the snake photos. Have I let you down before?"

"No," she admitted. "Okay, I'll try. But if it's too hard, I'll back away."

I had her now. I held the door open. "We'll come right back in if it's too difficult for you."

Mollified, Penny swept past me, close enough I smelled the musky scent of her fear. I followed close behind her as the wind whipped her hair against my face. We were less than a dozen feet from the edge. She walked stiffly, slowly to the edge, as though she were walking a pirate's plank to her death, on her way to a deep sea full of awaiting sharks. I briefly wondered what the scientific name was for a shark phobia, although living in North Alabama didn't provide an opportunity to work with such a fear, even in the unlikely event that I encountered a patient with such a phobia.

Silently, I put on lipstick and slapped on eyeliner before slipping on my thick leather gloves. Three feet from the edge, Penny abruptly halted.

"I don't think I can do it."

"You're almost there," I whispered, almost like a caress. "Here, I'll hold your hand."

I stepped beside her and took her hand. She glanced down at our entwined palms, surprise flickering across her face at the feel of my gloves.

"It's a little chilly," I explained quickly, pulling her forward.

Her breath drew in sharply, but she swallowed hard and took another step forward. "There's a box out here."

"I brought you a little surprise," I replied brightly. "A reward for being so courageous."

Luckily, the box appeared inert at the moment. Perhaps what was inside had fallen asleep, now that it wasn't being jostled around.

"But you have to go all the way to the edge to earn the treat," I encouraged.

Penny nodded, her gaze fixated on the ledge and not me. "Just walk to the edge, look down for one second, and then come back. Right?"

"Absolutely," I lied.

We walked forward. I don't know who gripped hands the tightest, me in my excitement, or Penny in her fear.

We arrived, and she looked down.

"It's . . . it's not so bad."

Liar. Her whole body trembled, and her teeth chattered. I felt the microtug in my palm as she prepared to retreat.

"Good girl," I gushed. "Now for your surprise. Close your eyes a moment."

I let go of her hand and gently positioned our bodies so that she faced me with her back to the ledge. Only then did I open the box lid, carefully extracting the rattler by its throat.

Penny must have sensed something was up, a primal instinct alerting her to danger. Her eyes flew open, immediately taking in the sight of the snake writhing in my hand. The rattlesnake's tail rumbled a warning, its cool body smacking the left side of Penny's neck and throat.

Her mouth opened, and a strangled gurgling sound escaped. She was too terrified to even scream. Instead, the almost silent choking noise sounded like what happened during sleep paralysis. Where lungs and chest muscles seized, and your body was cemented in place, unable to escape danger.

Penny suddenly found her legs and began stumbling backward, her eyes fixated upon the poisonous serpent. Under the full moon's light, her pale eyes mirrored the black, pointed fangs of the rattlesnake.

One step, then another. She was so close to falling. Just one more step. My heart picked up its pace, thumping almost painfully against my shirt.

Penny's ankles knocked against the six-inch-high raised bricks of the ledge. Her arms flapped like a whirligig as her slim body careened to one side. That would not do. She needed to go backward, not sideways. I thrust the snake into her face.

Penny arched away from the object of her terror, completely losing her balance. The snake's fangs pierced through the flesh of her neck. As both feet slipped from beneath their solid mooring, I pushed her chest to move her trajectory downward. She toppled over, and I released the snake so that it fell on top of her body as both descended to the waiting concrete below. Strangely enough, Penny found her voice in this final death tumble. But the scream was fractured by swirling wind, which disbursed it in several directions at once, weakening its volume. The scream cut off abruptly as body met pavement with a satisfying thump.

I quickly stepped away from the ledge and scanned the area where we'd been standing. Luckily, no one was about. I headed to the door, using my cell phone as a flashlight to check the ground. Nothing incriminating could remain, not even a footstep. After grabbing the empty cardboard box, I entered the building, locking the door behind me. It was difficult, but I tamped down the urge to run out to check Penny's motionless body. Odds were that she'd never survive the snake-bite coupled with the fall, but I needed to make sure. Step by step, I kept my eyes peeled for anything Penny might have dropped along the way but found nothing. I continued all the way to the basement, tossed the box into the incinerator bin, and then reentered the silent stairwell to the first floor of the hospital.

In case I ran into anybody, I stuffed my gloved hands in my jacket as I made my way to a rarely used side door. Outside, it had begun to mist. My breathing became hard and erratic, forming small vapor clouds in the chilly air. The back side of the building was poorly lit, and it took me several moments to locate the lump of broken flesh. I scurried to it, bent down, and lowered my ear until it almost brushed against Penny's mouth.

Not even the faintest trace of breath tickled my ear. Blood pooled about her head, and her skull appeared misshapen. Penny Thorpe had most definitely bit the dust. My work here was done. I straightened and carefully left the area, leaving no trace and ensuring once again that there were no witnesses. My only regret was that this time, there would be no bell left behind. No memento mori for survivors to reflect on their own mortality, their own weaknesses, which could lead to a similar fate that the victims had met.

Only the powerful survived.

Chapter 19
DELLA

I walked past the Normal Exterminator van that featured a charming mural of an intrusion of cockroaches lying on their backs, wiggling their six legs in agonized death throes. Seemed the former Officer Eckeridge had found himself a new career.

His house featured a wraparound porch, a common design element in the older neighborhood of quaint homes located in the oldest section of town. The cozy, friendly homes on the magnolia-lined street made my heart pinch. Only two days staying in a motel, and I missed my aunt Sylvie, missed my old room painted buttercup yellow, the handmade quilts and piles of books by my bed, sitting together in the den crafting cinnamon brooms, the air infused with the scents of herbs and candles.

I inhaled deeply and painted a false smile on my face before knocking on the door, confident he must have been inside eating a quick lunch before making another house call. Moments later, Brady opened it, a scowl on his face that only deepened when he recognized who'd interrupted his lunch.

"You," he said with a sneer. "What are you doing here?"

"Sorry for bothering you," I began. "I was in the neighborhood and thought I'd drop by to apologize for the unpleasantries at Dad's barbecue fund-raiser."

His eyes narrowed, and his lower lip bulged out. "How'd you know this was my house?"

I blinked a moment. "Your name's on the mailbox?"

The suspicion in his eyes melted, but not the hostility.

"I really am sorry. It's just that . . . well, being around my father for any length of time puts me on edge. I shouldn't have lashed out at you like I did."

"You called me a dirty cop and a smarmy bastard," he said flatly.

Getting Brady to open up and trust me was not going to be easy.

"I shouldn't have said that. Dad filled my head with a bunch of nonsense and poisoned me against you. But really, there's no justification for the way he cheated you all those years ago. You thought you'd purchased insurance from Dad, and in your time of need he blew you off."

Brady's faced darkened at the memory. "That rat bastard. I'd paid my premiums in full and on time for over a decade, and first time I file a claim . . . *boom* . . . they denied me for nonpayment."

"It must have been terrible."

"And even when he got caught with his hand in the cookie jar, Hunter had the gall to act as if he'd done nothing wrong. 'I'll take care of it,' he'd say, or, 'Don't worry, Brady. I'll get your roof fixed pronto.'" Brady snorted. "Took me two years to get the whole thing settled in court and have the insurance company reimburse me for the loss."

I shook my head in apparent sympathy. "Dad's hurt a lot of people."

"Not the least of which was you," he said gruffly, all hostility gone as he recalled the tragedy. "I knew your mom. She was a nice lady."

"I miss her," I said past the tight constriction of my throat. "And I wonder what Jimmy would have been like as a grown man. If he'd had the chance."

Brady shifted uncomfortably in the doorway. "Course you miss them. I never meant to imply that you didn't at that barbecue the other day."

I waved at the inviting rocking chairs. "It's so nice out today. Can we sit and talk a few minutes?"

"About what?"

"Just a few questions about that night they were killed."

"My lawyer don't want me talking about any of those old cases." A cagey expression crossed his face. I was fixing to lose him.

"I won't ask anything about the witness statements," I hastened to assure him.

I held my breath and waited. Brady sighed and stepped out of the doorway. "I only got five minutes. You ask anything about my case, I ain't sayin' a word."

"Deal."

We settled side by side in the chairs. "You were the arresting officer."

"Correct."

"What did my dad say when you arrested him? Was he . . . angry, upset?"

"Belligerent. Me and my partner, Andy Westman, found him over at Carolyn Merton's trailer. Soon as Hunter came to the door and saw me, he started hollering that I was harassing him. That I was leading a vendetta against him for personal reasons."

Yep. That sounded like my dad.

"I tried to explain the situation, that his wife and son had been killed, but he didn't act like he understood. He'd gotten his dander up that I was there arresting him. I flat out told Hunter he was in trouble big time and we were taking him to the station for questioning. We had a scuffle getting him into the squad car, even after he was warned we could charge him for resisting arrest. Bullheaded man wouldn't listen."

Brady was casting my dad in the worst light possible—a selfish, surly man who didn't seem to care that his wife and son were murdered.

But given what I knew of Brady, it was entirely possible that he'd abused his position as a cop and had acted like a bully, taunting my father and provoking him into a fight. Brady's next words confirmed my opinion as he puffed out his chest and smirked.

"I told Hunter he was way worse than a damn thief—he was a murderer. Then, at the station, he clammed up, demanded a lawyer. Only the guilty do that."

"And right there you decided he was guilty? Before an investigation had even started?" I kept my voice light, nonaccusatory, but Brady shot me a suspicious look.

"Didn't matter what I thought. Facts were that he'd taken out an extra life insurance policy on all of y'all. No one else had motive to kill you."

"I'm keeping an open mind, Brady. But I've got to say, if you and the other cops already had your minds made up on Dad's guilt, then how hard did you really look for other suspects?"

Brady abruptly stood and glared down at me. "We thoroughly searched your home for evidence."

"Not much left of it after the fire," I noted.

"Man was covering his tracks."

"Besides the obvious motive, what else convinced you Dad was guilty?"

"People say he was planning on leaving your mother for Carolyn Merton, that she was going to be his new meal ticket. Did you know that?"

"From everything I've read and heard, that's merely speculation. My parents had serious problems, and the word *divorce* was often tossed around at home by both of them. I'd say it was inevitable, and Mom had about concluded that she'd had enough."

"Even so, your mother would have had excellent grounds to take Hunter to the cleaners for adultery. He wouldn't be the first man to kill an ex to prevent paying child support."

"More speculation," I said mildly. "Plenty of acrimonious divorces without husbands resorting to murder."

I also stood, unwilling to allow Brady to physically hover above me. The man liked to intimidate. "Don't you ever wonder if you might be wrong?" I asked. "Especially now?"

Confusion slackened the tense set of his jaw. "Huh?"

"What with all the other murders that've come to light. Normal has a serial killer."

He snorted. "And again, your dad's a prime suspect. He was stupid enough to leave incriminating evidence behind."

I blinked. Nathan had told me that the found bells weren't public knowledge, but Brady still had connections with other cops, and it wasn't surprising they would talk freely to him.

"The bells? There's that," I conceded. "But I'm not a hundred percent convinced." I tried to articulate the dark wisps of doubt that clouded my mind and judgment. "Mom's and Jimmy's stabbings were brutal. Different from Melanie's drowning. Surely the method's different enough to question if the killer is the same person."

Brady folded his arms across his chest. "I'm not buying that. And you can't dispute the evidence of the bells. They once belonged to your mother."

"The engraved one did for sure, but maybe the killer had stolen that bell after the house fire. It was chaotic back then. So many people treading in and out of the house. Anyone could have taken that bell." *Including you,* I thought.

"You're stretching," Brady argued.

"Maybe. But the whole case against Dad was circumstantial."

"Doesn't matter. Enough of it added up to know it was Hunter that did it."

"Oh, it matters," I assured him. "Carolyn Merton's testimony—the one you coerced her into making—was another brick in the circumstantial theory that was thrown out by the courts."

Brady flushed but didn't back down from his position. "A travesty of justice they let that man out of prison. He still belongs on death row."

"Luckily, you aren't the judge and jury." I stepped around him. "Thank you for your time. I've heard enough."

When I was halfway to my car, Brady decided to have the last word. "Don't let that man pull the wool over your eyes," he called out. "As long as Hunter Stallings is roaming the streets, you're in danger."

I waved casually at Brady as I climbed into my car and pulled out of the driveway. But inside, I was far from calm. Once again, I found myself driving to the outskirts of town and then farther, past Uncle Vic's place. At our old ruined homestead, I stopped my car on the shoulder of the road and got out. Beautiful, sunshiny days like today only made the place appear more sinister and desolate.

I got out of the car and picked my way through the familiar charred structure that remained. Why was I continually drawn back here to relive my brief childhood period over and over? There were no answers to be found in the rotten boards and bits of broken tile and bricks. No comfort in the ugly, ravished debris. Last time I'd come, I'd vowed to either prove Dad was guilty or find the real killer. Now I had to face the possibility that I might never discover the killer's identity. All my life, the masked man might elude me. I'd live in this limbo existence, a gray expanse of doubt and confusion—a scarred woman who shrank from the color red and lived a half life in semireclusion.

Damn it, no. I was sick of it, sick of me. I kicked at the ground, scattering rotten shards of old wood. Nathan was right. Why the hell was I hanging around this place? Maybe I wasn't ready yet to move away from Normal, but I could take a baby step forward. I was supposedly on vacation. What was stopping me from driving four hundred miles south to Gulf Shores for a couple days?

Nothing but my own fears. Dr. Pennington wouldn't care if I missed our appointment this week. He'd be all for me striking out on my own and conquering my demons. I'd drive late at night to avoid traffic and viewing the red taillights of other vehicles. And if I saw anything red, I'd repeat the mantra Dr. Pennington had suggested, *cold blue waters*, and I would survive.

I practically skipped back to my car, already planning what to pack and arranging for a motel, which should be no problem in the off-season. Should I invite Aunt Sylvie? No, I quickly rejected the idea. Not because I was still angry with her, but because this trip would be for me, a declaration of forward progress.

My phone rang, and I checked the screen before answering. Aunt Sylvie had called several times, but I didn't want to speak with her yet. I'd texted her that I was fine and would contact her later. The break from each other would do us both good. I'd leaned on her support too much and for too long. She'd made it unhealthily easy for me to do so. A little distance helped me to see that truth, as well as a few subtle hints from Dr. Pennington.

It wasn't Aunt Sylvie on the line. I swiped my screen. "Hello?"

"Della? Sorry to bother you. This is Linda Bowen at the hospital. I know you're on vacation, but could you possibly stop by and see me a few minutes today?"

Was I in some sort of trouble? Linda's voice was tight, laced with stress. Unease jittered in my belly. "Of course I can. Is there a problem?"

"Yes. Not with you, but . . . just come."

"I can be there in ten minutes."

The sooner I got this over with, the less I'd worry.

My unease skyrocketed to anxiety at the sight of at least a dozen police cars parked in the emergency lanes by the front lobby entrance. More were parked by a side entrance, blue lights flashing. Worse, a stretcher covered with tarp was being loaded into a black sedan marked *County Coroner*.

Another death. Hardly news at a hospital—unless suspicious circumstances were involved. Nathan had said that all three victims had once had a connection to the hospital. Significant, but on the outside realm of coincidence. This fourth victim, if killed by the same person as the others, directly tied in the hospital.

But who? And why? I shuddered as I recalled my brush with the strange man wearing a stolen janitor's uniform. I might have been within a hair's breadth of becoming this fourth victim. This was why I'd been called in. I was to be questioned about the incident.

Sure enough, when I entered Mrs. Bowen's office, Detective Josh Adams was there, seated at the conference table and scribbling notes. From the exhausted frown lines etched on Linda's face, I surmised he'd been grilling her. She bestowed a wan smile and gestured for me to take a seat across from the detective.

"Miss Stallings," he said, the edges of his lips raising in a slight smirk. "Glad you could join us."

I couldn't help a swift glance of reproach at Linda. She could have warned me that Adams was lying in wait. Or maybe he hadn't given her the opportunity.

"What's going on?" I asked. "Why are all the cops back here again?"

"A patient from the psychiatric ward was found dead this morning," Linda explained. "When the woman, Penelope Thorpe, failed to show for either breakfast or her morning therapy session, a search was conducted. A nurse found her body on the west grounds."

"Directly above the body was an open window on the sixth floor," Adams cut in. "An initial inspection revealed a crushed skull, which would be consistent with a fall from that height."

I hugged my arms around my chest. That poor soul. "Was it a suicide then?"

"That's what we're trying to determine. If she jumped, or if she was pushed."

"She did have a history of prior suicide attempts," Linda said. "The hospital will conduct a thorough investigation on how a patient with strong suicidal tendencies was left unsupervised. We cannot allow such a tragedy to occur again."

The detective practically rolled his eyes at Linda's comment. "I'm sure your hospital's managerial team is deeply concerned about every patient's welfare. Not to mention potential lawsuits from the woman's family. Word is, there's been a significant decline in patient admissions and a number of current patients leaving."

Linda stiffened in her chair at the head of the table. "That's not within my purview as Human Resources director. I'll have to refer you to—"

Adams waved her off, his gaze affixed on me. "There was also an injury found on the woman's neck," he said. "Speculation on the scene is that it's a bite from a poisonous snake. There's a small puncture mark and swelling of the wound."

I couldn't stop the shudder of revulsion that coursed through me. How unlucky could one person get?

"That's . . . horrible," I managed.

Adams stared me down. "I read the incident report about the unknown man you'd encountered. We want you to come down to the police station and work with a forensics artist so we can have a composite sketch drawn. We very much want to speak with this person of interest."

If Linda weren't listening to us, I'd have given Adams a smirk of my own. *Guess you've found a new suspect that has nothing to do with my dad,* I'd have sniped. But she was there, so I stayed on my best behavior. "Of course," I told him coolly. "Anything I can do to help the police."

Adams tucked his notebook into his shirt pocket. "Good. He'll be available in about thirty minutes or so."

Without another word, he strolled out of the room.

"I dislike that man," Linda said. "Intensely."

"Join the club."

"Sorry I didn't have a chance to give you a heads-up. The detective came in right after I'd phoned you."

"Then that's not why you'd called? Is anything else wrong?"

Linda ran a hand down her face. "This whole morning—actually, the entire past two weeks—has been nothing but trouble."

"I hated to hear there's been another death. Do you think it was a suicide?"

"We might never know for sure."

"Sounds like you have no confidence in Detective Adams, or the entire local police force for that matter."

"You, as well as anyone, know that not all crimes get solved. Not even the most evil or notorious ones."

I sucked in my breath. "Does this mean you're not one of the majority around here who believe Dad killed my mom and brother? That he only got off on a technicality?"

"I'd never presume to judge. If the courts ruled there was insufficient evidence to keep your father incarcerated, then only the real killer knows for sure who he is and why he did it."

I soaked in her words. *The real killer.* Would I never find him?

"You worked with my mom. Did she have any enemies that you know of?"

Linda shook her head. "Everyone here liked and respected Mary. She was professional, fair, and an all-around nice person."

I nodded and clasped my hands in front of me. "It's odd, isn't it? Four deaths tied to women at this hospital. My mom had a connection too."

"Huh. I hadn't thought of that." Linda tilted her head to the side. "An employee instead of a patient, though. Interesting."

I shook off the melancholy that threatened to envelop me. "Probably a coincidence. Anyway, what did you want to see me about?"

I desperately hoped they weren't going to change my work hours, citing the potential danger of night shifts. Maybe one day, I'd be ready to switch, but not yet. And it wasn't like I was the only person working nights—my brain began to kick in with defensive reasoning to shore my position.

"It's a delicate matter. And please know that you are completely free not to respond. Really, I shouldn't even be asking."

The wheels in my brain ground to a halt. She wasn't going to ask me to give up my night hours. I waited for her to continue as she drew a deep breath.

"Have you picked up on any strange behaviors or activities with employees?"

"No. I rarely even see people except one of the maintenance men occasionally—or I'll say hello to a lab tech or nurse as we pass in the hallway." Which was pretty much the whole point of my unusual hours for data-entry work.

Linda tapped her fingers on her desk and scrutinized me, as though debating whether to proceed. This was so out of character with the efficient, confident manager I was used to seeing.

"You don't really think an employee has anything to do with the murders, do you?" I asked. "I'd be more suspicious of unauthorized persons in the building. Like the man I'd encountered dressed in a janitor's uniform."

"That was really weird. I hope the police artist's drawing helps solve that mystery. In the meantime, security has reprogrammed all the locks and hired additional personnel to patrol all the buildings."

"That's good to hear. I'll feel safer when I return to work this weekend."

Linda still appeared troubled. "Besides the ones you encounter at night, has any other employee made you feel uneasy? Do you feel unsafe here?"

What the hell was she getting at? My contact with others was minimal except for my sessions with Dr. Pennington. But Linda didn't know about those. Unless . . . "David Nelson isn't exactly my favorite person. He's been condescending in the past. As far as feeling afraid goes—I imagine we're all a bit uneasy these days. Are you worried that I'll crack under the pressure of everything that's been going on? I realize my sudden request for time off might cause you to have doubts about me. It's true I've been under a lot of stress lately, but I'm coping."

She did not appear reassured, and I swallowed hard, fighting to hide my nervousness. I'd planned on apartment hunting the next couple of days, excited about the prospect of at last getting my own place. But I couldn't do that without steady paychecks coming in.

"I do a good job," I continued in a rush. "And this was the first time I'd asked for any time off. You can check my record. I've probably taken no more than three sick days in all the years I've worked here."

"Your job performance isn't an issue."

"Is Human Resources about to start layoffs? I've heard the hospital fears a financial catastrophe because of all the bad press." Administrative staff would be the first to get let go. As a nurse, Libbie should at least be safe. I didn't have a child depending on me, but I still needed the money.

"Please, Mrs. Bowen. I—I need this job." If I had to grovel, I'd put away my pride and strong need for privacy. "I realize you may have concerns about my . . . my mental well-being, but I'm coping with everything. Really. I've even started going back into counseling with Dr. Pennington."

"You don't have to tell me, but"—she paused a heartbeat—"are you pleased with the quality of care you're receiving?"

I hadn't expected that particular question. Maybe recent events had everyone, even managers, questioning not only the safety but also the quality of mental health care provided by Normal Hospital. "Yes. So far, so good."

"Very well. If anything changes, if anything even the slightest bit unusual makes you uncomfortable, I hope you'll come to me."

"Yes, of course."

Linda nodded and smiled kindly. "Just so you know, your job security was never in question. There will always be a place here for Mary Stallings's daughter."

Despite Linda's assurances, I couldn't completely quiet the rumble of disquiet her words had caused. I drove to the police station, mulling over our conversation and trying to pick apart what had been said and what had been left unsaid. I couldn't help feeling that I was missing something important, something hidden in the minefield of her words.

Chapter 20

DR. PENNINGTON

This had to stop. It was getting out of control.

Not an hour after Penelope Thorpe's broken body had been discovered, Detective Adams had come around to my office, demanding to review her health records. I delayed him, citing that releasing them would be a violation of federal HIPAA laws. Under HIPAA, only Thorpe's next of kin had a right to read her health records. He, of course, pointed out that I'd let him review Melanie Mickelson's files. I'd argued that hers was an obvious case of murder while Thorpe's was not. In return, he'd claimed that state law provided law enforcement officers the right to access health records in the course of a serious investigation.

I told him to come back with a subpoena and make a written request with the hospital's legal department. I'd immediately delved into Penelope Thorpe's computer and paper records and expunged all mention of her fear of snakes and heights. As far as I knew, these deletions were undetectable unless my computer was seized and the hard drive examined by a computer forensics expert.

But why would anyone take such drastic action? Detective Adams might not like me—he didn't appear to like anyone (nor they him)—but he had no grounds to violate my privacy in such a high-handed manner. And after all, accessing all my patients' computer health files would be hard for a judge to legally grant.

Yet I couldn't merely sit back and allow the situation to continue. Everything had to be reined in, locked up tight and suppressed.

As if I needed further aggravation, I was also paid a visit today by the Human Resources director, Linda Bowen. So many pointed questions. Gayla—dear, trusting, loyal Gayla—had saved me for the time being, waltzing into my office and claiming I had several phone calls that simply must be taken.

But I was on borrowed time unless I immediately contained the damage and prevented new breaches. The seconds ticked away in my brain like a perpetual metronome. Click, click, click—a steady, unending, maddening pace.

Chapter 21

DELLA

I'd put off visiting Aunt Sylvie long enough. After my quick two-day trip to the beach, I was ready to see her, intent on mending fences. I'd just finished meeting with the police artist, and he'd sketched a remarkable likeness of the mysterious Myers. So now it was time to face Aunt Sylvie.

She invited me in with a wide smile and ushered me to the kitchen for tea. Her hands trembled as she set her cup of licorice tea down on the saucer, and the china rattled, betraying her nervousness at the sudden visit. Her long silver hair was dispiritedly plaited to one side, and her bare face was etched with deep lines I'd never noticed until now.

"You can ask me anything you'd like, Della," she said. "I owe you that much."

Did I ever have questions. How long had the affair lasted? Were she and Dad in love back then? Why the hell had she betrayed her sister? What had she ever seen in my father? Was their relationship the reason she'd never married anyone?

Yet I hesitated. Would hearing the answers really smooth over the hurt? I feared it would only make their affair more painful for me.

"You said Mom never knew. That's what matters. I guess the only other thing I want to know is . . . do you still love Dad?"

"God, no!"

The horrified revulsion on her face would have been comical in other circumstances. But not about this. Never about this old wound. "Then if it's okay with you, I don't ever want to talk about it."

"Suits me." She sighed. "Although I should defer to whatever your therapist deems best. If Dr. Pennington believes family therapy to discuss this would be helpful, I'm willing."

"God, no!" I said, mimicking her previous words.

We shared an uneasy laugh, and Aunt Sylvie clasped my hand. "I've missed you. But I can see the break was good for you. Even your face looks fresh and rosy."

I patted my slightly sunburned face. "The trip to Gulf Shores was amazing. Empowering."

"I'm so proud of you." Sylvie's eyes filmed over. "I sheltered you too much as you were growing up. I see now that I might have done more harm than good."

"You were wonderful. I don't know what I would have done without you."

"Lived with your uncle Vic and Mabel."

I gave a dramatic shudder, and we laughed again. But I recalled my conversation with him the day he helped me escape from the fundraising barbecue. "But he's really not that bad, you know? Uncle Vic's a good guy."

"Right. Just a little . . . rigid, shall we say? We all do the best we can."

I withdrew my hand and sipped my tea. "While we're being so open, I should tell you that I've put a deposit down on an apartment this morning. I'll move into it the first week in December."

Aunt Sylvie slowly nodded. "It's progress. Huge progress. But I'll miss you."

"I'll miss you too. It'll be good for both of us, though."

I stood and impulsively gave her a hug. "Gotta run an errand before work."

I left the warmth of our kitchen and got in my car with a lighter heart. The plastic bag filled with beach sand and shells lay on the passenger seat. It might be foolish, but Mom and Jimmy loved visiting Gulf Shores, and I wanted to sprinkle the beach mementos over the ugly ruins of our old home. I drove through town and then farther out, passing Uncle Vic's place and then to the property I'd inherited. A rusty truck was pulled over to the side of the road in front of the ruins.

Who else wanted to visit this lonely, ugly place?

A man wearing a blue windbreaker jacket was bent over at the waist, placing stakes around the property. Small orange flags waved in the crisp breeze. Indignation swept over me. Who the hell did he think he was, marking my property without permission? If it was a county worker on official business, he wouldn't be driving an unmarked truck.

I pulled in behind his car and got out, slamming the door. The man looked up, familiar blue eyes meeting my outraged gaze.

"Dad? What are you doing here?" I rushed over to where he stood.

He held up a map and industrial tape measure. "Vic saw a couple hunters round here yesterday. So I got this land plat from the county courthouse. Nobody's surveyed the area in years. Thought I'd better mark the borders to keep trespassers out."

Suspicion buzzed my mind like circling hornets. "Don't think those flags will deter men with shotguns."

"They can't use ignorance as a defense if I catch them either."

"Why do you care? Not like they can do any further damage to this place."

"Because it's mine; that's reason enough."

"No, it's mine, not yours, Dad. This property belongs to me."

"Then you should take better care of it."

"What the . . ." I waved an arm to indicate the charred house remains. "Can't get any worse than this."

"It doesn't have to be this way. This all needs to be bulldozed under. Give the place a new, fresh look. What do you say, Della? It's time to rebuild from the rubble."

Rebuild? I regarded him quizzically. "I'm not planning on building out here."

"Someone should live here. Keep an eye out on our property."

"*My* property," I reminded him. "And I don't lose any sleep over the occasional trespasser."

"Encroachment's a serious matter."

"Okay, Dad. What gives?"

Wide, exaggerated innocent eyes met mine. "I'm doing this for you," he said, managing to act offended.

I crossed my arms and waited.

"I've got a little money saved—"

"From all those people who donated to your legal fund?"

"Right. Anyway, it's enough to buy a used double-wide. I could set it up here. Keep an eye on things for you."

"First of all, you've suckered all those donors. They thought their money was going to aid an innocent man fighting the state to be compensated for wrongful imprisonment."

Dad bristled. "Some of that money went to my lawyer. You can't expect me to give every penny to some bloodsucking attorney. A man's got to live."

"Worn out your welcome already with Uncle Vic?"

"No. But I'm tired of being dependent on my little brother. And I'm tired of being preached to. He and Mabel go to church twice during the week and all day Sunday. They expect me to go with them too." His lower lip stuck out in a petulant pout. "It's cramping my style."

"I bet." I took a stab in the dark as to why his style was being cramped. "Heard you have a new girlfriend."

"Heard you have a new boyfriend." Dad's mouth twisted. "A cop, no less."

Word sure got around fast in Normal. "He's a friend. That's all. Besides, that's not the point. I don't need you or anyone else camped out on my property. I'm in no danger of having it whisked away."

"Why let it sit here unused? I bought this land."

"And your attorney signed it over to me when you went to prison."

"Only to protect my assets from being sold at auction. But I'm back now."

"It's in my name, not yours."

"A technicality. Guess I'll need to bring this up with my current lawyer."

I gaped at him. "Are you threatening me with a lawsuit?"

"C'mon, Delly-girl. Let's not argue. We should settle this between ourselves."

The gall of this man. "This land was bought with money that Mom's dad gave her. You had nothing to do with it."

A muscle in Dad's jaw tightened. "I see your aunt Sylvie's been running her fat mouth. Not that it matters where the money originated. Your mom and I were married; therefore, this will legally be considered communal property."

"File your lawsuit then. You'll lose."

"I don't want to fight you in court. Be reasonable. I'll bear the expense of cleaning up this place. It'll save you money in the long run and provide me with a rent-free place to live until I get back on my feet."

"No." I pivoted on my heel, needing to put distance between us. Arguing with Dad was useless and only upset me.

"At least consider knocking down the ruins. They're a public hazard. You're lucky no one's sued you over them."

I spun back around. "Are you seriously going to lecture me on my civic duty? Coming from you, that's rich. I can guess the real reason you want to clean up here. Those ruins are a reminder to you. Everyone passing by here remembers the crime. Remembers you. They're an embarrassment to be bulldozed under and buried beneath the earth's scorched surface."

Dad paled under the onslaught of my accusation. For the first time in my life, I saw him at a loss to defend himself. I marched to my car and left without a backward glance. It was no more than what he deserved. I sped down the road, fuming at his outrageous move to reclaim the land. Until his threat, I hadn't even realized how much that place meant to me. Losing it would be like losing Mom and Jimmy all over again—losing what brief happy childhood memories still remained. My own father wanted to jerk out from under me that last link to the old life that I still clung to.

Let him file his damn lawsuit. I'd hire my own attorney.

The baggie of sand and shells still lay on the car seat beside me, mocking my good intentions for the day. I picked it up and flung it onto the back seat, out of sight.

My mood had not much improved by the time I reached work. Good thing I had weird night hours. I didn't have to wear a mask of fake calm and make small talk with coworkers. The hospital was mercifully quiet and forlorn as I walked to my office and turned on the computer. My in-box was full, and I intended to stay busy. By the time my shift ended, my anger would have cooled, and I would be able to consider Dad's threat in a more rational frame of mind.

The monitor came to life, and I stared at my screen saver. The solemn face of Grand Duchess Anastasia Romanov stared back at me. In this particular photo, she was a prisoner, awaiting an uncertain fate as her country bled from inner turmoil. Could she have possessed any inkling of the undignified, horrific, bloody fate of her own family? I hoped she had not. Hoped she'd been blissfully ignorant right up until the very end, when her Bolshevik captors opened fire on all of them in the basement of the fortress ominously named the House of Special

Purpose. By all accounts, her inept jailers had made the ordeal even more horrific with their grotesque bungling.

Yeah, that girl had it bad. Put my own problems in better perspective. I shook off my morbid obsession with the Romanovs and set to work. It wasn't until I stood to stretch an hour later that my eyes caught sight of a wicker basket atop the file cabinet. I picked it up and surveyed the contents—a bag of dill pickle potato chips, packets of hot cocoa mix, and several chocolate caramel candy bars. All my favorites. A scribbled note from Knox was tucked into the goodies: *Welcome back, Della.*

How sweet. He always noticed the smallest details. First break, I'd take him the new jar of hand cream I'd brought.

I returned to work. Data entry was backed up from my brief time off, and the first four hours flew by in a haze. I'd actually missed the work, missed the structure and routine of a job. The time off had been needed, but I was ready to move forward.

At 4:15 a.m., only forty-five minutes before my shift ended, I finally finished my last assignment. By the time I made a cup of cocoa, used the bathroom, and left the hand cream with Knox, I'd returned to my office with just enough time left to catch up on emails and shut down my computer.

Satisfied, I headed out, thinking of my earlier run-in with Dad. Although I despised his high-handed manner, maybe he was right. Wasn't it finally time to destroy what was left of our old home and move on? Having him live there couldn't hurt anything. I could still come and go as I wished. And it would be a kindness on my part to help out Uncle Vic. He couldn't enjoy having his brother constantly underfoot any more than Dad disliked the arrangement. I wouldn't immediately call Dad, though. I didn't want him to think he could intimidate me. If I was lucky, Dad would win his lawsuit against the State of Alabama and leave Normal a rich man—free to start a new life far from here, far from me.

I passed by the deserted smallpox wing, still ruminating on my options, when I heard a swish of air and a door softly closing. I froze, straining to hear more.

Moments later came a shuffling and a creak, as though someone had sat on a mattress. The noise appeared to originate from a small corridor off the main hallway.

A loud clanging crash erupted, followed by a rolling tinkle—the distinctive tinny note of a bell.

Time warped and contorted, a train hurtling to the past. I was eight years old again, frozen on the staircase and weighted down with dread. Red painted our den in streaks and puddles, great slashes of crimson on the floors, the walls, my mom and little brother. The masked man slowly began to turn his head toward me.

Run!

I violently shook my head, tossing away the delusion, the urgent need to flee. I was a grown woman now, not a vulnerable child at the mercy of a monster. I removed my cell phone from my back pocket and pulled up hospital security's number on speed dial. There would be a guard stationed in the ER, which was much closer to me than Knox, who'd be making his rounds in one of the east buildings right now.

"Anybody there?" I called out, my finger still poised over the security speed dial button. I walked into the corridor and stared at a closed door off to the side.

No one answered. I started to call out once more, but the door flew open, crashing against the tiled wall. A man shot out of the room.

It was him. The same man I'd seen before and who I'd described to the police artist. Tall, pale, and emaciated, scraggly brown hair pulled back in a ponytail. Our gazes locked. His eyes were unnaturally wide, the whites showing above and below his pupils. Red streaks of broken blood vessels slashed across the dull yellow of his eyeballs.

I fell back against the wall as he ran past me, my breath ragged in the sudden silence. Hands shaking, I called security.

"Stay where you are," they warned. "Don't try to follow him."

As if.

I stood in the hallway and waited for their arrival. Only a trace odor of musk remained as evidence that the man actually existed. What was he up to?

I crept closer to the open doorway and caught a glimpse of a cheap cot and thin mattress that took up most of the small enclosed room. On the opposite wall from the cot were a toilet and basin. It looked more like a prison cell than a private hospital room.

Security would arrive any second. That frightened, desperate man wasn't returning. I walked closer, curious as a cat. I wouldn't touch anything in the room or disturb the potential crime scene. What was the harm?

At the entrance, I stopped, my gaze flickering over the room. The smell of musk was stronger here, mixed with unpleasant aromas of old food and stale sweat. Strewn across one end of the cot were empty food containers, a few dirty clothes, magazines, and papers. My gaze dropped lower. Under the mattress was a small brass bell upended on its side.

Chapter 22

DELLA

I stared at the maleficent object. The brass bell itself was approximately three inches high and attached to a wooden handle almost twice that size. It appeared cheap, a garden-variety object that could be purchased at a dollar store, certainly not collector's quality. The brass was weathered and dull, the handle nicked and unpolished. I couldn't imagine my mother seeing any beauty in it, even in a new, pristine state. The only reason to save it would be if it had been a gift and held sentimental value.

My palms itched to pick it up and examine it closer, but I knew better than to contaminate possible evidence. I dared not even enter the room for fear of leaving behind hair and fiber remnants.

Growing horror pressed upon me, and I rubbed the goose bumps on my arms. Was the man, who less than one minute ago had passed within a few feet of me, a serial killer? How long had he camped out in deserted sections of the hospital and abducted female patients?

What was his connection to my mother? Had he taken a perverted obsession with her when she'd worked here so long ago?

Running footsteps hammered from a distance, and my scalp prickled. If it was the killer returning, I was trapped in a dead-end hallway. It went against every instinct, but safety lay in racing toward the main hallway and whoever approached. It was the only path of escape. Surprisingly, my legs—which had turned to jelly moments ago—responded to my body's urgent demand to flee.

At the intersection with the main passage, I swiftly turned to the right—the direction toward the emergency room, from which help most likely would arrive.

Empty. No security guard approached. Footsteps again approached, and I swiveled my head to the left and glimpsed a familiar figure.

"Knox!" I called out in relief. "Thank God, it's you."

Concern blazed in his wide eyes as he approached and scanned my body head to toe. Glancing over my shoulder, he searched the area behind me for danger. "Are you okay? What happened? A security alarm sounded over the radio."

"I saw that guy again. The one parading as Myers." I pointed behind me. "He's been living in a locked room back there."

Knox skirted around me and headed down the corridor.

"Better not go in there," I cautioned. "Might be a crime scene."

Knox discarded my warning and entered the open doorway. "I'll be careful."

The sound of more footsteps rang out, and two security guards rounded a corner. I waved at them. "Over here!"

Quickly, I made my way to the room. "Security's almost here."

Knox bent over the bed, examining the strewn trash. He didn't turn to face me. "Come take a look at this."

I uneasily glanced over my shoulder and then entered. "We shouldn't be in here."

Knox merely pointed at the cot, and I followed his gaze. Newspaper photos and clippings were interspersed among the rubbish: "Hospital Patient Missing," "Additional Bodies Discovered at Hatchet Lake," "Another Death Investigated at Normal Hospital, Possible Connection to Prior Murders Explored."

A snapshot of a grinning Melanie Mickelson slammed into me, along with two other photos I recognized as Susan Battles and Willow Forsyth. Knox removed a handkerchief from his pocket, lifted the papers to view the clippings underneath, and then gave a soft whistle.

"You're going to get us in trouble," I said with a hiss. Judging from the noise outside, the security men were almost upon us now.

I tamped down my nervousness and bent lower, my body crowded against Knox in the tiny room. I peered closely at the older, more faded newsprint. Gray pixilated ink swirled and instantly arranged into an old, familiar pattern. It took several long moments for my brain to register what my heart had instantly recognized.

Mom.

Before us lay a work photo some reporter had snapped at a public meeting several months before her death. Short bobbed hair and an elegant profile of classic, proportioned features were on display as she leaned attentively forward at a conference table.

"Hey!"

We both jumped as two men appeared in the doorway. Both wore crackling and buzzing two-way radios clipped to their belts.

"Which way did the man run?" one of the uniformed guards asked.

"All I know is he turned left out of here toward the elevators by outpatient surgery."

The guard left, briskly updating other members of security on the situation. The remaining guard, an "Officer Albright" on his uniform shirt pocket, ordered us from the room.

"You shouldn't be in there," he admonished. "We might need to secure the room to gather evidence. Come on out."

Knox pointed at the clippings. "Looks like the guy had an unhealthy interest in the murder victims."

Albright's face grew even more grim. "All the more reason to get out."

I had no wish to remain in the suffocating cell, and we both hustled into the hallway.

"All the exits have been sealed," Albright assured us. "He won't get away."

I thought of Nathan and his displeasure when hospital security had fumbled about disclosing my first encounter with the possible killer. "Has anyone alerted the Normal Police Department?" I asked.

"They're en route," Albright assured me. "We'll comb every inch of the hospital if we need to. What alerted you to the suspect's presence?"

"I heard a door close and then what sounded like a bell fall to the floor. A moment later, he came tearing out of the room and ran past me without a word."

Another hospital security guard arrived, and Albright quickly filled him in.

"You stay here and watch the room," the new guy, evidently a supervisor, ordered Albright. "Don't let anyone else enter until the police come." He gestured to Knox and me. "Come with me. I want a statement for my records before the police arrive."

I had a feeling I'd be repeating my story over a dozen times before I was free to go home.

We followed the man, who introduced himself as Avery Lumpkin, to a large room in the administrative wing, which featured four cubicles; a wall of closed-circuit TVs that monitored the lobby, emergency room, and parking lot; and a hodgepodge of blinking electronic equipment I assumed were some sort of radio scanners. Lumpkin guided us to a small office, where David Nelson awaited. He indicated we take a seat across from his desk and typed on a computer keyboard as I repeated my story. Bet he didn't think I was a delusional pain in the ass anymore. Too bad he'd never taken me seriously to begin with. I continued relating what had happened, and Knox chimed in on arriving at the scene. As I described what we'd found in the room, the shock of seeing my mother's photo, a sudden trembling seized my body, and my teeth chattered.

Nelson's office was set to a comfortable temperature, but it might as well have been a freezing meat locker for all the good it did me. I huddled in the chair, wrapping my arms around my waist, seeking my own body warmth to ward off a chill that jabbed bone deep. Voices swirled around me, faint and distorted, as though I were in the bottom of a deep, dark well.

Della?

. . . not well

in shock . . .

. . . call a doctor

get her warm . . .

call a family member . . .

Della? Can you hear me?

I wanted to rise up and tell them I was okay, but my head was so very heavy, and my neck too weak to support its weight. Someone wrapped a wool blanket across my shoulders, and I gratefully absorbed its warmth and its protective shield against the exposed flesh of my arms. A sense of déjà vu enveloped me as my mind flashed back to the pink cheerfulness of my Hello Kitty comforter—that cotton fabric that had provided so much comfort to me during that fateful night.

"I'm okay," I managed to mumble. I forced my eyelids open and provided a wan smile.

Knox patted my hand. "Your aunt Sylvie's on her way to drive you home."

Nelson pressed a Styrofoam cup into my numbed hands. "Heard you like cocoa. This should help."

I straightened in my chair and took a tentative sip, allowing the hot melted sugar and chocolate to fortify me. By the time I'd finished, the trembling ended, and my mind was clear. My cheeks flushed over my display of weakness. I wanted the attention off of me. "Did they catch the guy yet?" I asked.

Nelson settled back at his desk and regarded me sympathetically. "Police have him in custody and are taking him down to the station for questioning." He cleared his throat. "I apologize for not believing you weeks ago when you were suspicious someone was here that shouldn't be."

"I'm just glad it's over. I—I wonder if he might have been the one that killed my mother and brother. He had all those clippings." But why had he done it? My head swirled with questions.

"The police will get to the bottom of this," Nelson reassured me. "If he's guilty, they'll make sure he's locked away."

Locked away. Like they'd done to my father? It was beginning to look more and more like Dad had been innocent all along.

David Nelson had a lot more faith in the cops than I did. But at least I trusted Nathan. There was that at least.

Chapter 23

DET. NATHAN WHITT

The suspect was fingerprinted, booked, and—for now—charged with trespassing. Adams and I studied his priors. And it was a long list.

Jack Jenkins was a fifty-six-year-old male who had been arrested for three assaults, several theft of property violations, and almost a dozen burglaries over a span of nearly four decades. A veteran with a history of substance abuse and mental health issues, Jenkins had a deeply troubled past. But much, much more interesting to us was that he'd been a patient at Normal Hospital during roughly the same period of time that Susan Battles and Willow Forsyth had also been patients.

"From the dates of his various arrests, he lived just fifteen miles south of here in Beauregard at the time of the Stallings murders," I said.

Instead of looking pleased at the news, Adams scowled. "His past assaults were bar brawls. Going from that to serial killer is a huge leap. Besides, why would he kill that family? Hunter Stallings was the one with motive and opportunity."

"Maybe we can dig the motive from him. Could be he'd gone to burglarize the house, accidentally awakened the mother, and then killed her to avoid being identified later. As far as the kid goes, he was in the wrong place at the wrong time."

"You don't believe that," Adams scoffed.

He was right. The stabbings were too personal, and the killer had chased Della through the woods to murder her as well—not something a surprised burglar would likely do. "I'm just throwing out scenarios," I said.

"I still say Hunter Stallings killed his wife and son. And I think Della Stallings knows it too. I'd love to have a reason to bring her into the interrogation room and have a go at her."

"You're wrong about Della," I said, much more vehemently than I'd meant to. I forced a note of calm into my voice. "I've questioned Della, and she knows nothing more about the killer than we do. She's cooperated every step of the way in our investigation. Matter of fact, I suspect that part of her might always wonder if her father tried to kill her that night."

"No, she won't." Adams shot me a severe frown. "Because we're going to solve this case once and for all. No more doubts. Let's go talk to Jenkins."

We proceeded to the brightly lit holding room, where the overhead fluorescent bars spotlighted the suspect's gaunt face. Patches of bare scalp gleamed beneath his brown hair and highlighted its threads of silver, all pulled back into a messy ponytail. He gazed at us warily, but with resignation and no fear. Jenkins was no stranger to police interrogation.

"How long have you been camping out at the hospital?" Adams asked, plunging right into the questioning.

"I reckon it's been about two years."

I let out a low whistle. "How the hell did you not get caught before now?"

Jenkins smiled sardonically. "Nobody ever really sees a janitor. You put on the uniform and keep a mop or broom on hand, and it's like—presto—you're invisible."

"I don't think you're giving yourself enough credit. Any employee at the hospital help you cover your tracks?"

"Nah. It's all on me." He drummed his fingers on the table. His nails were yellowed, and slivers of black were embedded at the tips. A stench of cigarettes and sweat clung to him. Bathing was either not a high priority or a bit of a risky undertaking when living underground.

Adams brushed this aside and went in for the kill. "What were you doing with that bell and the newspaper clippings on the Stallings case?"

"Bell?" Confusion momentarily flickered across his face. "Don't rightly recollect it. But I picked up odds and ends on my outings at night. Whatever caught my fancy, or whatever I thought might come in useful one day. You know, aspirin, candy bars, little trinkets like pens and candles. And—I'll admit it—whatever cash might be lying around."

"I don't believe you." Adams mouth was set in a tight line.

"Why would I lie? You caught me. Gig's up. Truth be told, I was getting a bit tired of the whole thing. Never talking to nobody or getting to go nowhere." He shrugged and then clasped his hands together, leaning forward. "Say, I could really use a cigarette. Can you help a fella out?"

Adams ignored the request. "What about all the newspaper clippings you stored? You're mighty interested in the murders."

"What newspaper clippings? I just had a bunch of old newspapers and books to read."

"Do you know Hunter Stallings?" I asked, changing tactics.

"Never met him personally. Just read what was in the papers."

"What about his daughter, Della Stallings?" Adams interjected.

Annoyance clawed at me. Without Della, who knows how long Jenkins would have continued to stay hidden? But I said nothing. The more I defended Della, the more Adams would dig in his heels and continue believing she knew something she wasn't telling.

"Don't know her either."

"Of course you do. She's the one who found you tonight."

Jenkins eyes widened. "That so? Well, I'll be damned. Had no idea who she was."

Adams made a click of disgust, and I took the opportunity to veer the conversation away from Della. "And did you know Susan Battles or Willow Forsyth?"

For the first time, Jenkins drew into himself and stared down at his clasped hands. "Why you asking me all these questions about the murders? I dunno anything about them."

We might be starting to lose him. "You want a cigarette? Talk to me about those women. We already know you were a patient at the hospital at the same time they were."

"Maybe." Jenkins wet his lips. "I sure could use a pack of smokes and a Coke."

Adams opened his mouth, and I could tell he was about to object. I caught his eye and slightly shook my head. But he spoke into the two-way radio he'd laid on the table and ordered someone to bring the items.

"I smoke Pall Mall unfiltered—" Jenkins began.

"You'll take what's available," Adams interrupted. "Now tell us about the women."

Jenkins pushed his chair back and folded his arms, clearly holding out until his smokes arrived. Adams rolled his eyes but didn't push him. Less than a minute later, a uniformed cop arrived with the requested treats. Jenkins's eyes brightened, and he hurriedly took a cigarette from the pack, lit it, and then inhaled long and deep. After several puffs, Adams tried again.

"Talk to us about the women."

Jenkins popped the lid on the soda and gulped half of it down. At length, he set the can on the table.

"I knew Susan best. We were both patients in the mental ward. I had a problem with PTSD and Susan . . . well, she was just messed up.

Scared of everything, even her own shadow. Had a thing about being cooped up inside too."

"Claustrophobic?" I asked.

Jenkins jabbed his cigarette toward me. "Exactly. She complained that sometimes she felt like the walls of the hospital were closing in on her so tight she couldn't breathe. So I suggested we sneak out a bit at night. Told her the fresh air would do her good. And it did. We'd sit on the rooftop and smoke a few cigarettes. Sometimes her friend Willow came along for the ride."

"What did you talk about?" I asked.

"Nothing special." Jenkins drew on the cigarette and then exhaled smoke rings. "You know, nurses we liked or didn't like. Things we were going to do once we got out."

"Did you have a romantic relationship with her?" Adams asked.

"Nah. I wouldn't even say we were friends. Just fellow patients, passing the time."

"Did you ever try to get in touch with Susan or Willow after your release?"

"Nope. I finished my thirty days of treatment and went back home. Back to my wife and my shitty job at the chicken plant."

"Why the hell should we believe anything you say?" Adams asked.

The wariness returned to Jenkins's eyes. "You can't seriously believe I killed them. I've never hurt nobody. Well, except for a few tussles when I was younger and wild with booze."

"The coincidences are beginning to pile up," Adams said. "You knew two of the victims, you've been roaming the hospital at night, and we caught you with the clippings and that bell."

Damn it, Adams shouldn't have mentioned the bell. Gross incompetence.

"What is it with that bell? What's the big deal?"

Adams backtracked, obviously realizing he'd spoken out of turn. "We ask the questions around here, not you. Did you know Melanie Mickelson?"

"No."

"Don't lie to us," I warned him. "If we find out you've withheld anything . . ."

"I'm not lying. I swear it." Jenkins's hands trembled as he stubbed out his cigarette and drew another one from the pack.

"Maybe you didn't murder anyone," I said. "But maybe you know who did. Maybe you burglarized the Stallings home and stole some things for somebody else."

"I don't know nothing about any of this shit. All I'm guilty of is trespassing and stealing."

"So that's your story, and you're sticking to it," Adams commented with a sneer.

"That's the truth. You think I'm some stupid nobody that you can pin this on and solve your case. Is that it? Well, it ain't happening. I know my rights, and I ain't talking no more without a lawyer."

"Your call." Adams shoved away from the table and got to his feet.

Damn it. He'd pushed Jenkins too far, too fast. I'd have to work on Jenkins. Visit him in his cell and bring him cigarettes and sodas, ease into gaining his confidence to try to discover what, if anything, he knew that might help solve these murders. I had a feeling there was something he could tell me.

Chapter 24

DELLA

I entered the police station, my nerves stretched taut at the sight of uniformed cops bustling everywhere. Some of Dad's mistrust of them had evidently rubbed off on me, although there was one particular cop who had managed to earn my trust. I picked my way through the crowded lobby and approached the receptionist.

"I'd like to see Officer Nathan Whitt, please."

She didn't crack even a ghost of a welcoming smile. "He expecting you?"

"Sort of," I lied. It had only been a few days since the arrest of the hospital's mystery intruder, a vagrant by the name of Jack Jenkins. News media reports on Jenkins were rife with speculation, but very few facts had leaked about his possible link with recent and past murders, none of which had been enlightening. I was hoping Nathan would cast me a few tidbits.

The woman frowned, and I half expected her to dismiss me without even checking with Nathan.

"What's the nature of this business?" she demanded.

I debated playing the sympathy card and claiming that Nathan was investigating my family's murders, which was indirectly true, but I went with, "It's personal."

She shoved a sign-in sheet at me, and I found a seat and began filling it out, feeling ridiculous. I had no legitimate claim to Officer Whitt's time. If he'd wanted to tell me anything, he'd have called. Frankly, it surprised me. The night of Jenkins's arrest, I'd seen him for a moment as Aunt Sylvie and I exited the hospital. He and two other officers were carrying what I assumed to be evidence bags. His eyes had locked with mine, and he'd immediately come over and spoken, asking whether I was okay.

So why hadn't he contacted me since then? I'd even texted him two days ago asking for information. He'd responded with only a brusque comment about being busy.

Maybe in my mind, I'd built what was a mere acquaintance into a friendship. Not like I had much experience in the friendship arena. But Libbie and I had met twice in the past week, and her concern about my well-being after discovering Jenkins had been evident. And I had my aunt Sylvie and my sessions with Dr. Pennington. A pathetically small circle of people I could count on, but I was coping.

I stopped writing on the form and abruptly stood. Who was I kidding? Nathan wasn't going to divulge any confidential information to me. I wasn't important enough in his eyes. His silence had made that clear. I returned the clipboard to the receptionist and strode for the door.

A chill breeze blasted me as I walked outside, head down to avoid the wind, ignoring a group of men headed into the station.

"Della?"

My head snapped forward. Nathan waved and held up a finger, motioning for me to wait. He told his coworkers he'd be a moment and walked to where I stood.

"Has something else happened?" he asked. "More trouble?"

"I came to see you."

"What about?" His eyes shifted to the station door, as though he wished he were walking through them. Away from troublesome me.

"Thought you could update me on the Jack Jenkins investigation."

Nathan shrugged. "He was arrested and is being held without bond pending trial."

"Everyone in Normal knows that," I gritted through my teeth. "I was hoping you could tell me something that hasn't been reported on the news every night. What about the bell? And the clippings? What does Jenkins have to say about them being in his possession?"

"Says he has no knowledge of how they got there. He's been pretty closed mouth, considering the seriousness of the charges. The guy's been depressed, either sleeping or mooning about in his cell. We've put him on suicide watch."

I hadn't even considered that the man might kill himself, taking all his secrets to the grave. This was the worst possible scenario I could have imagined. "What else? Has he mentioned my mother?"

"No." Nathan scanned the area around us, checking to make sure the coast was clear. "Why don't we talk in my car? It's warmer and more private."

Maybe Nathan was going to throw me a few crumbs after all. I followed him to one of the many police cars parked in the rear of the station, and we climbed inside. Nathan positioned an arm across the back of his seat and faced me.

"What I'm about to tell you is in confidence. You can't repeat it," he warned.

"You can trust me. It's not like I'm a reporter."

He nodded and resumed talking. "When asked about the names of particular victims, Jenkins claims to be innocent."

"Hardly surprising. I could have guessed that."

"Here's where it gets interesting. He's been secretly camping out at the hospital for almost two years."

"Two years?" I sputtered. "How could he have gotten away with it for so long?"

"That's something Nelson's going to have to account for. I have a feeling heads are going to roll at the hospital."

"As they should."

"In all fairness, providing security there must be a nightmare. All those unoccupied buildings and a sprawling campus out in the middle of nowhere."

"The whole place is archaic," I agreed. "A relic from the seventies. Still seems incredible, though, that he escaped notice for so long." I pondered what Nathan told me. "But what about the time line? There are victims that date back a lot further than two years."

"Jenkins is originally from Beauregard, so he's always been in close proximity to our town, with the exception of time spent in the military. After a dishonorable discharge from the army, he had a run of bad luck—lost his job at a chicken plant, lost his wife, lost his home. And he's had a string of arrests."

"His arrest record was aired on the news. Tell me something new."

"I can tell you we've collected DNA samples from him and are thoroughly investigating the matter. You understand I can't give you any more details. I won't be responsible for jeopardizing this case."

My hands clenched into fists, but I couldn't argue against his reason. "Just tell me this. Do *you* think Jenkins killed those women?" I swallowed hard. "Do you think he killed my mom and brother?"

He laid his hands on top of mine and gently pried my fingers loose. I stared down at his hands, the rough palms and long fingers as they stroked my exposed wrists and palms. "It's possible. We don't know for sure. It'll take time to uncover the truth. Sorry I haven't talked to you sooner," he said gruffly. "I really have been busy. I promise I'm doing all I can to get the answers you need."

Sucking in my breath, I gave him a nod. "Okay, thanks." I opened the car door, and Nathan called after me.

"Be safe, Della."

I gave him a rueful smile. "You always say that."

"I do?"

"You do. It's not like I want trouble, you know. It just always seems to find me."

~

Nathan's words stayed with me as I drove to the coffee shop where I'd promised to meet Dad before work. Why the warning again to stay safe? Did he have doubts about Jenkins's guilt? The tiny seeds of doubt I harbored niggled away at me, but I deliberately tamped them down. Even if what I was experiencing was a false sense of safety, what good would worrying do me?

I parked by Uncle Vic's truck. Dad had beat me here. I entered the coffee shop, where a crowd was gathered around my father. He rocked back on his chair's legs, a wide grin pasted on his handsome face. People were falling all over themselves to speak with him now that it appeared Jenkins was responsible for the latest victims.

I approached the convivial group, who were joking and laughing. Dad jumped to his feet and threw an arm over my shoulder. I did my best not to cringe at his outward act of solidarity between us.

"Excuse us, folks," he said. "I want to enjoy a little private time with my favorite girl."

I offered everyone a half-hearted smile as he guided me to a booth in the back. I'd been avoiding him, unsure what to say regarding recent events. Since we'd last talked, I'd only called him once, letting him know that I'd changed my mind and he was welcome to set up his trailer on my property. Emphasis on *my*.

Dad left to go place our orders and returned shortly afterward, placing a steaming cup of cocoa before me on the table. "See? I remember what my girl likes."

Again, I fought to hide my annoyance with his exuberant endearments. Was there something deep down wrong with me? I couldn't connect with him, my own father, who'd served almost two decades on death row for a crime that he most likely hadn't committed. People in town appeared willing to give him the benefit of the doubt. Shouldn't I be able to do the same?

"Told you it wasn't me that did those killings," Dad said without preamble. "And as far as that Jack Jenkins dude goes, I've never seen him, never heard of him. Guess everyone owes me an apology."

I stiffened in my chair. This conversation was going to be as awkward as I feared. "Sorry," I said tightly. "Looks like you're back in the good graces of the townsfolk."

"People are quick to judge on circumstantial evidence, even though the guy might be as innocent as me. At least I'm in the clear for now."

I silently sipped my cocoa, and he quirked a brow at me. "Don't you have anything else to say to your old dad?"

"I said I was sorry. It wasn't like I wanted you to be guilty."

Dad grinned, the old salesman persona never far below the surface. "Actions speak louder than words."

And here it comes. The inevitable request for a favor. I set down my drink. "What do you want?" I asked flatly.

"My lawyer says it's going to be a few more weeks before a judge hears my civil suit. Can you loan me some money? Just a little to tide me over. My double-wide is bought and paid for, but I need money for groceries and utilities."

"How much?"

"About three thousand?" he asked hopefully.

"That's a lot of groceries."

"Come on, now. I got lots of expenses getting settled. I'll never ask you for another dime. I promise."

Bullshit. I closed my eyes, picturing my savings account drying up to a near-zero balance. At least my apartment deposit and first

217

three months of rent were already paid for in advance. But maybe, just maybe this time he was ready to settle down and do right. If almost two decades on death row hadn't instilled a lesson in him, nothing would. I'd give him this last chance.

"I can swing it, but after that, you're on your own. Maybe it's time you got a j-o-b. You know, a regular nine-to-five that provides a steady paycheck."

"I'm familiar with the concept." His tone turned to one of injured self-pity. "You don't realize how hard it is to find a decent job with a prison history."

"Can't your arrest record be expunged?"

"Still leaves me with an almost twenty-year employment gap that can't be explained." He shook his head. "Sure was hoping Linda Bowen would offer me a decent job."

Guilt twisted my gut as I recalled telling Linda that I'd rather not have Dad working in the same building as me.

"I figured she'd help me out since she and Mary were old friends, but she wouldn't budge from her position that there were no openings."

I'd have to rectify the situation, explain to Mrs. Bowen that I'd changed my mind. "Try again," I urged Dad. "I'll talk to her for you."

Dad snorted. "Well, that would be a neat trick."

I cocked my head to the side at the unexpected response. "What do you mean?"

"Guess you haven't heard the latest today. Linda Bowen died late last night. When she didn't show up for work this morning, or answer phone calls and texts, one of her employees went to her home. After getting no response from her knocks, she called the police. The cops broke in her house and found her body at the bottom of the stairs. Apparently, she'd taken a tumble sometime last evening and suffered a fatal brain hemorrhage."

I sucked in a breath, stunned at the news. "That's terrible! Do they think it was an accident?"

"Yeah. There were a couple toys on the stairs that'd been left behind when her grandchildren visited last weekend. Cops think she stumbled on one of them and lost her footing."

Her death shocked and saddened me. We hadn't been close, but she was a nice lady. An old friend of my mother who I could count on at work if needed. A connection to my past. "I hate this," I said, turning my gaze to the window.

"These things happen," Dad said with a shrug. "Maybe the new HR director who takes her place will offer me a job."

I faced him, dumbfounded by his callousness.

At my expression, he held up a hand as though to ward off my disgust. "I know, I know. That sounded harsh. But that's life. You gotta keep moving on and surviving as best you can. Speaking of which, I better run and attend to business. Harley and Steve are going to help me work on clearing my property this afternoon."

"*My* property," I corrected.

"Right, well . . ." He stood and hovered above me. "About that money . . ."

With a sigh, I collected my purse and yanked out the checkbook. "Don't cash this until tomorrow," I said, writing the check. "I've got to transfer money from savings to checking."

"You got it," he said, beaming. "See you soon."

I watched as he stopped by several tables on his way out, speaking to everyone, lighthearted as a child let out of school early. He was whistling as he walked out the door. I finished my drink and headed to the door myself.

"Oh, miss!"

I turned to find a teenage girl waving her arms at me. She hurried over and handed me a slip of paper.

"What's this?"

"The bill. Your dad said he forgot his wallet, and you'd pay for the drinks on your way out."

Son of a bitch. I withdrew my wallet and handed over the cash. Once outside I shook my head and mumbled to myself. "Unbelievable. Thanks a lot, Dad."

Some father-daughter reconciliation this had been. But what had I expected? It was too late for us.

At least he probably wasn't a murderer after all, I consoled myself.

Chapter 25

DR. PENNINGTON

Wasn't it wonderful when everything miraculously fell into place?

Just when you thought your world was about to implode and all was bleak despair, the tide turned. At the exact moment when a tsunami wave crested above your trembling body, blocking out the sun's light, and when the roar of its rising power was crushing your ears, crushing your soul—it inexplicably receded and left you afloat in calm waters.

I studied my computer monitor, pleased to note that hospital admissions had risen considerably since the arrest of Jack Jenkins. And I no longer had to worry about Linda Bowen hounding me with questions. Could this day get any better?

Gayla knocked, then entered my office carrying two cups of coffee and a stack of paper tucked under her right elbow.

"How did you know that's exactly what I needed?" I said by way of greeting, smiling broadly at my plain, elderly secretary. "What would I do without you, Gayla?"

She returned my smile with her customary reserved self-assurance and took a seat across my desk. "Why, I suspect you'd be up the creek without a paddle."

Debbie Herbert

"Indeed," I replied, my smile dialing down a notch. Her homespun homilies irked me.

Gayla handed me my coffee cup, untucked the papers under her arm, and then laid them on the table, dividing them into two separate stacks. "Take this, for example," she said, sliding the stacks toward me.

"You're certainly chipper and on the ball this morning." Inwardly I sighed, not in the mood to read one of her tedious, painstaking reports on trivial matters such as my itemized travel expenses or a quarterly analysis of some miscellaneous office activity. But I often humored Gayla. She was my most loyal and staunchest advocate here at the hospital. So I donned my glasses and glanced down.

At first, I was confused. Why had she printed out hard copies of Penelope Thorpe's intake diagnosis records? And why two copies, as they were exactly alike? I looked up, quirking an eyebrow.

Gayla sipped her coffee. "Go to page three on both reports and view the highlighted text on the second printout. Everything should be crystal clear to you then."

I flipped through the pages and read several paragraphs highlighted in yellow. My heart jackhammered in my chest, and my hands began to tremble. I dared not look back up at Gayla until I had my panic under control. *Don't show fear—it's a sign of weakness.* That had been drilled into me from an early age. Carefully, I laid my hands flat on my desk and drew several deep breaths.

"Well, Doctor?" she asked at last.

I feigned ignorance as I faced her. "Well, what?"

Annoyance momentarily blazed through her normal exterior calm. Gayla jabbed a wrinkled finger at the incriminating report. She had old-lady hands, wrinkled and shot through with blue veins that bulged against crepe-thin skin. But she kept her nails short and manicured with an appropriate coat of light pink polish. Always one who took care of the smallest details, that woman.

Obviously, I hadn't credited her intelligence enough.

"The discrepancy is obvious," Gayla began, speaking in her meticulous, detached manner. I'd always mistaken that tone for a certain arrogance and cool professionalism. But Gayla had unplumbed depths, a layer of deceit that ran deep to the bone. Too late, I saw that now.

"The report on your left makes no mention of Ms. Thorpe's phobias. That's the version currently on file in your computer and that matches the paper copy in Ms. Thorpe's official medical chart."

"Correct." I kept my expression neutral, my mind racing. I'd destroyed the original paper version. I was sure of it.

Gayla offered a tight, triumphant smile. "But I'm extremely thorough, Dr. Pennington. And not one prone to rely on hard copies forwarded outside of my office and stored elsewhere. I always, *always* make extra copies of your reports and store them in my office. In case there's ever an emergency or glitch in the system."

"You're a clever woman."

"Indeed," she said, mimicking my earlier reply to her quip.

I waved a hand over the incriminating papers. It was worth an effort to pretend ignorance and brazen it out. "I have no explanation, of course. Although, in the end, I don't see that it matters."

Gayla snorted. "Bet it matters to the police. How interesting that this patient's death involved both of her phobias—snakes and a fear of heights."

"Coincidence," I said, all the while realizing that Detective Adams would pounce on this tidbit.

"A mighty big one. And then there's the evidence that you've tampered with the report. I'm sure a computer forensics expert could verify that fact."

"Obviously, someone else has been meddling with my computer if that's true. I can only think of one person, besides myself, who knows the password. Except, my dear Gayla, *you*."

"Nice try. But no one's going to buy that, and you know it. Questions will be raised. Do you really want an investigation into your background, Ira?"

I felt like someone had slid a bag of ice down my spine. My mouth worked, but no sound emerged from the tight knot in my chest that was a vise on my lungs and throat.

"If you continue scanning those papers, you'll find another patient report that's been similarly altered. Melanie Mickelson, as you know, had a fear of large bodies of water. And again, the information on your computer and the hard copies sent to microfilm don't relay that fact. Only my copy reflects the patient's particular phobia. Yet another woman whose death resulted from her greatest fear."

A potent miasma hung in the charged space between us. My ears tingled and pulsed with its toxic weight. My head swam at the surreal nature of her words. This had to be a dream. Loyal, deferential Ms. Pouncey surely was not implying I was guilty of these heinous murders, was she?

"What exactly are you accusing me of doing?"

"I'm not accusing you of anything. It's up to the police to investigate the evidence and draw their own conclusions."

I pictured Detective Adams's glee at Gayla's providing him this information. Young and ambitious, he'd be eager to arrest me and make a name for himself in the process. Whether or not I was innocent of murder might be immaterial to him.

"I'd like to retire," Gayla continued, flipping back into a conversational, genial tone. "Comfortably. I've worked at this hospital for over forty years, serving both you and the mental health director prior to you. I'm smarter than either of you ever have credited me for, and I'm ready to at last reap a little financial compensation of my own. You understand what I'm saying?"

I managed a glum nod. "How much?"

"One hundred thousand dollars," she answered crisply. "For starters."

Starters? She intended to bleed me dry. I'd never be free of Gayla as long as she lived. "You've grossly overestimated my financial worth. I don't have that kind of money."

"Nonsense. After all the years you've drawn a huge salary at this hospital, I'm confident you have this amount available. But if not, then you better find a means of obtaining it. I expect my money by the end of the business day tomorrow."

"I need more time. I don't have it readily available."

"Not my problem."

"Be reasonable. Give me at least a week or two. I'll need to sell off some stocks and other assets."

Her eyes crackled with annoyance, and I rushed to convince her to wait. "I'll write you a check immediately for twenty-five thousand," I said. "A show of good faith."

"Cash only. And the rest is due in one week. Again, I'll only accept cash." Gayla glanced at her watch as she rose to her feet. "If you leave now, you can withdraw the twenty-five thousand dollars before the bank closes. I'll be in my office waiting."

The woman had me—at least for now.

Chapter 26

DELLA

Four thirty, and darkness was falling rapidly, obscuring the gray clouds of a chilly day. I pulled into the hospital lot and parked, idly drumming my fingers on the steering wheel as I listened to the radio. My appointment with Dr. Pennington wasn't until five o'clock, so I had a few minutes to relax before heading inside. It was nice of him to accommodate my schedule with these late appointments. Once our hour-long sessions ended, I had plenty of time to grab dinner in the hospital cafeteria or make a run to a fast-food place before my shift started at seven o'clock.

A few staff members were already leaving work for the day. An elderly lady emerged from the main entrance, carrying a large cardboard container. I recognized that face, so I collected my purse and got out of the car. I hurried to her even though I wondered whether she'd be offended and brush off my offer to help.

"Let me help you with that, Ms. Pouncey."

I held out my arms, and to my surprise, she deposited the box without protest. I'd always found Gayla Pouncey a bit intimidating with her stern business suits, overly formal manners, and perfectly coiffed hair.

"I was hoping you'd offer. Thank you, Della. You must be on your way for your appointment with Dr. Pennington."

Irritated at her lack of discretion, I cast a quick glance around us. Thankfully, no other employees were within earshot.

"Don't worry. I made sure we wouldn't be overheard. I can be very discreet." She gave a secretive smile, as though she'd vocalized some private joke that I wasn't privy to understanding.

Inside the open box were a number of framed photos, a few books, and a stack of greeting cards. "You doing a spring cleaning of your office?" I asked.

"A permanent cleaning. Today's my last day. As of this moment, I am officially retired."

My brows rose at her pronouncement. Gayla had been a fixture at the hospital, one that had been there forever and that would remain until her dying day. "That's wonderful. Congratulations, Ms. Pouncey. I'm sure you'll be missed."

She frowned but said nothing. Again, I tried to make conversation. "So what do you have planned for retirement? Spending time with grandchildren? Traveling?"

"I plan on getting as far from Normal as possible. All I want is to live my life in comparative ease and on my own terms."

"Like . . . no more waking up to an alarm clock, getting dressed in suits, and attending boring meetings?" I guessed.

"And pandering to men who think they are so much smarter than me."

I regarded her set, scowling face and wondered whether she and Dr. Pennington had had a falling-out of some sort. But it was none of my business, so I didn't ask. We reached the end of the sidewalk, and she pointed at a nearby gray sedan. "There's my car."

I followed her and placed the box in the back seat. Gayla looked back over her shoulder at the hospital.

"Everything okay?" I asked. "Miss the hospital already?"

She shuddered beneath her heavy woolen coat. "Not on your life."

I shifted on the balls of my feet and cleared my throat. "Well, then. I wish you well, Ms. Pouncey. Happy retirement."

Instead of climbing inside, Gayla leaned against the car door. "I knew your mother. Did I ever mention that? Nice lady. Mary hired me back in the day and always expedited my promotions. Odd how both HR directors met such unlikely, violent deaths."

Her observation startled me. "You think there's a connection?"

Gayla affixed me with a cool stare. "And because I respected Mary, I'm going to give you fair warning. You need to be very, very careful. Jack Jenkins's arrest changes nothing."

It was my turn to shudder. For the second time today, I'd been issued a warning that I might be in danger.

"There are strange goings-on here at the hospital," she continued in her detached, crisp voice. "It's not safe here. Especially at night. Especially for you."

"But why—"

Gayla got in her car and turned the keys in the ignition. "And as far as Ira Pennington goes? I'd suggest you find a new doctor. Immediately."

"Ms. Pouncey, stop. Please tell me why—"

She slammed the door shut and, with a squeal of tires, backed out of the parking space so fast I had to jump out of the way to prevent my toes being run over.

Talk about a dramatic retirement exit.

I watched as she hightailed it out of the parking lot and took the turn onto the county road so fast that her car momentarily jackknifed and then straightened as she sped away into the darkness.

What the hell had all that been about?

I walked into the hospital and took a seat in the lobby, trying to absorb the dire words Gayla had unexpectedly sprung on me. Although I normally wasn't one to enjoy being among a crowd, I found comfort in the number of people coming and going in the lobby, attending to business as usual. Since Jenkins's arrest, the presence of cops milling about was gone. Hospital employees, patients, and even the community had appeared to settle down to normalcy, secure in the knowledge they were again safe.

Bits of red floated by—a jacket, a cup, a book—random odds and ends sporting the chaos of color. They speared my consciousness like jagged spikes of aggression, but I didn't close my eyes, and I didn't run away.

This was progress. No matter Gayla Pouncey's beef with her former boss, Dr. Pennington was doing me good. Either that, or I was finally willing to deal with my phobia and move forward with my life.

Despite my pat on the back over the state of my mental health, Gayla's words still ate away inside, confirming my intuition that things were still not quite right. Something unseen in the shadows had shifted. My world had altered, and there was no going back to the way things used to be.

I no longer enjoyed working here, and every time I left my office, I expected to run into another Jack Jenkins. Maybe that feeling would pass in time, maybe not. But I no longer felt safe working the night shift, even though Knox checked in on me periodically as he made his rounds. Too bad the hospital was the best-paying employer in town. Until, or if, I was ready to relocate to a larger town, I was stuck in this job.

Yet it was within my power to change a few things in my environment. I pulled out my phone and opened the email app. Buddy Harris, Linda Bowen's longtime assistant, would more than likely be promoted to HR director, so I addressed my email to him, requesting that I'd like a transfer to first shift as soon as possible. Did he know why I had such odd hours for data entry? Harris, or whoever replaced Linda, probably would want to end the arrangement we'd had anyway. I couldn't imagine my request being denied.

At 4:45 p.m., I hit send, hoping that Harris would read my email before he left work today, or would at least get to it first thing in the morning. With any luck, tonight would be my last night shift. I returned my phone to my purse and crossed the lobby to the back stairwell. Would people on day shift wonder why I never took elevators? I'd claim it was for the exercise. That should work.

I ascended the stairs, remembering my encounter with Melanie Mickelson, remembering Gayla's words of warning. With each step, my heart felt heavier, and dread fatigued my muscles. By the time I reached the fifth floor and pushed open the doorway, I felt like I'd run a marathon.

Why had Gayla tried to warn me off seeing Dr. Pennington? Perhaps it was sour grapes, some bad blood between the two of them. Maybe she'd been forced to retire and was bitter. I couldn't deny I'd never really warmed up to the man. There was a certain coldness in his dark eyes that only warmed when I described how it felt to experience the color red. Then the coldness was replaced by an unnerving interest. The wall of reserve he maintained between us made it difficult to confide. I'd never been to another psychiatrist, though. That reserve might have been standard practice to avoid igniting inappropriate emotions between doctor and patient.

But did my distaste for Dr. Pennington matter as long as I continued to improve in my coping mechanisms? Maybe my progress would be faster, less stressful, with someone else. There was no law that said I had to stay with this doctor. There were plenty of clinics nearby in Huntsville, and I was now able and willing to make the trip.

Dr. Pennington's office suite was as gloomy as the cold, gray day had been. All of Gayla's personal effects had been removed, and the lights above her desk turned off, leaving the reception area dark and empty. It contained an aura of austere coldness that matched the personality of Dr. Pennington. He came to the door and beckoned me inside, only a sliver of a clinical smile crossing his implacable face. It was hardly welcoming.

You don't have to go in for this session. You don't have to submit to his scrutiny. You don't have to squirm under the hawkish gleam of his eyes as you describe your misery.

I stood at the threshold, hesitating.

Chapter 27

DR. PENNINGTON

The moment Della stepped foot in my office, I knew Gayla had warned her off me. I'd seen them speaking in the parking lot and the way Gayla had kept glancing back at my office window as she'd spoken to Della. But how much had she said?

Della spoke at last. "I came by to tell you that I won't be needing your counseling any longer."

"I see. That's certainly your prerogative. May I ask whether you feel that you're no longer in need of any counseling at all?"

She hesitated, and I knew the answer before she spoke. Della wasn't giving up on counseling—she just didn't want *me* as her doctor anymore.

"Come into my office, and let's discuss it," I said, providing what I hoped was a warm, encouraging smile. "Consider it an exit interview. I require a twenty-four-hour cancellation notice for nonresidential patients, which means your insurance company will be billed for the hour regardless whether or not you attend. And since you're here—"

"If you could just provide me the names of a few doctors in Huntsville you recommend, given my history."

I did not let my smile slip one iota. "Of course. I'll be happy to do so. Might as well come inside my office and have a seat while I gather the information."

"I'm in no hurry."

"There's no need to allow a gap in your treatment, Della. The sooner you have those names and numbers, the sooner you can transition to a new doctor. You've made such good progress. We don't want you to regress now, do we?"

I turned my back on her and entered my office, giving her no choice but to follow me inside. Della was much too polite to walk away from my entirely reasonable request. I settled behind my desk, which was strewn with a pile of medical journals.

I needed to find out what Gayla Pouncey had said to her.

"Let me pull up a list of my colleagues in Huntsville." I pretended to be absorbed in the task. "Saw you ran into my former secretary as she was leaving."

"Yeah, she surprised me. I didn't think Ms. Pouncey would ever retire."

"It was rather sudden. Did she mention that?"

"No."

"Frankly, I'm a bit concerned. Her decision seemed rushed and out of character." I scribbled down a couple of names and numbers. "Did she appear agitated to you?"

Della chewed at her lower lip. "You could say that. I don't think she feels safe here anymore, not after everything that's happened."

"Even though Jenkins is in custody?"

"She warned me to be careful, that this place is still dangerous."

I scrunched my brows together, as though confused by Pouncey's logic. "But the ordeal is over. Did she give a particular reason why?"

"No. She just said to beware of . . ." A guilty flush stained Della's cheeks.

"Beware of whom?" I asked softly. "Me?"

Della mutely held my gaze, clearly unwilling to divulge more.

"I have to admit there was a great deal of tension in the office the past couple of weeks." I shook my head and gave a heavy sigh. "Something—I'm not sure what—rattled Ms. Pouncey, caused her to be edgy and mistrustful with everyone on staff. Such an abrupt personality change makes me wonder about the state of her mental health."

"I had the impression that the two of you might have had a falling-out of some sort," Della admitted. She tapped an index finger against her lips, as though considering their conversation in a new light. A light that I hoped would offset Gayla's poisoned words and ease Della's misgivings about me.

"Perhaps I, or one of Ms. Pouncey's coworkers, can check on her in a couple of weeks. Make sure that she's doing fine."

"That's nice of you."

I laid down my pen and shoved the paper across the desk. "Here are a couple of doctors I recommend. They have experience working with patients suffering from phobias. Unless you'd like to continue working with me? I do know your history, after all. But, of course, it's entirely your choice."

Della folded the paper and tucked it into her purse. "My mind's already made up, Dr. Pennington. I'm making several changes in my life, and I believe that a new doctor in a new environment is what I need." She rose to her feet and extended a hand. "Thank you for all your counsel over the years."

I also stood and accepted her offered hand. It was small and warm against my own.

"Very well then," I said graciously. "I wish you all the best. Good luck."

She left, and I watched the delicate curve of her hips as she walked away, seemingly eager to make her escape.

Better keep running, little girl. Della Stallings would need all the luck she could get.

Chapter 28

DELLA

I still couldn't shake the sense of impending doom Gayla had imparted. Was the woman crazy as Dr. Pennington had implied? Was I crazy?

We're all mad here.

The *Alice's Adventures in Wonderland* quote seemed apt for Normal Hospital. I couldn't help smiling at that as I fired up my computer, briefly glanced at Anastasia Romanov on my screen saver, and then set to work. Staying busy was the best medicine. My fingers danced on the keyboard, brain focused on hard data—objective bits of letters and numbers that held no mysterious, hidden meaning. It was numbing. It was freeing. Only the tightening in my shoulders and the ache in my right wrist clued me in that the hours were rushing by.

"Aren't you a busy bee?"

I gasped at the unexpected interruption and tore my eyes from the screen. Knox stood in the doorway, smiling down at me.

"You scared me," I admitted.

"Sorry. Didn't realize you were so wrapped up in what you were doing. It's forty-five minutes past your usual break time, so I thought I'd do a check-in."

I frowned, irritated at the intrusion and his protective manner. But that was unfair; Knox's presence had been a comfort to me these past few weeks until Jenkins was caught. "I'm perfectly fine," I answered crisply. I laid my fingers back on the keyboard, a subtle hint that I wanted to be left alone and continue working. I liked the guy, but I had work to finish right now.

He either didn't notice or didn't care that I preferred not to talk tonight. Knox sat on the small metal stool beside me and stretched out his legs. "Us night workers have to stick together, right?"

"Right." I slid my gaze to the computer. Knox ignored my not-so-subtle sign.

"You know, I'd miss you if you ever left."

My head snapped up. "What makes you say that?"

"Just stating a fact."

No way Knox could possibly know I'd put in a transfer request mere hours ago. Or could he? The hospital could be a *Peyton Place* full of gossip, but this was ridiculous. I searched his eyes for a clue, but they were a blank canvas.

"I'd miss you, too," I said breezily, suddenly uncomfortable. Knox's stretched-out legs blocked my path to the door. The air felt thick and suffocating. Too intimate. Surely he wasn't going to embarrass us both by wanting more than—

Knox drew a deep breath and stuck his hands in his pockets. "Uh, I was wondering if you'd like to go out to dinner sometime?"

"Not like a . . . you aren't suggesting a date, are you?" Knox was almost twice my age, and there was zero chemistry between us. Not on my end anyway.

A flush darkened his cheeks. "Guess you're interested in that cop you been talking to lately. Nathan Whitt."

Again, an odd stirring prickled down my spine. "I've mentioned him to you?"

"Several times."

I couldn't recall a single occasion when I'd done so. Knox apparently paid close attention to my every comment. I didn't answer his original question. Let him think Nathan and I were a thing. That way I'd avoid an awkward conversation. "How's your back tonight?" I asked, changing the topic.

"'Bout the usual. Can't complain."

"Good."

An awkward silence fell. I cleared my throat. "If you don't mind . . ." I waved a hand over my keyboard.

"I'll get out of your way then." Knox pushed to his feet, and a stab of guilt sliced through my gut. The man had been nothing but kind to me, and I'd hurt his feelings.

"See you later," I said cheerily, trying to make up for my lack of interest in a date. "Thanks for stopping by."

He didn't even look at me as he left. Moments later, the forlorn squeak of his mop bucket sounded as it rolled down the hall. I'd pop in on Knox on my way out this morning and speak a minute, let him see we were still friends, even if I wasn't interested in dating him. Guilt assuaged, I returned to work but found I had a hard time concentrating. Not an hour later, I temporarily called it quits and dug out change from my purse. A stroll to the vending machines and a hot cup of cocoa might do the trick in regaining focus.

Knox was in the vending room, and I started to back away, hoping he hadn't seen me. But he caught my reflection in the glass and waved.

"Looks like we both needed a break at the same time."

"A short break for me." I stepped into the room and shoved quarters down the drink machine slot. "Got to get back to it. Busy night."

As I stood watching a cup fill with mocha-colored liquid, Knox sidled close beside me, close enough I could smell sweat mingled with a pine industrial cleaner.

"Sure you don't want to give me a chance, Della?" he asked huskily, his breath fanning my hair. "I know you so well. More than you realize."

What the hell was that supposed to mean? I couldn't look at him. If I turned toward Knox, my mouth would be within inches of his. I retrieved my drink and stepped to the side. He knew too much, presumed too much. Tomorrow morning I'd beg Buddy Harris in person for that immediate transfer.

"I'm only interested in you as a friend. Sorry."

He ran a hand through his hair and sighed. "That's okay. You've made your decision."

We both exited the vending room and silently headed down the hallway, a new awkwardness between us. As I turned near my office, Knox cleared his throat.

"Can you stop by my office? Just for a minute? You've always been so kind to me, bringing me gifts and all. So I made a little something for you with my own hands." He spoke and smiled in the easy way he'd sported before he'd asked me out. "Hope you like it."

How could I refuse?

"Just for a minute. Then I really do have to get back to work."

Reluctantly, I continued walking beside him. His pace grew slower, and he rubbed his lower back with one hand.

"Tough night, huh?"

"Yeah. Think I'll clock out early." He glanced down the west-wing tunnel. "You mind if we swing over to a room down this way? I left my cart there and don't feel like returning to get it before I leave."

"Of course. Or if you want, I can get it for you and bring it to your office."

"No sense in you losing any more time."

Our footsteps echoed eerily in the tomb-like acoustics. Knox grabbed his key ring and unlocked a door set off in a small alcove to one side of the tunnel. "It's in here," he said, unlocking the door. He winced and rubbed his lower back again. "Spasms are getting worse."

"Let me get the cart for you." I pushed past him and entered the room.

Crimson painted the walls and floors with an aggressive saturation of its pulsing hue. The wash of red walloped the back of my retinas, blinding my eyes and choking the breath from my lungs. An overpowering odor of bleach burned my nose, and I also detected the stench of something metallic and earthy.

What kind of hell was this? I swayed, suddenly dizzy and weak kneed. Darkness formed around the edge of my vision, a black veil that snuffed the swarming red. My limbs grew weaker, and my body threatened to collapse. I closed my hands into fists and fought against the light-headed sensation but was powerless to stop the onslaught. Black coated my entire vision. I was falling into a dark abyss.

And at that moment, when I believed I'd freefall forever into inky oblivion, a painful tug on my arms pulled me from it.

I tried to escape the painful grip on my arms, but it was useless. The ebony void in my mind lightened to ash, to pewter, then to light oyster pearl. I was floating into the fluorescent light overhead in an out-of-body fugue state.

I didn't know who I was or where I was or why I was there. I only knew that everything happening was very, very wrong, and I was in imminent danger.

The dizziness began to fade, and pressure pinched at the delicate flesh encircling my wrists. I became one with my body again, staring down at large hands binding my own smaller ones with zip ties.

I should run. I should scream. I should stop this. My brain scrambled to swim out of its fog, screaming messages that my body was incapable of obeying.

A familiar face stared at me. Familiar and yet terrifyingly altered with malevolence. There was the same arrangement of physical features—long face, dark eyes, full lips. Yet now they appeared exaggerated and sinister.

The long horsey face was of a deforming length, the full lips redolent with perverted sensuality, the dark eyes aglow with macabre promise.

I licked my dry lips. "Wh—what are you doing?"

"Della, Della, my sweet Della," Knox purred, caressing each syllable with deliberate care. He swept a hand over the room. "If only you cared about me as I did for you, this would not have been necessary."

He paused, bending his knees to the floor and zip-tying my ankles to the leg of something I sat upon, although I had no clear recollection of how I'd gone from standing to sitting.

"When you made it clear that you didn't want me," he continued, "I realized, with a sad heart, that it was at last time to prepare this room for you. For your correction."

Correction? What the hell was he babbling about? Terror completely cleared what was left of my mental fog, lasering through the haze of confusion. Something was terribly wrong with Knox, an insanity he'd hidden behind a veneer of normalcy. A damaged, demented man hidden behind a cloak of friendship.

He meant me harm.

I strained my arms and legs against their bindings, but I was too late to save myself. All the martial arts training in the world was useless to me now that I was restrained. I pictured my teacher, towering above me after he'd flattened me on my back with a surprise attack. I'd held up my hands in surrender. *You got me,* I'd said. He'd shaken his head. *Stay calm. Think. You always have options.*

Options.

Knox grunted in satisfaction as he tested the tightness of the last ankle restraint and began to raise his head. The moment his face was level with mine, I threw all my weight forward, headbutting his nose with brute force.

Bone and cartilage cracked, and blood gushed from his nostrils, a cherry-red stream set against the pale flesh of his face. Bile rose in my throat at the onslaught of fresh blood. Knox screamed and scrambled backward, crab-like on the slick floor. How had a mere nosebleed coated the ground so quickly? I stared at the concrete floor completely striated with strands of red from wall to wall. It had been freshly mopped with blood.

"You hurt me," Knox accused with astonished pique. Clearly, he'd not been expecting a fight.

"Let me go," I demanded, infusing my voice with a confidence I was far from feeling. "This is crazy. You're going to get in trouble."

"Only if I get caught. Which I won't." He dug a handkerchief from his pocket and pressed it against his nose. Blood blossomed on the white cotton fabric.

"Why are you doing this? What do you want?" If I had these answers, perhaps I could reason with Knox, appeal to whatever part of him had once liked me and been my friend.

"I'm correcting your weakness. I'd been willing to overlook your phobia at first. You noticed me. You were nice to me. We were friends. I wanted more, and I thought you did too."

"We're still friends," I hastened to reassure him. "It's not too late. Release me, and everything will be okay. You can get help."

"Help?" He cocked his head to one side, brows furrowed.

"Counseling. It's helped me. Dr. Pennington's been—"

Knox threw back his head and laughed. "Ira's helped you? *Ira!*"

"I take it you aren't a fan?"

He waggled a finger at me, face lit with a secret amusement. "He has his methods, and I have mine. You'll find mine are more drastic."

What drastic measures did Knox have planned for this so-called correction? My eyes grew unfocused, and his face blurred as a wave of dizziness threatened to overtake me. There was no reasoning with a madman.

Knox stuffed the blood-soaked handkerchief in his pocket. "Look what you've done. I'm going to have to wash my face and get a clean towel. Maybe I'll pop a couple of aspirin too. While I'm gone, I want you to have a good look around, Della. I've gone to quite a bit of trouble for you. Over the last few weeks, I've slowly gathered pints of blood. A little here and there, so no one noticed anything missing."

He knelt before me, careful to stay out of striking range, and spoke in a deep, taunting tone. "What does this room remind you of, Della? Do you think Anastasia Romanov was in a similar dungeon when she faced execution? Did she see the blood of her family splattered all over the four walls and floor—just like you did the night your mom and brother were stabbed to death?"

Horror strangled my heart like a vise and tightened my chest.

Stop.

I must have said it aloud. Knox chuckled and rose to his feet. "Stop? We've only just begun."

I gulped in air and screamed. Over and over.

Knox paused at the door, his face twisted in anger, an expression I'd never seen on him before. He raised a fist at me. "Stop it."

I was startled into submission, the sound of my screams still echoing and bouncing around in my head.

"Nobody's going to hear you way down in the bowels of this place. But you're annoying the fuck out of me." He plucked the stained handkerchief from his pocket. "Want me to gag you with this?"

I shook my head, nausea roiling inside.

"Then shut up."

Abruptly, he left. The door slammed shut, followed by the click of a key engaging a lock mechanism.

This couldn't be happening. My gaze swept the windowless room, trying to purge my mind of the angry red opaqueness staining the stark white walls. If I wanted to escape, I'd have to keep my shit together. I needed to find a weapon and search for a possible means of escape. But there was only one way in and out—and Knox held the key.

I guessed that I was trapped in an old surgical room. Against one wall was a tall wooden cabinet encased in thick glass. Silver instruments lined its shelves—scalpels, clamps, and other menacing equipment. Sharp, pointy things designed to cut through flesh and tendons and nerves. I tugged harder at the zip ties but only succeeded in cutting my skin, the plastic digging into the flesh of my ankles and hands. Glancing down, I saw that I wasn't in a chair. Knox had strapped me into what appeared to be a rusted gurney. My scalp prickled with dread. Did he plan to lay me flat on the gurney and torture me with those archaic surgical devices?

It seemed Knox had only been gone seconds when the rattle of keys sounded outside the door. He stepped back in. He'd changed into a new set of maintenance uniform shirt and pants and held a clean washcloth to his nose. A medical mask hung around his neck. His hair was damp around the temples, as though he'd splashed his face with water. In one hand he held a metal folding chair.

"I apologize for my vulgar language earlier," he said, plopping the chair down in front of me. He climbed onto it, resting his elbows against the chair's backrest. "Let me explain why you're here and what's about to go down."

Suddenly, I wasn't so sure I wanted to know his plans for me. "I hurt your feelings," I rushed in to say. "I'm—"

"My feelings don't matter anymore. The correction is all for you, to help you face and conquer your phobia, to get rid of your one weakness." He pulled something from his pocket and swiped it across his mouth. Careless swipes of dark plum slashed his lower and upper lips. Then he ran a stubby black liner around both eyes.

"Wh—what are you doing?"

He pursed his lips together and then popped them back open, a diva trying to evenly distribute newly applied lipstick. It was bizarre—clownish and terrifying. In all these years, I'd never known him. Not really. He had this secret face, this secret life I'd never suspected.

I squeezed my eyes shut and shuddered. "Please don't do this." I forced my eyes back open to face him, pleading for mercy. "I'm sorry,

Knox. Truly. I—I might not be interested in you in a romantic way"—
I figured it wouldn't be believable if I abruptly turned around and
declared myself in love with him—"but we're friends, right? And friends
don't hurt each other."

Anger again flickered in his dark eyes. I'd said the wrong thing.

Chapter 29

THE CORRECTOR

Friends?

Not hardly. At this point, she'd say anything to escape this room, to escape from me.

Della's eyes appeared desperate, unnaturally wide. More than ever, their unusual green color was striking. It was her only real beauty, but a stunner nonetheless. I'd worked around Della for years not paying her much notice. She tended to blend into her environment—average height, common hair color, and bland clothing. Plus, she mostly kept her head down and arms crossed, emitting don't-fuck-with-me vibes like a neon sign.

Everyone in this small town knew her background, of course. She was a tragic figure, the daughter of a convicted killer and, essentially, an orphan in the world. The one who everyone claimed had escaped from a murderous butcher.

She would not escape tonight. Not until she'd been thoroughly tested and the correction process complete.

"Our idea of friendship is worlds apart," I told her, hardening my heart at her obvious fear. "You keep disappointing me, Della."

"How? What have I done?"

I held out a hand and ticked off the reasons why with my fingers. "Strike one: you're leaving night shift, and I'll never get to see you much. Strike two: you're quitting your treatment with Ira Pennington." I continued past her bewildered gasp of air at that revelation. "And strike three: your obvious feelings for a cop. That's inexcusably bad taste right there."

"How do you know I quit my sessions with Dr. Pennington?" she demanded hoarsely. "That happened only hours ago. You must be stalking me, following me everywhere at the hospital."

I shrugged. "I don't have to follow you, not literally. Here, I'll demonstrate." I dug out my cell phone, selected the audio file Ira had uploaded, and pressed play.

My mind's already made up, Dr. Pennington. Her recorded voice rang out loud and tinny. *I'm making several changes in my life, and I believe that a new doctor in a new environment is what I need. Thank you for*—I tapped the icon to stop the playback.

"You get the idea," I said with a grin.

Her cheeks flushed with anger, dissolving her fear. "How dare you listen in? You have no right. Those conversations are supposed to be private."

"There should be no secrets between us. Such a shame. I so enjoyed your therapy sessions." I glanced thoughtfully at my cell phone as I started to tuck it away. "Which reminds me, I'll need your phone."

"I left it on my desk."

"Forgive me if I don't believe you." I reached toward Della to pat down her jeans pockets, and she jerked away from my touch, almost toppling over onto the bloody floor. I quickly felt the outline of her ass and slim hips as I searched. Nothing there.

Della glared at me. "Told you I didn't have it."

Could she have it tucked away in her bra? I pulled up my phone's speed dial screen. There were only two numbers listed there, and hers was the first. I tapped the icon. Seconds later, the shrill ringtone sounded. Della's face crumpled as I located the source of the noise.

"Well, isn't this clever," I said with a chuckle as I plucked her phone from her shirt. She wore one of those new fancy workout tops with a sleek hidden phone panel sewn into the sleeve. "Ah, don't look so sad, Della. The way your hands are bound, you'd have never been able to reach it anyway and call for help."

Tears ran down her cheeks, but she lifted her chin. "Bastard," she spit out.

"No need for that," I chided, although I rather enjoyed her show of spirit. It boded well if she were to have any chance of surviving the next few hours or days—however long it took to break her spirit and test her true mettle.

I held up her phone. "What's your password?" I teased. "Never mind. I remember. It's AnaR1918, the year of Anastasia's execution. Very clever. Considering your obsession with the dead duchess, I believe you'll appreciate everything I have planned this evening. Too bad it's October—there'd have been poetic justice if it was July seventeenth, the same date that she died. But, then again, nothing's perfect. Your circumstances aren't an exact mirror of her killing."

Della regarded me wordlessly, defiance still evident in the jut of her chin. I flipped through her text messages and mentally reminded myself that before her shift ended, I needed to return to her office, sign off on her computer, and confiscate her purse. "Nothing new from lover boy," I noted.

"Nathan's not my *lover boy*, you asshole."

Such hostility. "You've brought all this on yourself. I could have overlooked your weaknesses if you'd stayed with me. If you'd chosen me. Surely you see that, don't you, Della?"

She refused to answer my question, exhibiting a childish stubbornness I found oddly endearing. Maybe the real question tonight was whether I'd survive this correction without falling weak and showing mercy. If we both survived one another, I'd take her away, far from Normal. Some remote hideaway where she'd feel free to adore me and appreciate my power and all I'd done to make her strong.

I patted her thigh. "I'm going to leave you alone now in this room I've prepared for the first phase of your correction. Remember, no one can hear you through these thick walls. Nobody will be around. Not for hours. Ready? Don't worry. I'll be back for you, Della. I won't be far at all. Well, you'll see. Don't want to ruin the surprise I have in store."

I laughed at my little inside joke, then brushed her cheeks with my fingertips, marveling at their smooth softness dampened with tears.

I recalled what Nonnie used to say at times like these: *Don't worry, my precious. This will hurt me more than it hurts you, but it's for your own good. Be strong.*

Chapter 30
DELLA

My shoulders slumped with relief as Knox disappeared behind the door, tensing again as I heard the click of the key locking. I'd been granted only a momentary reprieve from whatever torture he'd devised.

Waiting was the worst. It provided time to take in every detail of Knox's macabre work, time to smell and see every nuance of the blood-drenched room and contemplate what was yet to come.

What had Dr. Pennington taught me? To counterbalance the effect of red with a new suggestion for my mind. Create new neural pathways. I closed my eyes. *Cold water. Deep, cold blue waters.* A whisper of relief cooled the red fever. I opened my eyes, determined to draw on this lifeline as I faced what I was up against.

Red pulsed and vibrated with an energy both life giving and life draining, sanguine and sinister. My temples pounded with its heavy beat, drumming against my skull in hammerblows, silent and lethal. Brain tissue absorbed the pressure wave of silence that had its own sound if you listened long enough and close enough—a thick heaviness that rumbled like thunder. My mind grew obese with terror from the weight of silence.

Cold water. Crisp, icy, and dripping wet. I imagined plunging into the deep blue waters of Hatchet Lake. I swam underwater like a mermaid, never wanting to emerge from the cold cocoon of safety. But something long and dark and lifeless drifted ever closer toward me. The black silhouette took shape—arms, legs, and long hair floating like a black cloud. A sudden undertow rippled through the water, and the body rolled closer. A pale face floated within an arm's length, facing me with empty black holes where eyes should have been. I tried to swim away, but more bodies popped up all around me, blocking my exit. I'd stumbled upon an aquatic graveyard of murder victims.

My eyes sprang open, and I was once again trapped in a burning red nightmare, surrounded above and below and on all sides by slick satin ribbons of death that gleamed as though possessed by a diabolical spirit. But better to face this known, familiar enemy than the suffocating underwater miasma of Hatchet Lake that I'd conjured.

Where had Knox gathered all this blood? Had it been collected from other victims forced to endure his corrective measures? More likely he'd filched it from the hospital's blood bank. My eyes were drawn to the wet floor, patterned by mop grooves of blood. I pictured Knox painstakingly covering every inch of ground, drawing a malignant mandala.

The floor design started at the wall with ever enclosing circles. I was situated dead center in the room. Beneath my feet was a drainage hole. I guessed that decades ago, once the day's surgeries were complete, a janitor would enter and hose down spilled blood along with any other body fluids or tissue that had carelessly ended up on the floor. Is this how Knox would cover his tracks later, leaving behind no evidence I'd ever been here? My blood would mix with bleach and water, spiraling down the drain. He'd take what remained, my bones and organs and flesh, and throw it into the hospital's fiery incinerator.

Vanished without a trace. So what if by some miracle forensic experts scoured this very room with a luminol test? This was a hospital. Traces of blood would be expected everywhere.

And as far as the incinerator—would my bones be completely transformed to ash? I had no clue. I bit the inside of my mouth hard, concentrating on the pain, on my here-and-now predicament. Grisly contemplation about the eventual disposal of my body would do no good. Somehow, I'd come up with an exit plan. I'd done so at only eight years old with a killer breathing down my neck. I was older and stronger now, so I sure as hell could manage it again.

I drew in a shaky breath and then gasped at a new smell wafting through the room. Had my thoughts about the incinerator conjured an olfactory hallucination? I inhaled deeply, testing the air. No, this was real. Acrid and instantly distinct. I searched for the source.

High on the wall to my right, wisps of smoke curled through a small vent. Was Knox responsible for this? *Don't be stupid—of course he is,* I answered myself. He'd set a fire on the other side of the wall and was deliberately fanning the smoke toward me. The real question was, Did he plan on killing me through asphyxiation?

That method didn't seem personal enough, though, not like slicing me open with a scalpel and forcing me to watch the blood burst from the cuts and then slowly seep from the flesh wounds. He'd do that over and over until the knife carved deeper and deeper, gashing muscle and organs.

No. I had to force my mind from wandering down these twisted paths. He'd said tonight was a test or a correction or some such idiocy. The smoke was a deliberate reminder of my family's home that was burned to the ground on that long-ago night.

"The fire's drawing closer, Della." Knox's singsong voice spilled through the vent. "The flames are licking at your heels. Hot and fast. You can't outrun it."

The smoke grew thicker, and I swore it felt as though a blast of heat scorched through my clothes. Whether that was a result from the power of suggestion or Knox turning up the thermometer, only he knew the answer.

"Are you enjoying this?" I yelled with a bravado I was far from feeling.

As best as I could manage while bound to the gurney, I scanned the room for a camera, twisting my body in all directions. I didn't spot one, but that didn't mean it wasn't well hidden in the bookcase or that he hadn't found some other means to view my terror.

The only way to know for sure was to turn the tables and test *him*. I pasted a wide, fake grin on my face and extended my middle finger, slowly turning all around the room, straining against the gurney, testing all the angles. Knox didn't respond, so I guessed he wasn't watching. I explored the area around my ties, searching for sharp bits of metal with my fingers.

I coughed, the smoke irritating my lungs. Tears streamed down from my stinging eyes.

A maniacal scream burst through the vent, ping-ponging around the tiny chamber. What the hell was happening on the other side of the wall? Was there another hostage in another room? I stiffened, desperately wishing my hands were free so I could clamp them over my ears. My search for a weapon or a way to break free grew more frantic. My index finger pricked a dull rusty point, and I traced the outline of what felt like a nail or small coil. I squeezed it between two fingers and worked it back and forth. It broke free from the gurney, and I turned the pointed end toward the plastic tie and seesawed.

It was too smoky, and my eyes were too watery to see whether I'd made any progress. I stopped and felt along the edge of the tie. I'd barely made a dent. The piece of metal was too dull to be of any use. I blinked, barely making out the edges of the cabinet. I cried tears of frustration. To be seated within a few feet from shelves littered with sharp objects and yet not be able to reach them. Their silver silhouettes taunted me through the ashy haze. Smoke obliterated the omnipresent red, but the cost to my eyes and lungs was too high a price to pay for the mental relief.

The screaming abruptly stopped. I narrowed my eyes and looked up toward the ceiling. The smoke had ceased pouring through the vent. Did this mean Knox would be returning shortly? I tugged at my bindings, screaming as they cut through my already tender flesh.

Loud voices filled my ears. It took several seconds for me to register that one of them was my own voice.

"What happens when you see the color red?" Dr. Pennington asks.

"I dissolve under its heat," I hear myself explain. "It absorbs me. Everything and everyone loses their boundaries until they're covered by a red wash of rage. I'm powerless against it."

That bastard. Knox must have stolen recordings of all my sessions with Dr. Pennington. Equal measures of anger and humiliation swirled inside.

A whirring noise erupted directly above my head, and the smoke began to lift, spiraling upward into the ventilation system. I tried to brace myself for whatever was coming next, but when it came, it utterly destroyed me.

Fractured light flickered through the vent, followed by an unexplained clicking sound.

"Look behind you, Della," Knox instructed from some hidden place.

Click.

I twisted my torso. Against the back wall was a huge projected photo of a bloody corpse. I blinked at the horrific image.

"You recognize her, don't you?" Knox cooed.

And all at once, I did—the shoulder-length bobbed hair, the pearl button earrings, the silhouette of her profile—the details coalesced and formed the horrible, undeniable truth. I whimpered at her ruined flesh.

Click.

It disappeared, and another image was projected onto the wall. Dirty-blond hair, chubby cheeks, and lifeless, staring eyes. Jimmy. I took in the sight of multiple knife wounds that had punctured his small chest. Like Mom, each stab had been circled and numbered. These were photos from the coroner's office that had been displayed at trial.

Click.

A grainy newspaper photo of me in the arms of a firefighter as he carried me from the yard. My legs dangled free from the Hello Kitty comforter draped over my shoulders. A piece of bone broke through the skin of my twisted right ankle.

Click.

A whirring sounded, and then the wall went black. The slideshow from hell was over. An uncontrollable trembling swept through my entire body, and my teeth chattered. It felt as though I might have been trapped in a storage freezer instead of this cramped room. *Nothing you haven't seen before,* I reminded myself. *Get a grip.* Breathe in, breathe out. Breathe in, breathe out. Breathe in . . .

A key rattled in the door, and Knox entered, shaking his head. "Doesn't look like you fared too well this round."

"You bastard! You sick, sick bastard. I've seen those photos before. You're not going to break me."

"You have to admit the enlarged image against a blood-splattered wall enhances their grisly effectiveness," he said.

I wouldn't give him the pleasure. Abruptly, I shifted the conversation. "What was all that screaming about?"

Knox pulled the folding chair across from me and sat. "It's a special recording I made. A mixture of losers—Melanie, Penny, and others."

I stared into his monstrous eyes, fear sparking up and down my limbs. How could I never have guessed this man, a person I'd thought of as a friend, had killed so many people? From the casual way he'd tossed their names out, they meant nothing to him. No regrets, no compassion.

I worked past the tight spasms burning the back of my throat. "You killed all those women."

"They were losers. Weak people."

"Those bodies by Hatchet Lake . . . you killed them too?"

"I've been doing this a long, long time."

A creeping dread of suspicion formed. "How long?"

"Years." A knowing smile lit his face, his eyes goading me on. "More than a decade even."

I didn't want to know any more. It was too much to take in all at once.

"Come on now, Della. You can do better. Keep guessing."

My lips were numb, my tongue heavy. I wasn't sure I was even capable of speech. "Y—you?" I whispered.

"I took no pleasure in that one. Not that I do in any corrections. But Mary Stallings was different."

I found my voice and screamed, an animal sound of rage and grief. "Why? *Why?*"

"Your mom found out something she wasn't supposed to. Stuck her nose where it didn't belong. I had no choice."

Sobs erupted down deep from my soul, and I shook with anguish. A memory surfaced of my little brother being tucked in at bedtime, dressed in Batman pajamas and smelling like baby shampoo and soap. Then I remembered the last time I'd seen him, bloodied and crying, clinging to our dying mother. He'd never had a chance against this evil. Never had a chance to grow into an adult and experience life.

"What about Jimmy?" I cried. "He was just a baby!"

"Wrong place, wrong time. Tough luck for that little kid."

Knox's voice held as much regret as a lump of coal. I wanted to kill him. To make him suffer like he'd made Mom and Jimmy suffer. I strained against my bindings, sure that my fury would give me enough strength to set me free. But I succeeded only in having the zip ties more thoroughly embedded in the skin of my wrists and ankles. And through it all, Knox sat still, utterly calm and utterly lacking in human warmth.

I stopped trying to break loose and slumped down in the gurney. "It was you behind the mask that night. You chased me to the woods and tried to kill me too."

"You were a skittish, gangly colt with your skinny little girl legs pumping. Running wild in the night. I didn't have time to chase you through the woods. Your screams were drawing attention, and I had to get away."

"And then you let my dad rot on death row for what you'd done. All those years, I believed him guilty. And the whole time, he was innocent."

Knox grinned and rocked back in his seat. "Those bells sure worked out convenient. I was going to just take one at first from the collection on display. You know, a memento to remember that night. But they were so pretty that I decided to help myself to several. Later, I had the brilliant idea to plant them on the bodies of all the weak women who'd failed my tests. In the end, doing that led the cops straight back to your father."

I bowed my head, not wanting him to witness my devastation. If I didn't survive him, and it looked like I wouldn't, I wanted to leave behind a clue that Knox was a killer. Some trace to lead authorities to him. I'd never get the chance to apologize to my dad, though, never get to tell him how sorry I was for believing the worst about him.

My poor aunt Sylvie. She'd be out of her mind with worry in a few hours when I didn't return home. And when the hours stretched into days and weeks, she'd know the worst had happened and that I'd never come home again. It would devastate her to lose yet another member of her family. I was so grateful that I'd forgiven her one lapse of judgment and that we'd moved on from the sins of the past. For Sylvie's sake, I hoped my body would eventually be found and that the police would arrest my killer.

Knox pinched my chin up and forced me to look at him. "You haven't already given up hope, have you? How disappointing. I thought you had more spirit."

"You're crazy," I said with a hiss, wishing I could destroy him like he'd destroyed Mom and Jimmy. "I hate you."

He smiled. "Good. Maybe that hatred will give you strength."

I had to admit he was right on that score. If I wanted to avenge my family's murders or lead police to the real killer in Normal, I would need my wits.

"What do I have to do?" I asked grimly. I'd been too dazed and frightened to understand his earlier babbling. "What do you mean about going through a correction?"

His eyes lit with approval. "Once I learn a person's deepest fear, I set up an environment to watch their terror as they face it. Like I said—it's good for you. Makes you stronger. And you must be strong, Della. No one has ever passed the correction, but you might."

I pushed aside thoughts of my family for the moment. My best chance of living depended on gathering all the knowledge I could, including his usual method of operation. "Melanie Mickelson drowned. So I take it she was afraid of water?"

"Right. You catch on quick. Penny was afraid of heights and snakes, so I took her to the top of the building and surprised her with a rattler. Others were afraid of things like the dark or enclosed spaces. Ordinary, run-of-the-mill type of stuff. But you take the cake. Chromophobia, fear of a damn color. You're rare, Della. Rare and special."

"Yeah, that's me. Rare." I tamped down a wave of bitterness and fear. I needed to focus on escaping, or at least surviving this night. "Go on. How does someone pass your corrections test?"

"For the others, passing my test meant facing their fear without flinching. No crying or pleading or trying-to-run-away bullshit. But I'll make it easier for you. Endure this without becoming a drooling idiot, and I'll let you go."

"You'd release me? I find that hard to believe," I scoffed. He never meant to offer me or anyone else a real chance of escape. This was all

Debbie Herbert

part of his game. He was toying with us for his own amusement, dangling false hope like a carrot to make the torture last longer.

"What would keep me from killing you once I was free?" I asked.

I was rewarded to see a quick spark of anger cross his features. Knox smiled, but it was tight and forced this time.

"You won't. You'll learn to respect me, and then we'll run away together. Somewhere remote and safe."

I returned the same tight smile he'd given me. He was either lying or delusional. I hoped he was delusional. Because if he thought I'd docilely agree to running off with him after all this was over, I'd use that to my advantage and kill him at the first opportunity.

"You're on," I whispered.

Chapter 31

THE CORRECTOR

I wiped off my makeup as I walked through the tunnel and then exited it. At five o'clock in the morning, the main hospital wing was beginning to stir to life. Elevators pinged, and a few lab techs and nurses roamed the halls. Occasionally, the beams of car headlights in the parking lot pierced through the floor-to-ceiling glass panels of the lobby. As usual, not a single person paid me any notice, although sometimes, like today, that oversight worked to my advantage.

The six-inch blade of my knife pressed against my outer right thigh. Its bone handle protruded from my pants pocket, but I covered it with a cleaning rag. Doubtful that anyone suspected me of wrongdoing, but I had to play it safe. This correction was my most important one ever, and I couldn't allow anything to stand in my way. Before entering Della's office, I slipped on a pair of latex gloves. Even if someone saw that, it was hardly suspicious behavior in a hospital environment.

Like the master chess player that I was, I'd planned a strategy to cover my tracks. I'd throw her purse in the waste bin on my trolley and then later toss it into the incinerator. Then, before closing Della's computer, I'd spend a few minutes entering keystrokes on her current project. This would place Della on her jobsite until she'd finished the end of her shift and lead police to believe she went missing on her way to the parking lot. In the meantime, I'd spend a good thirty minutes in the ER waiting room, mopping floors, making a point to engage in conversation with the security guard, and placing myself in view of the CCTV camera, thus securing my alibi at this crucial time span.

In the meantime, Della was locked up tight and stewing in the red room. All was well.

I stepped into her office and blinked at an unexpected, unwelcome sight.

Officer Nathan Whitt sat at Della's desk. I recognized him, having studied from afar all the cops that had been brought into the hospital after Melanie's and Penny's deaths. He wheeled around to face me, then slowly stood and glanced at the lettering on my uniform shirt. "Knox Wilkes?"

My fist closed over the knife handle. This was bad. Very, very bad. But I couldn't afford to be stupid and panic. Just . . . stay prepared. Nathan stood a good four to six inches above me. His dress shirt was crisp and slightly tight around a muscular chest and biceps. In a fight, the physical advantage belonged to him. His face was clean shaven and his eyes piercing. Resentment flooded over me, and I felt my face darken with the emotion. This was the man that Della preferred. If not for him, I'd have had an easier time winning her affection.

"Where's Della?" he demanded, placing his hands on his hips and narrowing his eyes.

Why the intimidation tactic? A sense of foreboding prickled my scalp. "No clue. I stopped by to see how she was doing."

"She didn't close out her computer, and her purse is still here."

I shrugged. "Must be on a bathroom break."

I began backing out of the doorway, but Whitt followed.

"Most people are ready to leave work the second they can." Whitt glanced at the wall clock. "It's already a few minutes after five o'clock."

"She'll probably be back in a minute." I turned my back on him and grabbed my janitor's cart to get the hell away. Nothing I could do now about Della's purse or closing out her computer. Damn Nathan Whitt.

"Actually, I came to see you. I just stopped by Della's office first to see if she wanted to go out for breakfast."

I slowly turned around. "You came to see me?"

"Had a long talk an hour ago with Jack Jenkins." Whitt paused, searching my face.

I said nothing.

"You remember Jack, don't you?"

My forehead broke out in a sweat. "The intruder Della found. Yeah."

"Guy finally ratted you out, Wilkes. Claimed you knew he was living on these premises illegally. Said you even brought him food and helped keep him hidden from the cops and the hospital's security guards."

"He's lying," I said flatly. The cops had nothing on me. It was my word against Jenkins's. Too bad framing him with the bell and newspaper clippings appeared not enough to keep the heat off me.

Whitt stepped forward, shoving his face near mine. "Why would you do that? Why would you harbor a criminal, knowing that women in this hospital were being kidnapped and killed?"

"I didn't."

"So you say."

We silently stared at one another. Beads of perspiration rolled down my forehead and stung my eyes. I dared not move or speak, afraid of giving myself away. The clock on the wall in Della's office clicked loudly, and I was aware of the hospital's background noises increasing as more employees arrived to begin their shifts. Another hour or two and the place would really be hopping.

Whitt spoke at last. "Maybe you'd be more forthcoming down at the station."

"Are you arresting me?"

"No. Not yet. Are you refusing to cooperate with the investigation?"

"There's nothing to tell."

Whitt took a step back and folded his arms across his broad chest. "Why don't we just wait here together for Della's return?"

My heart jackhammered in my chest, so strong I marveled that Whitt didn't see it beating against my shirt. He knew something. Or, at the very least, suspected I was involved in no good.

"I've got work to do," I mumbled. "Tell Della I said hello."

"Not so fast." Whitt grabbed my arm. "What's that on your shirt? Blood?"

I followed his gaze and saw a single, incriminating stripe of blood on my left sleeve. How had I missed that?

"And what's that on your face?" He peered closer at me. "Your mouth is stained red, and you have traces of black streaks running down your face."

I hadn't done a good enough job removing the makeup. "What can I say? I've been working all night, and it's a dirty job."

"And your nose is swollen. You been in a fight?"

"No. I fell." I tried to back away, but he kept coming at me. I bumped into the doorframe and winced as the knife nicked my thigh. My hand involuntarily rubbed the injury. Whitt's gaze lowered, and he saw the knife handle.

"Why are you carrying a weapon?"

"Protection."

Nathan shook his head. "I don't like what I'm seeing here. We're going down to the station."

I felt everything begin to fall apart. I didn't think. I reacted. My right arm swung upward, plunging the knife into the Adam's apple of Whitt's neck. His eyes widened with surprise, and his hands dropped to his sides as he began to stagger backward. I twisted my knife to enlarge the wound channel as I pulled it out of his neck.

Blood gushed from Whitt, and I stuffed the knife in my cart, appalled at the mess. I'd killed a police officer. They'd stop at nothing now to find me, to kill me. I needed to get the hell away from here.

My best chance of escape was to flee this room, this hospital, this town, and this state. It wasn't like I didn't have a contingency plan in place for just such an emergency. And I did have one person I could count on to help me in my time of need.

Whitt fell to the ground, gurgling blood. I almost left the cart and ran, but good sense prevailed. I noticed my shoes had stepped in his blood, leaving a trail of footprints. I removed them and wiped up the mess with a rag. Quickly, I left the room and headed toward the tunnels. Lady Luck was with me. Not a soul was in sight. In the basement, I took everything off the cart and threw it all into the incinerator. I changed clothes yet again from my stash of uniforms in the basement locker and ditched the cart.

I pumped myself up, tamping down the panic. *You got this. They can prove nothing. You've been on the run before.*

The worst of it though was that I couldn't leave a loose end. There was no time to finish Della's correction. No time to make her love me. There went my hopes of a happy future with the only woman who'd ever noticed me and been nice.

Della had to die.

Chapter 32

DELLA

He'd be back.

And this time Knox would kill me. That, or make me wish I were dead. If I were going to escape, it would have to be now. Right now. And to do that, I needed to clear my mind of what might await and instead focus on a plan.

An odd calm settled over me. Again my gaze drifted to the surgical cabinet. Therein lay my best chance. Everything I needed was inside it. There was nothing else in the room except for me, the gurney, and a light bulb blazing overhead. I examined the gurney more closely.

I twisted my torso 180 degrees to the right and saw where my swollen and bloody wrist was zip-tied to a metal coil behind me. Twisting to the other side, I observed my left hand also secured to a coil. My left ankle was bound to my right ankle, and only my right ankle was secured against a metal leg. Wheels were attached to the feet of the gurney. If I could maneuver it toward the cabinet, then I could try to strike my feet against the glass and break it open. It would hurt like hell if glass shards cut through my ankles and legs, but it could be no worse than whatever Knox had in store for me. Once the cabinet was open, I'd have to somehow grasp an instrument with either my toes or fingers and then try to cut free one hand. No doubt I'd probably cut an artery or two in the blind attempt, but again it was better than passively waiting for Knox to return and torture me.

But could I move this old contraption? I managed to move my right ankle down the gurney leg and then experimentally swung my legs and hips forward and began to pump them back and forth. Excruciating pain shot from my wrists with each forward thrust, burning and pinching. I ignored the agony. The thing wasn't moving. I stretched forward as far as I possibly could until my shoulder muscles screamed. I pointed my toes and made contact with the floor. I scooted my toes across the slick floor in a macabre ballet. The wheels on the gurney squeaked and then rolled forward an inch. It worked!

I redoubled my efforts. Sweat rolled down my face, stinging my eyes. My breath seesawed in my chest, and yet I continued because giving up meant certain death. Over and over, I pumped my legs and rose up on my toes, desperate to get closer. At length, I had to pause for a moment to catch my breath and assess my progress. I'd managed to move the gurney only two feet. I had another two feet to go. Tears of rage and fear flowed down my cheeks, but I resumed the painful, strenuous crawl.

I had no idea how long it took or how much time I had left before Knox returned, but I finally drew within striking range. Bracing myself for pain, I drove my feet through the glass. I screamed as a long shard sliced through the flesh of my left calf like hot butter and lodged inside. Somehow, I had to work through the pain—keep going.

Now came the most difficult part. After another agonizing series of thrusts, I placed my back to the cabinet and began to search. My fingers were numb from the lack of blood flow, and I fumbled about the broken glass. A quick sharp pain split my left index finger. I craned my neck over my shoulder and saw a scalpel sticking from the swollen digit.

Okay, that was one way to locate a weapon. I pulled my stuck finger to the edge of the shelf. It took several attempts, but I extracted the scalpel from it and then grasped it in my hand. It was just long enough that when I curled it backward, the sharp edges cut at the zip tie.

It also cut at my wrist, but I was beyond caring about the pain. Would Knox open the door at any moment? I couldn't hear past the rush of blood pounding in my ears. I concentrated on the operation at hand. The tie broke at last, and I cried out with relief. Blood spurted from a severed vein. In short order, I sliced off the ties on my other hand and feet.

My eyes swam with tiny black specks, and I felt punch drunk from the loss of blood. I needed to stanch the flow. In the bottom cabinet drawer, I found rolls of cloth bandages and did my best to wrap my wrists with numb fingers. When Knox returned, I'd give him a fight to remember, win or lose.

I paced the chamber to increase the blood flow to my feet and con-templated the best way to escape Knox. I could either sit back on the gurney and take him by surprise when he drew close, or I could spring on him the moment he entered the door.

I chose the latter. He was bound to notice the shattered glass of the cabinets the moment he entered the room. But the scalpel was so short that I'd have to jump on Knox to ensure I cut him. With one deft move to the side, he could escape my first parry and overpower me. I needed something longer.

There was nothing in the cabinets that could fit the bill. I turned my attention to the rusted gurney. On its side was an old rod, a lever that must have served to adjust the bed height. I kicked at it until the rusted metal joint where it was attached broke in two. Metal clanged on the floor. I gathered it up and gripped it in my stiffened fingers, felt its solid form peppered with gritty rust and imagined the tetanus toxic soup of that rust eating into my open wounds. Still a small price to pay for a chance at freedom.

There was one final step I could take to momentarily disorient my captor. I climbed atop the gurney and smashed the overhead bulb with the rod. It shattered, spraying bits of glass everywhere. The room plunged into total darkness. Unease tingled up and down my spine. Had I done the right thing?

I shook off my misgivings and took position against the wall by the door. I waited, wondering what in the hell Knox was up to. What if he never returned? What if I died here in this dark, forgotten room? I might not be discovered for years. I imagined some unlucky janitor unlocking the door and discovering my rotted corpse. Death by dehydration and starvation. Probably a slow, painful way to go.

I kept my focus on the door, both wanting Knox to return and dreading the moment of reckoning. It could have been an hour, it could have been ten minutes, but at last the sound of running footsteps reverberated from beyond my locked room. I held the rod in my right hand and a backup scalpel in my left in case the first blow at Knox didn't knock him out when he lunged at me. The scalpel would be quick and, hopefully, lethal. I'd aim for the most vulnerable area available—eyes, throat, or heart.

A key jangled in the lock. I raised the metal rod and crouched like an animal awaiting its prey. The door creaked open, and I was assailed by sudden doubt. What if this wasn't Knox? What if it were instead a cop searching for me?

No, no. There could be no hesitation.

The tall figure of a man was backlit. The faint scent of industrial cleaner with an even tinier trace of a familiar scent. Chamomile. From the hand cream I'd given him. Knox pushed through and then paused at the room's unexpected darkness. Adrenaline surged through me as I raised the rod and brought it down full force across the side of his face.

For an instant, he turned toward me. His eyes widened, and his mouth parted in an O of surprise. Again, I lifted my weapon. The rod whistled through the air and thwacked the center of his face, striking his already broken nose. He howled as the weapon bent. The rusted rod fell and rattled about on the floor. I held my breath waiting to see whether Knox fell down or lunged at me.

He toppled against the wall, hitting the back of his head with a satisfying thump. This was it. This was my chance. I hurtled forward. Light blinded my eyes. One step, two steps. When I was halfway through the door, his hand seized my left ankle. I tried to kick it loose, but he gripped it tighter. I screamed, hoping that someone—anyone—might hear. Knox gave a vicious tug, and I began to fall.

The scalpel. Don't drop it. Slice him and keep slicing until he lets go.

Stars burst behind my eyelids as my back and head hit the hard tile. Knox loomed over my body, where I lay sprawled on the floor, close enough that his breath warmed my face. It smelled of cherry TUMS. His dark eyes gleamed with wounded offense.

"You hurt me, Della," he said in the tone of a surprised child who doesn't understand why he's been punished.

Now!

I clenched the scalpel and jabbed it into the nearest flesh available—the side of his belly. Knox roared with pain and began to roll away. I saw my opportunity and took it. I scrambled to my knees and again raised the scalpel, this time slicing open one of his eyes.

Knox curled on the floor, screaming and writhing, holding both hands to his ruined face. I backed away, careful to make sure he didn't grab an ankle again and send me tumbling. Finally, I turned my back on him and ran.

The tunnel hallway was deserted but well lit and, blessedly, a monochromatic wash of pale green with not a speck of red marring any surface. My feet were clumsy beneath me, yet I kept stumbling forward, ever closer to freedom. At the end of the tunnel, I risked a look back.

Knox loped down the hall, blood smeared over half his face. A Frankenstein that could not, would not, die. This wasn't over. Twenty feet ahead, the tunnel ended by an elevator and stairwell. I momentarily slowed, debating my best option.

The light above the elevator glowed, and the metal unit hummed and vibrated in a rapid descent. Help had arrived! Were the police already searching for me, or would it be a hospital employee? I desperately hoped it was Nathan. Perhaps all the cops were searching for me, although I couldn't be sure whether I'd been missing long enough. For all I knew, I could have only been imprisoned an hour even if it had felt like days. As I reached the elevator, the steel doors parted. A familiar figure emerged, the last person I expected.

Dr. Pennington, immaculate in his white jacket and navy-blue trousers, stepped out of the elevator and halted in surprise at the sight of my bloody dishevelment. A severe frown creased his haughty face.

"Where's Knox?" he demanded. His gaze dropped to the scalpel still gripped in my hand.

Blood dripped from the sharp implement onto the waxed, pristine floors. *Plop, plop, plop.* I grew dizzy staring at the garnet droplets splashing abstract designs.

"Have you hurt my brother?"

Brother. The word bounced round and round in my head. Such a simple, common kind of word, but my brain was slow to decipher the obvious meaning. Brothers? Knox and Dr. Pennington?

He turned his head to the side where Knox still loped forward, almost upon us. The danger had not passed. Dr. Pennington stood rooted, blocking my path to the elevator. Was he friend or foe? *Blood's thicker than water,* the old adage warned.

I made a sudden dash to the stairwell.

Blinding pain seared my scalp, as though someone were ripping the skin off my head. Was it Pennington or Knox? The scalpel clattered to the ground, and a worn boot kicked it from my reach. Knox. While he'd been down on the ground, clutching his face, I should have taken my weapon and cut out his heart.

Knox's arm locked around my neck from behind, and I lowered my chin defensively into the crook of his elbow, protecting my throat from crushing pressure against the vessels in my neck. I kicked at his shins. But no blow ever seemed to fell him.

"Let her go," Pennington demanded. "Don't be stupid. Don't kill her."

"She hurt me," Knox groaned. "Hurt me bad."

"I can see that," Pennington said in a calming, soothing voice. "You need medical attention. I'll walk you to the ER."

"No! I'll get in trouble again. They'll call the cops."

"The cops are already here, Knox. They're swarming the place. I got wind of a possible disturbance at the hospital while listening to my police scanner. I guessed you might be down here. You used one of the rooms down here before. What was her name? Ellen York."

"She didn't make it," Knox whimpered.

My skin crawled at the mention of a new name, a new victim. Had Ira Pennington known all this time that his brother was abducting and killing women? Why had he never stopped him? No wonder I could never fully trust my doctor. There was something fundamentally broken about the man. If I were to escape, it was up to me. I hadn't taken years of martial arts classes for nothing. Escaping from rear choke holds was a scenario I had practiced many times.

I placed both of my hands atop Knox's bent elbow and pressed his arm in toward my body, creating a pressure point for leverage. I spread my legs wide and took a large step to the right, in the same direction of his right arm. Next, I began to swing the full weight of my body toward the right, maintaining pressure on his elbow joint as I turned.

You'll need at least a good, solid 180-degree turn to break free, my instructor had warned. *After that, you can either run or attack back.*

I broke free of Knox and didn't hesitate. I fisted my right hand and slammed it into his exposed, vulnerable kidney area, in the exact spot I'd earlier sliced open with the scalpel. Inhuman screaming rent the air, and he went down, hard. Ira rushed to his side. Above me, hospital sirens exploded to life. Shouts and footsteps sounded from the stairwell.

"I don't want to go to prison," Knox said with a moan. All the fight and anger had gone out of him, and he lay helpless on the floor. The monster was no longer a threat. I stood transfixed at the sight of him whimpering like a wounded child.

Pennington cradled Knox's head in his arms; his white jacket became smeared with red. "Maybe they can help you in prison. I never could."

I glared at Pennington. "You knew," I spat out. "All this time. You knew. And you didn't stop him."

"I wasn't positive," he said.

"Stop defending him. It's despicable. *You're* despicable." I was flummoxed. How could such a highly educated man, whose career had been spent healing patients, turn a blind eye to the danger Knox posed?

"He's my brother," Pennington said simply. "I didn't want to believe he was a murderer."

His words rang false in my ears. Pennington was only out to save his own ass.

"It didn't have to end this way," Knox said, suddenly lucid and staring directly at me. "We could have been together."

"Never."

"Why? Because of Nathan Whitt? Because that's not going to happen."

New fear seized and tightened my chest. "What do you mean?"

"He was in your office earlier." Knox's face twisted in a spasm of pain, and he clamped his mouth shut.

Three cops burst through the elevator door with drawn guns. Two-way radios crackled, and more footsteps sounded from the stairwell.

"Get back," one of them yelled at Ira.

Pennington stood and stepped backward, hands raised in surrender. "I came to help her." He nodded at me, but neither officer spared me a glance as they bent to the ground on either side of Knox.

"What did you do to Nathan?" I yelled at Knox.

Cuffs were slapped on his wrists, and he offered only passive resistance as cops jerked him to his feet. Knox met my glare.

"He's dead."

The pronouncement hit me like a gut punch. "Where is he? What have you done?"

"Officer Whitt?" One of the officers interrupted. "He's not dead. At least, he wasn't as of fifteen minutes ago. Who do you think alerted us?"

Thank God. My shoulders slumped with relief.

"Son of a bitch," Knox roared. "He should be dead."

"Shut up." A cop twisted his arm, and Knox whimpered. "Nonnie."

"Don't hurt him," Pennington said as they dragged his brother toward the elevator. He followed them onto the elevator, not even sparing me a backward glance. What would Ira have done if he'd found me in that locked room, either dead or barely alive? My bet was that he'd protect Knox as he'd always done, even if that meant permanently silencing me.

For the second time in my life, a cluster of uniformed police officers suddenly surrounded me. A middle-aged female cop with a kind demeanor draped an arm over my shoulder. "You've been through an ordeal. Let's get you to the ER."

"I'm okay. Where's Nathan? How bad is he hurt?"

She didn't evade my question or try to patronize me. "It's serious. Stab wound to the throat."

"I want to see him."

The woman nodded and pointed at the stairs. "This way will be quicker." Her gaze fell to my bloody ankles. "If you're up to it."

I ran to the stairs and began climbing, not wasting time answering. "What floor?" I asked.

"Outside your office. Docs were administering triage." Her breath grew ragged as she struggled to keep up with me. "Might be in surgery now, though."

At the main-level floor, I burst through the door and ran, pushing past cops. One of them tried to block my path, but the woman gestured for him to move aside. "She's with me. Where's . . ."

Down the hall, three doctors ran alongside a gurney, heading toward an open elevator door, where more cops stood guard at the entrance.

I cursed my clumsy feet, running as fast as my injuries allowed, finally glimpsing Nathan. One of the doctors held white gauze to his throat, stanching the flow of blood. Tubes and IVs were stuck in both arms, and his face was as white as the hospital linen he lay upon, but his eyes were open and alert.

I pulled up short, racked with remorse. This was my fault. Nathan had come searching for me and run straight into the evil that plagued my life. It'd been selfish of me to make a tentative stab at friendship. If not for me, this never would have happened.

His eyes caught mine, and he raised one trembling hand, mouthing something to the doctors. A cop waved me over, and I followed the procession of docs and cops into the elevator. I stood next to Nathan. He turned his face to the side, searching for me, and then raised a hand. He tried to smile but grimaced at the effort.

"You made it," he whispered, his voice raspy and strained.

"Don't try to talk," one of the doctors ordered Nathan.

"You're going to make it too," I said, hoping I spoke the truth. I bent over and touched his chest, unheeding of the red bloom soaking the front of his shirt. His hand found mine, and I clasped it with both of mine. His skin was cold and clammy between my palms.

I didn't let go.

Not even when the elevator door swung open. I held on to the very last second. Until the grave-faced doctors whisked him away for surgery. The adrenaline that had fueled me since Knox's attack left my body in a swoosh. I sank to my knees. Darkness gathered at the corners of my eyes and spread inward until only a pinprick of light remained.

A voice sounded somewhere above. "She's going into shock."

Chapter 33

THE CORRECTOR

In the interrogation room, I squinted my eyes against the unrelenting glare of the overhead fluorescent light. I'd seen Detective Josh Adams around the hospital before and immediately recognized his type. You could practically see ruthless ambition streaming from his abrupt gestures, clipped voice, and calculating eyes. Of course, the minute I was brought into the police station, it was Adams who took control of my questioning.

I'd dreaded this day of reckoning for so long, but now that it had arrived, I was surprised at the relief that came from unburdening my secrets. No wonder people said confession was good for the soul. It was true.

I spilled my guts to Adams, even for the crimes they wouldn't have otherwise been able to pin on me—shoving Linda Bowen down the stairs, Penny's fall from the rooftop, the existence of more bodies at the bottom of Hatchet Lake, the deaths of Mary Baines Stallings and her young son, James Ronald Stallings.

But my motives were my own. I'd protect my older brother, just as he'd always protected me as much as possible when we were younger.

I'd killed three people just for him—Mary, Jimmy, and Linda—so his secrets would remain hidden.

"You thought you were really clever, didn't you?" Adams said, smirking. "Stole those bells from the Stallings home and set up Jack Jenkins to take the fall for everything. But I've got you cornered now. I always get my man in the end."

I could tell Adams was practically salivating with eagerness to talk to the news media and demonstrate his own cleverness in order to advance his career. I expected a little gratitude, seeing as I was the one who'd provided the bombshell revelations to help solve a multitude of cold cases.

"Eluded all of you for decades," I shot back. "Jack Jenkins would have taken the rap for it all if not for one mistake."

"You're one cold motherfucker," Adams said. "Stabbing a four-year-old kid and then having the premeditated foresight to steal nearby objects for future use. You even placed those bells around the bodies of older victims we hadn't discovered yet."

He gave me too much credit. That night I'd stolen the bells . . . when they'd caught my eyes, my only thought was that they were pretty. Nonnie's house had been dark and dreary, nothing frilly or decorative. Later, when I lived on my own, my taste had run decidedly minimalistic. I had no talent or role model for how to make a home cheerful. But the Stallings house had been classy and cozy at the same time. And so I'd stolen the bells, thinking they would brighten up my place. I wasn't plotting to use them at some future time, but they sure did come in handy later.

I took no pleasure in these deaths. Why couldn't anyone understand?

"One more thing," Whitt said, speaking up at last. "Did you plant those cigar bands by Mickelson's body?"

I had nothing left to lose by answering. "Della's father came to see her one night at the hospital. I followed him out to the parking lot. He took out a cigar, peeled off the band, and tossed it on the ground before lighting up. When he drove away, I picked up the band. Figured it might eventually come in handy."

"What's the deal with the makeup?" Adams asked with his usual sneer.

This time, I didn't answer. Let them think what they would. The spark of connection I felt with Nonnie whenever I smeared the stuff on my face was my little secret.

"You're going to end up on death row," Adams continued. "Right where you belong."

"Like all you cops once thought Hunter Stallings had belonged?"

The detective's face flushed at the jab, and he motioned for the two guards at the door to take me back to my cell. They were none too gentle as they escorted me to the bowels of the county jail located directly behind the station. The other inmates in the holding cell stared as I took a seat on a bench near the barred gate. At some point, they'd put me in isolation. A smaller cell with better security until I was sentenced and delivered to death row at Holman Prison in Atmore, Alabama.

Maybe I'd get Hunter Stallings's old cell at Holman. I'd always felt a little guilty for that sucker over the years. But he deserved punishment. By all accounts, he hadn't been a good father to Della.

Della.

An image of her bleeding and bound to the gurney in the red room flashed in my mind. I had come so close to completing my mission. Now I'd never know whether the correction was successful. I liked to think that it would have been. After all, I'd put in so much time and preparation for our session. I'd stolen Ira's recordings of their therapy sessions and played them over and over, listening to every nuance of her voice as she described what happened the night she witnessed the killings. The same night I'd also chased her into the woods, intent on ending her life at age eight. A young girl running in her pajamas clutching a pink blanket in the darkness. It had been my duty to reverse all the damage I'd caused Della. But now she'd always be tainted by the past, her fear never fully eradicated. It would haunt her days and dreams. Della would keep running from the slightest tinge of red that seeped through her isolated world.

And as for me? The future stretched ahead, long and bleak. Every minute of every day would be a colorless suspension of time filled with stark grayness and stifling boredom.

The Department of Corrections was going to perform their own version of correction on me. I'd have to learn to accept the claustrophobic quarters and monotony of time as it slowly marched forward. The grim reaper would be a welcome visitor when at long last I'd draw my final, dying breath.

I huddled on the bench, whispering an old lie. *I fear nothing.*

But that wasn't quite true. I feared nothing *alive*—snakes, killers, heights, or the dark. But my dead nonnie? Even now I break out in a cold sweat at her memory. Everything she did was for my own good; it made me the man I was today. Still . . . I normally kept my thoughts of her locked tight.

It had been necessary to kill her in the end. Nonnie had taught me to search and destroy any weakness. Right up until the day I'd finally determined that my fear of her, of the daily corrections, was the only impediment to my strength.

I kept her memory buried in the darkest recesses of my brain, much as I'd dug down deep in the dirt of those remote Ohio woods. I'd laid my nonnie's body to rest beneath the cold, cold snow in a place sunlight never touched. Not now, not ever.

Chapter 34

DELLA

Two weeks later

Nathan yawned and ran a hand through his hair.

"You should have let me drive," I said. "You're trying to do too much."

"I'm fine. Can't a guy just be tired?" he asked with mock severity.

I bit my tongue. Arguing would do no good. Nathan had insisted on returning to work yesterday, only a couple of weeks after emergency surgery, even though the doctors had recommended a longer rest. I glanced at the scar on his neck, which was still red and raised. He caught my gaze and frowned.

"Stop. It's not your fault. We've been over this."

"Right."

I was trying my best. And I'd come a long way in a short time. I'd started working the day shift at Normal Community Hospital and had attended a therapy session with a new doctor in Huntsville. I liked him and had agreed to weekly sessions. Didn't mean the chromophobia had totally vanished yet. I still longed for a world purged of red, but I coped.

And if I occasionally awoke some nights, Knox chasing me in my dreams, sometimes as a black-masked hunter, sometimes as a bleeding, one-eyed monster, then who could blame me?

But if I could survive a night with a serial killer, I could beat my demons. Scars encircled my wrists and ankles, white scrapes and puckered skin, and another long scar snaked up one leg where broken glass had sliced through. New scars to join the old ankle injury from eighteen years earlier.

I ran a finger across the line of indented skin on my left wrist, shivering slightly at the physical reminder of my narrow escape.

Nathan must have caught my movement. He laid a hand over mine and squeezed. "You just worry about you. Everything going okay at work?"

"It's manageable. But if Pennington returns, I won't stay there, even if it means accepting another job somewhere else with less pay."

Normal Hospital had placed Dr. Pennington on administrative leave, pending the police investigation on the extent of his prior knowledge of the crimes his brother had committed. The hospital board was also concerned about the apparent leaking of patient information and what role Dr. Pennington might have played in that. If nothing else, in his position he bore the ultimate responsibility for safeguarding patient confidentiality. Knox Wilkes's computer and cell phone had been seized, and it was discovered that he had recordings of Pennington's recent therapy sessions saved on these devices.

"I don't see him ever returning there," Nathan said, his tone deepening with conviction.

I raised a brow. "Why? Has anything new developed?"

"You know I can't give you all the specifics, but we're closing in."

"Dr. Pennington had to be involved," I argued, not for the first time. "I heard him say Knox had used a hospital room before to hurt a woman named Ellen York."

"When questioned, Pennington claims he was guessing about his brother's role in that woman's disappearance—trying to get Knox to confess."

"I bet you anything one of the new skeletal remains belongs to that poor woman." An additional two remains had been discovered from dredging Hatchet Lake. "And I bet she was tortured by her worst fear in the process," I added, shivering as I always had at the knowledge of how close I'd come to meeting the same fate of the other victims.

"We're still embroiled in the legalities of obtaining medical records of all the known victims. We suspect tampering of the records and that there's missing information in the files, but we'll have that theory confirmed within days."

My pulse quickened. "Y'all found Gayla Pouncey, didn't you?"

Although he didn't directly answer my question, Nathan smiled with a grim satisfaction that informed me they had.

"Told you she knows something about her old boss."

"Your instincts are great."

I let out a snort. "Hardly. If they were so great, I'd have suspected Knox was a killer before he got to me." As always, my thoughts drew back to my mother. "But I still don't know what she found out that was so horrible Knox felt like he had to kill her."

"Could be that in her position as Human Resources director, she'd had to reprimand him over some job violation, and he'd been offended. Perhaps his behavior was so out of proportion to the minor slap on the wrist that your mom was alarmed and delved into his prior job history and found something disturbing. We're going through all the old microfiche reports from the hospital."

I slowly nodded. "She might have discovered he had an arrest record in Ohio. That makes as much sense as anything else. Or it could be he'd been watching her, as he had the patients, and decided something about her needed correction. Poor Jimmy was just in the wrong place at the wrong time."

In the end, Knox's motives weren't what concerned me. But his punishment did. He'd destroyed my family. Mom and Jimmy were gone. Dad had been falsely accused and imprisoned. And I had my own scars to bear.

I remembered Knox's pale face cartoonishly slashed with lipstick and eyeliner as he'd explained how I needed correcting to face my fears. Nathan had shared with me that Knox had told them about his grandmother's "corrective" sessions. I tried to feel sympathy for him in light of the past abuse that had so warped his mind, but I wasn't there yet. Maybe I never would be.

"We're closing in on every detail and meticulously documenting all the evidence. I promise you, Della, Knox Wilkes will never again be a free man."

"Because this time you have the right person in custody. And no Brady Eckeridge screwing up everything with his lies." I'd never forgive that dirty cop for intimidating witnesses and helping to send my father to prison. I'd grown up believing the worst about him. Dad was many things—but not a murderer. Somehow the two of us needed to reconcile our relationship.

And what if I'd had no Aunt Sylvie to take me in when my world fell apart as a child? I shuddered at the thought of Aunt Mabel raising me, even if Uncle Vic was a decent-enough guy.

At long last, Nathan cut through my meandering, twisting thoughts. "We've got company."

Dad wandered around the new construction on the old homestead property, carrying a stick and smoking a cigar while inspecting the newly poured cement. What was he doing here? A confusing pang of guilt and annoyance shot through me. He squatted near the slab, apparently taking a closer look at something. Nathan pulled into the yard, and I opened my car door.

"Aren't you getting out?" I asked him when he remained seated.

"Nah." He pocketed his car keys and avoided looking at me. "I'll let you and your dad have some privacy first."

I studied him, sure that I was missing something. "What's going on?"

"Hunter called me earlier," Nathan admitted sheepishly. "He'd like a few words alone with you today."

I didn't like the sound of that. Whenever Dad wanted alone time, that usually meant I left our meeting with a lighter wallet. "Suit yourself then. I just came for a quick look at the progress here."

Sighing inwardly, I approached Dad. What did he want this time? A loan to finish paying for the concrete slab he'd contracted for the trailer's foundation?

I picked my way over through discarded concrete bags and other construction detritus. Even though I'd visited a couple of times since the old ruins had been demolished and hauled away, it still felt strange. Even stranger now that a new structure would be taking its place.

"How's the work going?" I asked. "Is there a problem?"

Dad grinned and stood. "You're always direct. But no, there isn't any problem." He swept a hand over the site. "Everything's progressing nicely."

"That slab's huge. Guess you paid extra to have a porch."

"Not exactly." He pulled an oversize paper from his jacket and handed it to me.

"What's up?" I opened it, studying the architectural drawing of a house. My stomach dropped. Should have known Dad wouldn't be content with a used double-wide. Now he was going to insist on building a house.

Annoyed, I held the paper back out to him, but he wouldn't accept it. "I can't loan you any more money, Dad."

"I didn't ask you to."

"You mean the bank actually loaned you money? Wait a minute. If you think I'm going to cosign—"

"Paid cash up front."

"Really? That's . . . that's terrific," I stammered. The townsfolk must have come through in a big way donating him money. "Congratulations."

"No. I should be congratulating you."

He wasn't making sense. "For what?" I asked.

"The house is for you, not me."

A thousand questions bombarded me, but I couldn't manage a single word. What was his secret agenda? Because with Dad, there was always an angle.

"All yours, free and clear," he continued. "You'll need to look over that drawing, see if you want to make any changes to the layout before they start framing in a few days."

"But . . . how?"

"Won my lawsuit," he said with a grin. "The great State of Alabama compensated me for time falsely served."

I couldn't wrap my head around the sudden change in his fortune. "That's wonderful, Dad. But this should be your house then. I don't need—"

"Take it." His face grew to an unaccustomed seriousness. "Please. It's the least I can do. I've never been there for you growing up, and—"

"You were in prison."

"You and I both know I've never been much of a father, no matter the circumstances."

Again, I tried to return the drawing to him. "You should live here. Not me. It's your money."

"I've got plenty more of it," he said, waving me off.

"How much more?"

"Enough to start a new life in a new town. A place where no one knows my past."

"I didn't realize your reputation bothered you," I said slowly. Behind the toothy salesman's smile, he must have masked hurt and anger.

"Course it does." He smiled ruefully. "I do have feelings."

My throat clogged, and Dad's image grew splintered through the film of tears coating my eyes. I'd misjudged him for far too long. "I'm sorry. I—"

"Don't you dare keep apologizing."

Dad scanned the yard and shoved his hands in his pockets. "You know, it wasn't all bad here. We had good times too. Good memories. I hope . . . I hope you remember that."

I nodded. "When are you leaving?"

"ASAP. I'm not one to let the grass grow under my feet."

"Uncle Vic will miss you."

He snorted. "Vic's a good guy, but I've worn out my welcome. I don't want to impose anymore. He'd let me stay indefinitely if he got it in his head it was his Christian duty. But screw that. I don't want to be anyone's moral obligation."

I knew just what Dad meant. "Will you keep in touch with me?"

He stared straight ahead, not meeting my eyes. "You want me to?" he asked.

The air between us was charged, crackling with intensity. Thunderbolts of warring emotions clashed inside me—pain and peace, regret and hope, words spoken and unspoken, betrayal and redemption.

"Of course I want to stay in touch. You're my dad."

His eyes grew as watery as my own. "Well, then. It's a deal."

He managed a salute and a broken smile that in no way resembled his former mien of confident conviviality. He was just a regular man, ready to move on with his life. Dad cleared his throat and surprised me with a quick hug. "You take care of yourself, Delly-girl."

He turned away, and I watched him get in his truck and drive away, filled with a sadness I wouldn't have suspected. Nathan exited his car and strode to me.

"I take it Dad already told you the news," I said.

"Yeah. You okay?"

Without answering, I looked down where Dad had knelt by the concrete. Two rows of stick lines were scribbled across the flat service. I squatted on my haunches and saw he'd inscribed a message:

"Mary, Jimmy & Della I'm Sorry."

My fingers traced each letter of the etched apology, absorbing their meaning. I hadn't even realized this was what I needed. That all these years the little girl inside me blamed Dad for not being home that night. For not protecting Mom and Jimmy. For not protecting me.

"Let me borrow your car keys," I said thickly to Nathan.

Wordlessly, he pressed them into my hand. I dug a key blade into the semidry cement and began to write underneath Dad's words, delivering my own message:

"You're Forgiven."

Nathan placed a hand on my shoulder, its weight warm and comforting. For the first time, I accepted that tearing down the old ruins and building a new home was the right thing to do. My family was gone but never forgotten. I'd make new memories here, and they would soothe my violent past, blending out the sharp edges of remembered pain.

Epilogue

IRA

I packed the last of my bags and stuffed them into my Mercedes, perspiring like a lowly peasant. I'd done no wrong. Knox was the killer, but I'd accrued enough deceptions to warrant an arrest, both for things left unsaid and things gone unreported. For turning my eyes the other way, suspecting all the while that my younger brother was having his own kind of fun with the missing women. I was the only person in the world who understood what had driven Knox. Not because of my knowledge of psychiatry, but because we'd been raised in the same house by the same psychopathic grandmother.

But he'd had it so much worse than I. I was the product of her daughter's, Karen's, first marriage. My father died of cancer when I was only eight years old. Knox had come along two years later, born out of wedlock and unwanted. His biological father had promptly fled town for more uncomplicated pastures upon discovering that she was pregnant. Karen had spiraled downhill after the double blow. She'd turned to drugs to cope, and within a year of Knox's birth, social services had taken us away. Nonnie had stepped in to raise us. Unfortunately, I'd rather have taken my chances in foster care, but I'd had no say in the matter.

Knox had never had a chance with that hard, unyielding woman. I'd tried to help him as best I could. Shield him from abuse while I still lived at home. And years later when he'd called me late one night, asking for my help, I'd agreed.

We'd buried Nonnie together. I had no regrets on that score.

Detective Adams was hounding me daily now, convinced that I'd lied when I claimed no knowledge of what Knox had done. He'd never prove it. Knox would never betray me—of that I was certain. Gayla Pouncey hadn't contacted me for more money, no doubt realizing that blackmail was a dangerous game, one in which people could end up dead. She hadn't spoken to the police, either, and I didn't believe she ever would.

But even worse than the police harassment and the slight worry that my former secretary might yet spill the beans on me, I realized that my career here as a psychiatrist was dead in the water. With all of the press and police scrutiny, it was only a matter of time before the truth leaked out.

I returned inside my home and sighed at all the Gothic Revival antique furniture that I'd so painstakingly collected over the years. I'd have to leave them behind. They'd probably end up being sold at auction for a fraction of the price I'd paid. Most people found the dark rosewood, heavy velvets, intricate carvings, and throne-like chairs to be pretentious and uncomfortable. But the massive medieval pieces appealed to my refined senses as dignified and classic.

Of course, I'd also miss my elegant lake house, but it was mortgaged to the hilt, and I'd leave behind more debt than equity paid into it. I slipped inside my bedroom for one last lingering look. Moonlight slanted against the gleaming armoires and highlighted the stately four-poster bed elaborately carved with gargoyles and dragons. I'd enjoyed many a night here lying in bed and gazing at the killer view of Hatchet Lake from the bay window.

But walking inside the master walk-in closet pained me the most. There was only so much space inside the Mercedes, and over half of my custom-tailored suits and Italian leather shoes would need to be left behind with the furnishings. I'd considered packing everything up—wardrobe, furniture, and expensive tchotchkes—and having it shipped to a warehouse out of state, but that plan felt too risky. Best to cleanly cut all ties when starting over and remain untraceable.

The last time I'd been forced to pick up and move, I'd been a young man. Knox had needed me when he got into a bit of a pickle with local police in Ohio. Normal, Alabama, had felt like a world away from Cuyahoga Falls, and so I'd hatched a new life for us. One where I made a fantastic salary and was able to use my influence to get him a job in which his solitary nature was well suited. To prevent anyone from ever connecting me to Knox's unsavory background, I'd made sure to hide the fact that we were brothers. If he got into trouble again, no one would begin to question me as well.

The night maintenance work, with its lack of supervision and zero need of social skills, had been a brilliant idea. Knox had bought into it with enthusiasm. I'd agreed to share my computer and cell phone passwords so that he could listen in on therapy sessions and enjoy the same stories as I did. Only, I was innocent and in control of my impulses. Poor Knox couldn't contain his fascination to merely an intellectual delight; instead, he had to physically play out his dark cravings to murder our sick grandmother over and over again whenever she manifested into the physical form of a female stranger. He confessed to police it was all part of a correction process similar to the type he'd been forced to endure by Nonnie, but I guessed the truth. Even though he lacked the self-awareness to discern his motives.

I sighed and prepared to exit my home for the very last time. At the foyer, I paused and drank in the luxurious space I'd created. My heart pinched at the loss. I left the door standing wide open, unconcerned about burglars or utility bills. None of that was my problem anymore.

Being older made it so much more difficult to start over. Especially since this time, I thought I'd finally found roots. A picturesque place to eventually retire when my work began to bore me. A bedroom with a view of the calm lake that harbored dangerous secrets. A respected member of the community and able to keep watch over my younger brother from afar. A proper distance between us that allowed me to help Knox but not live with him in close quarters and be reminded of our dark childhoods.

I'd miss him. But for the rest of his life, he'd be well cared for at the state's lockdown psychiatric ward. Knox was a clever enough lad to get by and thrive. Maybe even clever enough to escape his confines one day. But he'd never find me.

So, on the bright side, I was responsibility-free of my younger sibling. Shed of any familial burden.

Hatchet Lake was Cimmerian and quiet in this middle hour between dusk and dawn—between past and present, and also between ruined dreams and new possibilities. The air held only a tinge of chill even though it was the first week in November. I'd be sad to leave the mild winters, but after all, I was headed farther south anyway. Snowy Ohio had never been entertained in my schemes for a new beginning.

With one final look at my vacated home, I started my Mercedes and began driving down the isolated dirt road. With every pothole, fabric bags and shoeboxes slid around and rattled in the back seat. I triple-checked the glove compartment, where wads of bills were locked up tight. I'd been squirreling away cash for months now for this move. Just in case.

Alabama was only a memory when dawn finally broke. Coral rays burst through a violet sky. I took that as a good omen. I crossed the state line into Florida, a sunshiny peninsula of flowers and gators and palm trees. Seemed like a good place to live, to start over.

The rest area bordering the two states was a safe enough distance from Normal for a short trip break. I pulled into the rest area and set the GPS on my new phone for Sunny Acres. They had an opening at their local mental health center for a seasoned psychiatrist. It would be a step down from chief of staff at a hospital, but still not bad for someone who didn't have a medical degree.

Not even an undergraduate degree.

Mary Stallings and Linda Bowen, as Human Resources directors, had been within a hair's breadth of discovering the truth. Both had responded to anonymous suspicions about my qualifications, and both had questioned me after being unable to verify the education and work experience claims listed on my résumé.

I'd confided that fact to Knox, and he'd taken it upon himself to handle the situation. My hands were clean, as was my conscience.

The world needed a self-made, clever man like me. Someone who was very, very invested in his patients and fascinated by the stories of their mad, mad inner worlds. Obsessions and phobias and psychoses were my passion.

More troubled people were out there, waiting. It was up to me to find them and distill all their crazy secrets.

ACKNOWLEDGMENTS

Many thanks to my editors Megha Parekh and Charlotte Herscher for all their help in making this story better. And also thanks to the entire Thomas & Mercer team for their solid support along the way. I'd also like to acknowledge my agent, Ann Leslie Tuttle of Dystel, Goderich & Bourret LLC, who has helped and cheered me in innumerable ways over my writing career.

ABOUT THE AUTHOR

Photo © 2013 One Six Photography

Debbie Herbert is an Amazon Charts, *Washington Post*, *USA Today*, and *Publishers Weekly* bestselling author who's always been fascinated by magic, romance, and Gothic stories. Married and living in Alabama, she roots for the Crimson Tide football team. Debbie enjoys recumbent bicycling and Jet Skiing with her husband. She has two grown sons, and the oldest has autism. Characters with autism frequently appear in her works—even when she doesn't plan on it.

For more information, visit www.debbieherbert.com and sign up for her newsletter to receive a free short story. Connect with her on Facebook at Debbie Herbert Author or Debbie Herbert's Readers and on Twitter @debherbertwrit.